ACCLAIM FOR CARRIE STUART PARKS

"I love Carrie Stuart Parks's skill in writing characters with hysterical humor, unwitting courage, and page-turning mystery. I hope my readers won't abandon me completely when they learn about her!"

—TERRI BLACKSTOCK, *USA TODAY* BESTSELLING AUTHOR OF *IF I RUN*, *IF I'M FOUND*, AND *IF I LIVE*

"Parks has created an intriguing female sleuth with depth, courage, and grit. The well-developed characters are complemented by a unique setting."

—*PUBLISHERS WEEKLY*, STARRED REVIEW FOR *PORTRAIT OF VENGEANCE*

"Parks does a wonderful job in creating mystery, leaving clues without giving anything away. *Portrait of Vengeance* is an intense novel that takes readers through the struggles one woman faces to come to terms with her past as a way of saving the future."

—*RT BOOK REVIEWS*, 4½ STARS, TOP PICK!

"Fans of Dee Henderson, DiAnn Mills, and Brandilyn Collins will flock to this suspenseful series."

—*LIBRARY JOURNAL*, STARRED REVIEW FOR *PORTRAIT OF VENGEANCE*

"Rich characters, a forensic artist's eye for detail, and plot twists—Carrie Stuart Parks hits all the right notes!"

—MARY BURTON, *NEW YORK TIMES* BESTSELLING AUTHOR

"I've always known Carrie as someone devoted to mastering her craft, be it forensics, fine art, public speaking, kick-butt dinners (but please, no more zucchini!), or writing suspenseful mystery novels with just the right touch of her characteristic wit. *When Death Draws Near* reflects

Carrie's way with all things creative: it's engaging, tightly woven, painstakingly researched, and a just plain fun read. Dive in!"

—FRANK PERETTI, *NEW YORK TIMES* BESTSELLING AUTHOR

"Carrie Stuart Parks is a riveting storyteller, and every book about forensic artist Gwen Marcey shines with authenticity from this real-life forensic artist. Her books are an automatic buy for me and stay on my keeper shelf. *When Death Draws Near* and every other Parks novel is highly recommended!"

—COLLEEN COBLE, *USA TODAY* BESTSELLING AUTHOR OF
MERMAID MOON AND THE ROCK HARBOR NOVELS

"Thank you so very much, Carrie Stuart Parks, for giving me a reading hangover! I highly recommend [*When Death Draws Near*], but only when you have several hours of uninterrupted time to read because you will NOT want to put it down. Fabulous job!"

—LYNETTE EASON, AWARD-WINNING, BESTSELLING
AUTHOR OF THE HIDDEN IDENTITY SERIES

"Parks, in her debut novel, has clearly done her research and never disappoints when it comes to crisp dialogue, characterization, or surprising twists and turns."

—PUBLISHERS WEEKLY, ON *A CRY FROM THE DUST*

"Besides having a resourceful and likable heroine, the book also features that rarest of characters: a villain you don't see coming, but whom you hate with relish . . . *A Cry from the Dust* will keep you hoping, praying, and guessing till the end."

—BOOKPAGE

FORMULA
OF
DECEPTION

OTHER BOOKS BY CARRIE STUART PARKS

THE GWEN MARCEY NOVELS

A Cry from the Dust

The Bones Will Speak

When Death Draws Near

Portrait of Vengeance

FORMULA
OF
DECEPTION

CARRIE STUART PARKS

THOMAS NELSON
Since 1798

Formula of Deception

© 2018 by Carrie Stuart Parks

Published in Nashville, Tennessee, by Thomas Nelson. Thomas Nelson is a registered trademark of HarperCollins Christian Publishing, Inc.

Thomas Nelson titles may be purchased in bulk for educational, business, fund-raising, or sales promotional use. For information, please email SpecialMarkets@ThomasNelson.com.

Unless otherwise noted, Scripture quotations are taken from the ESV® Bible (The Holy Bible, English Standard Version®), copyright © 2001 by Crossway, a publishing ministry of Good News Publishers. Used by permission. All rights reserved.

Publisher's Note: This novel is a work of fiction. Names, characters, places, and incidents are either products of the author's imagination or used fictitiously. All characters are fictional, and any similarity to people living or dead is purely coincidental.

Library of Congress Cataloging-in-Publication Data

Names: Parks, Carrie Stuart, author.
Title: Formula of deception / Carrie Stuart Parks.
Description: Nashville, Tennessee : Thomas Nelson, 2018.
Identifiers: LCCN 2018004759 | ISBN 9780718083854 (trade paper)
Subjects: | GSAFD: Mystery fiction. | Suspense fiction.
Classification: LCC PS3616.A75535 F67 2018 | DDC 813/.6--dc23 LC record available at https://lccn.loc.gov/2018004759

Printed in the United States of America

18 19 20 21 22 LSC 5 4 3 2 1

To four beautiful women: Karen Solem,
Amanda Bostic, Erin Healy, and Colleen
Coble. You all believed in me. Thank you.

FAMILY TREE

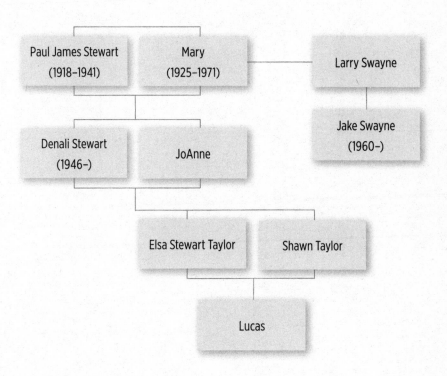

PROLOGUE

April 1, 1946
Alaska

The fountain pen in the man's hand skidded across the journal, leaving a blotch of ink like black blood. He gripped it tighter, but the surface rippled under his arm. "What the . . ." He shoved away from the heaving table and stumbled to his feet.

The floor shifted.

He put out his arms to steady himself.

The trembling increased, the floor rising and falling like earthen waves. The lantern on the table bounced and turned on its side. He lost his balance and dropped to his knees.

Earthquake.

The first rocks from the mountain above him clanged onto the metal roof of the Quonset hut. The shaking intensified. Metal plates and cups flew off the shelves, clattering on the wood flooring.

Heart pounding in his chest, he scrabbled for the door.

The crashing of rocks on steel grew, then increased to a roar. The ceiling bent inward, cracking the wooden surface.

A shriek tore from his throat.

The building shuddered and moaned. The door to the lab

smashed inward as boulders crushed that end of the hut. He crabbed sideways to avoid the tumbling rocks.

More stones slammed through the front door and broke through the windows.

He covered his ears, closed his eyes, and tried to pray.

The shaking stopped.

Slowly he tottered to his feet. The toppled lantern illuminated the shattered windows. Rocks blocked the openings. *Don't panic.* He could still get out. The rocks couldn't be that deep or the weight would have crushed the Quonset hut—as they had the adjacent lab.

Cold air from Alaska's violent winds blew around him. The williwaw's chill cut through his flannel shirt and stirred his shaggy hair, raising goose pimples on his arms. Harsh cries of seagulls carried through the remains of the ventilation opening over the door. He could see early-morning light.

"See?" The sound of his voice calmed him. "The avalanche didn't bury this side. I can get out."

He slipped on a coat, righted the chair, and sat at the table. Full daylight would come soon enough. He'd assess the damage then. The remnants of the hut would protect him from the weather, but many of his provisions were in the crushed lab.

He wouldn't have to wait very long for help. His partner would return within a day or two with a report on his meeting with the Supreme Command. There was a chance he'd even met General Douglas MacArthur.

He would, of course, have turned in the results of their own Operation Fair Cyan. The results of what they'd known two months ago, that is.

The new data was far more disturbing, but the experiment was over, and no one would ever hear about it. Or about the missing pair of rats. He'd made sure to hide all the details of their work.

He rose from his seat to straighten the cot, then knelt and withdrew a lockbox holding his personal possessions. Using the key he carried on a chain around his neck, he unlocked the lid. A photo of the love of his life rested underneath a service medal and ribbon bar. He pinned the medal to his khaki shirt, then kissed the photo once, then three more times before returning it to the box.

A strange crashing sound caught his attention.

He glanced up, then over to the clock still ticking in the corner. Even the seagulls sounded strange, squawking like a bunch of crows. He scratched the day-old whiskers on his cheek.

The crashing occurred again, followed by a loud hiss.

He stood and cocked his head to listen. He'd lived on this island long enough to be familiar with every sound.

The hiss grew, then another crash. The surf? Or maybe a large ship. Or maybe . . .

Tsunami. He slowly backed away from the door facing the ocean.

Frigid saltwater surged through the rocks blocking the entrance, covering his ankles.

He stumbled, dropped to one knee in the freezing water, then grabbed a chair and lunged to his feet.

The water rose to his thighs. He opened his mouth to scream.

The sea smashed through the rocks, crushing him against the wall.

CHAPTER 1

Murphy Andersen's mission to Kodiak Island was about to collide with her lies. She hadn't planned on getting in so deep.

But here she was in a dying Russian's bedroom, with a cop standing beside her.

The stench of Vasily Scherbakov's deteriorating flesh engulfed her. She blinked and breathed through her mouth.

"Cancer's a nasty way to die," Detective Elin Olsson whispered.

Boy howdy, you can say that again. "I'm used to such things. You know, messy crime scenes, dead bodies, stuff like that." *Liar.*

The Russian Orthodox priest standing beside the bed inspected Murphy from head to foot.

She'd already ducked her head and turned it sideways. They always stared at the scar first, the angry red one that split her eyebrow and continued down to her cheek. Her oversized glasses hid some of it, but not enough. She studied her scuffed shoe tips, waiting for his scrutiny to continue. Despite her cheerful scarf, he no doubt noted the threadbare navy blazer, stained shell blouse, and too-big khaki slacks.

A quick peek told her the audit was over. Here came part two. The priest spoke with a slight Russian accent. "But she is a child. A young girl."

Bingo. It never failed. It came from her short stature, thin

5

frame, and childlike face. Whenever she ordered a beer, servers always carded her. To some, looking young would be a compliment. But not to Murphy.

"You said you would bring an experienced artist. A . . . what do you call it? A forensic artist."

The priest didn't look so . . . priestly himself. She'd expected an elderly man wearing fancy embroidered layers of clothing, with a long gray beard reaching his stomach, and a big hat. And he should have an oversized ring, something for people to kiss.

This character appeared to be in his midthirties, with a brown beard, piercing dark eyes, and hair pulled into a hippie-style low ponytail. He wore a black cassock, a big cross, a brimless soft-sided cap, and lime-green tennis shoes.

Detective Olsson tucked a stray lock of white-blond hair behind her ear. "The regular forensic artist from the agency was tied up in a case in Montana, but I assure you, Father Ivanov, she's a trained forensic artist."

Okay, so Detective Olsson didn't know that she had fudged the truth. Murphy *was* an artist, and she had a decent portfolio of pencil portraits, and since her purse had been stolen with every last penny to her name, she needed the work.

When she had asked her landlady yesterday for an extension to pay the rent, Myra, against all of Murphy's protests, called the police to report the theft. And when Detective Olsson saw the portraits spread out on Murphy's kitchen table, her lies began in earnest. *Yes, I have experience in forensic art. Yes, at a police department in West Virginia. No, sorry, my credentials were in my purse. Yes, I'm available tomorrow.* How hard could forensic art be to someone already good at drawing figures? She spent quality time last night watching a YouTube video on the subject. She was practically an expert.

The priest turned to Vasily. *"Eta genshina budet risovat' litso mugzhiny kotorogo vy videli. Ya ne dal ey nikakoy informacii."*

He took the words right out of her mouth. She stared at the floor until she could control her grin. Too little sleep, not enough coffee, and her own nerves only led to the giggles. Once the mirth passed, she pulled up a chair to the bed, sat, and opened her art bag. She removed the packet of mug photos—provided by Detective Olsson—a pad of bristol paper, and a pencil.

"What did you tell him?" Murphy asked the priest.

"You are the art lady."

Detective Olsson smiled. "The priest has offered to translate for the interview."

That didn't sound good. Rather like watching a foreign-language film with subtitles. The actors always said more than what appeared on the screen. "Vasily doesn't speak any English?"

"His English is limited," Father Ivanov said. "He understands it better than he speaks it."

"I just hope you can understand my Virginia accent, y'all." Murphy smiled slightly at Vasily.

"I thought you said West Virginia?" Detective Olsson asked.

"That's where I worked." Murphy nodded quickly.

Detective Olsson looked at the priest. "Where is the woman who called this in? She seemed distraught."

"His caretaker, Irina. Yes, she was very upset. She's one of my parishioners. I wish she would have talked to me before calling you. She'll be in later today to look after Vasily. Do you want to interview her?"

"I do. I just want to be sure I cover all the bases."

The priest nodded.

Murphy's hard and uncomfortable chair was as spartan as Vasily's bedroom. A wooden icon of the Virgin Mary was the sole item on the wall. The furniture consisted of two straight-backed chairs, a nightstand covered with prescription bottles, and a metal cot. A faded piece of cadmium-red calico fabric blocked the closet, and a matching curtain sagged at the window.

Vasily lay on the bed, quilt pulled almost to his chin. His chalk-white skin stretched across his skull, and wisps of fine, light-brown hair haloed his head. His skeletal hands clutched the blanket while his sunken eyes watched her.

"Good morning, Vasily," Murphy said. "May I call you by your first name?" She was grateful when he nodded, considering she couldn't pronounce his last name.

"Well, Vasily, my name is Murphy Andersen. I've been asked to draw a portrait from your memory. I have no idea what you saw, other than Detective Olsson said it's a cold case."

"Technically, it's a new case from the past. The Alaska State Troopers have asked us to do the preliminary interviews." Detective Olsson moved to the foot of the bed. "We're taking your report seriously and have several technicians on their way. Maybe you could tell Murphy what you saw."

Vasily straightened slightly, adjusted his blanket, and began speaking in Russian, never taking his eyes from Murphy's face. He spoke for some time before pausing to cough. The priest held a glass of water to Vasily's lips.

The room was overheated. Murphy clamped her jaw shut to stop the yawn that threatened to emerge and peeked at her watch. The sun rose early and stayed up late in Alaska's June, and she'd been awake since 4:00 a.m., too nervous to sleep with the upcoming interview. Her eyelids felt like gravel pits.

Vasily took a sip of water from the priest, closed his eyes, then waved for Ivanov to translate.

She prepared to take notes.

8

The priest took the chair next to her. "Vasily hunted on various islands, first with his father and uncles, later alone. About ten years ago he was hunting on Ruuwaq Island when he stumbled across five men."

"Five men?" she asked. "No women?"

"No," Vasily answered, then waved Ivanov to continue.

The priest leaned forward. "He remembers one man's face as if it were yesterday."

"I see." She glanced at the blank paper. "And what were the men doing that was so memorable?"

"Doing?" The priest raised his eyebrows. "They weren't doing anything. They were dead."

"Dead. Of course, but are we talking about an accident? Murder?"

Father Ivanov spoke briefly to Vasily in Russian, listened to his reply, then said, "He says it looked like they killed each other with their bare hands."

CHAPTER 2

Heat rushed to Murphy's face and a buzzing started in her brain. She stared at the priest for a moment. "Okay then." She cleared her throat. *Remember, Sherlock Holmes never fainted.* "You saw five men. Am I drawing five composites?"

"No," Vasily said, then spoke to the priest for a moment.

The priest nodded, then looked at Murphy. "He'll describe the man he saw first, the one nearest to him. He glanced at all five bodies but only remembers that one face clearly. He fled the island after that."

"Okay, one drawing it is."

"If you could," Detective Olsson said, "maybe you could do a second drawing as well—a rough sketch of how all the men were arranged. The crime scene."

Nodding, she jotted a note to remind herself. The dying man stared at her expectantly, but somehow it seemed wrong to just jump into the description. "Mr. . . . ah . . . Vasily, let's start with your arrival on Ruuwaq Island that day. What kind of day was it?"

"Gray. Dark," Vasily answered.

"And how did you feel?" she asked.

He raised his eyebrows but answered, "Like hunting."

"Tell me about the island."

Vasily spoke for a time to Father Ivanov. The priest listened intently, bending forward in his chair, then turned to her. "He said the island is tiny, treeless, and mostly bordered by cliffs. The south side is low but is filled with treacherous rocks and currents. Because of that, few hunters bother with it. Vasily thought he could climb the cliff on the northeast side. With the icy conditions, it took him part of a day to reach the top. The land sloped to the ocean, with a rockslide on his right near the water. He saw nothing to hunt and was about to leave, but then he spotted piles of clothing near the rocks. The wind shifted and he smelled . . . death."

"Picture in your mind walking to the bodies. Mentally look around you. What's going on?"

"Wind cold in my face, light rain," Vasily answered.

"What did you hear?"

He spoke to the priest. "He could hear the ocean waves crashing and seagulls," Father Ivanov said.

"Now how were you feeling?"

Again Vasily spoke to the priest. Ivanov listened, then patted the man's hand before turning to her. "He said the wind was icy, but the cold filled his heart. He didn't want to look. He wanted to run away from that terrible place."

She understood. She would have hightailed it out of there the second she spotted the clothing. "I admire your bravery," she said to Vasily. "Tell me about the man you saw, the one you remember so clearly."

Vasily launched into more Russian. When he finished, Father Ivanov said, "He believes all five were Asian. The one he remembers was a small, thin man, possibly in his twenties. Black hair, medium skin color, big teeth."

"Big teeth?"

"I suspect he means the lips were drawn backward so he

could see all his teeth." Ivanov spoke to Vasily for a moment, then nodded.

"How long do you think they had been dead?"

Vasily spoke. "Not long time."

She tugged the packet of mug photos out of her art bag and handed them to Vasily. "Please go through these photos and find people who look like the man you saw. Point to the ones who look similar and I'll write it down."

The dying man took the mug shots and dumped them on the bed. Almost immediately he selected one and pointed at an oval face. She took the photo from him and made note of it. In different images he indicated a high forehead, coarse black hair combed backward, and almond-shaped eyes with epicanthic eye folds. The nose was average in length, though somewhat broad at the end. Rather thin lips rounded out his selection.

Murphy made a note that the lips were pulled away from the teeth and would be stretched out and flattened. She'd draw them fuller in the sketch. Vasily's face had grown even paler during the facial selection. He returned the unselected photos to the bag and gave it to her. She put it away, then opened her pad of paper to a clean sheet. "Could you sketch some stick figures to show how the bodies were lying?"

Vasily nodded. She handed him the sketchpad and pencil. With a few strokes, he drew five stick figures on the paper, then put an X on the body farthest from the others. "This one I saw best."

"Where were they in relation to the rockslide?"

Vasily drew a line across one side, then handed her the pad.

After studying the sketches, she asked, "Did you ever return to Ruuwaq Island?"

"No." His voice was a whisper.

"Why did you wait so long to tell anyone what you saw?"

The priest cleared his throat and glanced at Detective Olsson. "Vasily hasn't had the best relationship with law enforcement."

Pulling out a piece of drafting velum, Murphy placed it over Vasily's rough sketch and drew prone bodies, then held it up. "What should I change to make this look more like what you saw?"

He closed his eyes as if unwilling to revisit the scene, then pointed to two figures. He made his fingers into claws, then wrapped his hands around his throat to show strangulation.

"They were strangling each other?"

He nodded.

She changed the drawing.

Pointing to a third man, Vasily made his hand into a fist and struck the bed.

"This man was beaten? With a fist?" she asked.

Vasily nodded. "And rock."

Once again she made the changes, then turned the rockslide line into a drawing of rocks. "Now what should I change?" She held up the image.

"One rock by two men look like table."

She drew a rectangular rock parallel to the two men, then showed him the drawing. "Now what?"

"Nothing." Vasily shrank into his pillow.

She closed the sketchpad, removed her glasses, and took Vasily's hands in hers. "Vasily, thank you for sharing this memory. I'll take this home with me and bring the drawings back when I'm finished for you to correct. Was there anything else I should have asked you or you wanted to say?"

Vasily blinked at her several times, then started to talk. The Russian words tumbled over each other as he barely paused for breath.

Father Ivanov leaned backward in his chair, his gaze going from Vasily to Murphy.

Vasily didn't notice. He continued to speak, now with spittle forming at the corners of his mouth.

Murphy watched the man's face, nodding as if she understood what he was saying.

The flow of words ended and Vasily closed his eyes. "Thank you," he whispered. His skin had turned ashen, with delicate purple veins crossing his eyelids. His grip on her hands relaxed.

Her heart pounded in her ears. *Is he dead? Did I just kill him?*

A hand clutched her arm.

She jumped.

Detective Olsson tugged at her. "Come."

She put on her glasses, picked up the art bag, and allowed the other woman to lead her into the living room.

"What was that all about?" the detective asked.

"I don't know. Is he . . . ?"

"Dead? No, he's still breathing."

Murphy let out a breath she didn't know she'd been holding. "Maybe he was remembering more details—"

"No." Father Ivanov gently closed the bedroom door behind him and entered the living room. "Nothing new about the deaths. It was as if . . ." He stared upward, his eyes unfocused.

"As if what?" Detective Olsson asked.

"As if he needed to unburden himself of every evil deed he'd ever done."

Murphy shivered slightly. She was glad she didn't understand Russian.

"So, a final confession." The detective folded her arms.

"In the Russian Orthodox faith, you don't confess to the priest. You confess to God in the presence of the priest."

"Like I said—"

"No. This was . . . different." He shook his head, and his gaze sharpened on Murphy. "He seemed to want to share with *you*. He certainly opened up."

"I didn't do anything." Murphy shifted her weight from one leg to the other. "I think he just needed to have someone near, holding his hand."

Detective Olsson raised her eyebrows at the priest. "She has a point. I don't suppose you've been holding hands with the man . . ."

Father Ivanov stiffened. "It's not my place—"

She held up her hands. "Just pulling your chain, Father. We'll return with the completed drawings as soon as Murphy is finished. From what I understand, seeing the completed sketch usually triggers additional memories. Vasily may remember a whole lot more information."

The priest folded his arms. "That's good. I'll pray that your drawings turn out well."

She reached for the door. "Come on, Murphy, let's get those sketches done."

Murphy paused before leaving. "Thank you, Father Ivanov. I appreciate your translating." She could feel his gaze, not much less disapproving than when she'd arrived, on her back as she closed the front door.

Detective Olsson slipped into the police SUV and waited for her. Murphy climbed in, rubbing her hands together to warm them.

"After the caretaker reported this story to me three days ago," the detective said, "I followed up with Father Ivanov, then looked for missing-persons reports in that time frame. No luck. Not one, let alone five. Then I had to figure out where Vasily hunted. With the large number of islands in the Kodiak Archipelago, plus almost seventy in the Aleutian Island chain stretching across almost seventeen hundred miles, that was a lot of territory to cover."

"But he gave you the name."

Detective Olsson started the engine and pulled away from Vasily's tiny home. "Ruuwaq Island was what he called it, but that's not the official name. I called up all the pilots I knew and described the island. Butch Patterson, a retired trooper with Alaska Wildlife, finally came up with a possibility. I had him fly over the island yesterday to see if he could spot anything. He said the rockslide was there, but nothing else, at least that he could see from the air. He suggested I have Jake Swayne, his replacement, take Bertie, the crime-scene tech, out there tomorrow morning."

"Bertie?"

"Roberta Fisher, from Anchorage. State crime lab." She pulled out onto the street. "I told Bertie you were doing our sketches. She, ah, she's asked if you'd go with her."

"Why?"

"She said she needed help. I offered a couple of deputies, but none of them can even write their name legibly, let alone diagram a scene. I assume you've done crime-scene diagramming before."

"Of course." Murphy felt herself skidding down that slippery slope of lies.

Detective Olsson turned toward Murphy's apartment. The sun was well up in the cloudless sky in spite of the early hour.

"I suppose a boat ride—"

"Not boat. Floatplane."

"Oh."

"You're not afraid of flying in a small plane, are you?"

"I don't think so. I see them every day taking off and landing, but I've never flown in one." She thought for a moment. "Back to Ruuwaq, how did the men get on the island in the first place? Vasily didn't mention seeing a boat."

"Good question." They soon pulled up in front of Murphy's place. "Call me when you finish those drawings." The detective handed her a business card. "You can drop them off at the station, or I'll send someone to pick them up."

"I don't have a car, Detective, so sending someone would be a good idea."

"Call me Elin. How do you get around?"

"Bicycle." Murphy grabbed her art bag, stepped from the car, and closed the door.

Elin rolled down the passenger window. "I suppose that makes life simple. No car payment, no insurance, no maintenance." She waved and drove away.

"Yeah," Murphy muttered, "and no way anyone can find me."

CHAPTER 3

For the past year, Murphy had called the daylight basement of a single-wide trailer her home. The rent was cheap and the view priceless. Although the exterior of faded, avocado-green metal overlaid with rust was grim, her windows on one side opened to shimmering Mission Lake. Once she'd found out the name of the lake, she had to live here.

In the distance, just beyond a narrow spit of land, were Bird and Holiday Islands, rising out of the Woody Island Channel of the Gulf of Alaska. She never tired of watching the seagulls and bald eagles fish the lake, nor the changing light as it crossed the emerald-green land. Kodiak Island was a rain forest, and the seventy inches of rain that fell there each year provided a moody atmosphere that matched Murphy's outlook on life.

Myra Hampton, the landlord, a chain-smoking woman in her forties, provided a temperamental microwave, dorm-size refrigerator and freezer, hot plate, and Crock-Pot. Cooking for one person was as much fun as scrubbing floors, but Murphy had mastered the Crock-Pot and created interesting meals that could be divided up and frozen. Even experimental Crock-Pot failures smelled good and hid the odor of cigarette smoke that drifted down from above.

Her room had its own entrance, so she could come and go

without disturbing Myra's television game shows. Her landlady was generous enough to give her rides to town or the grocery store during the snowy days of winter. The studded tires on her bike helped on the icy days.

The only personal items she had brought with her to Kodiak were her necklace and a framed photograph of her identical twin sister, Dallas. Should anyone see it, they'd think it was Murphy. Before the scar.

Twice a month she delivered several small acrylic paintings of regional scenes and a selection of handmade sea glass jewelry to a downtown gift shop. They in turn sold them to tourists. She signed the art and jewelry *Taanga*, an Aleut word for water. The gallery owner ignored her obviously Caucasian appearance and sold them as created by a Native.

Murphy was grateful. The more layers between herself and her past, the better.

A marmalade-colored cat greeted her at the back door.

"Good morning, Mr. Brinkley." She unlocked the door and let the cat scurry into the basement in front of her. She had no idea of his real name. The small notch in his right ear proclaimed him a feral cat, but he'd claimed ownership of her and demanded kibble accordingly. After emptying the last of a bag of Cat Chow into his bowl, she pulled out her art supplies. "I got a job today."

The cat continued to crunch on the dry food.

"It's a cold case, just like on television." She placed the supplies on the small kitchen table in front of her. "I might be able to do a bit of research on my . . . mission as well. What's that you say?"

The cat ignored her.

"Yes. I did have to tell a tiny lie to get the job. Well, maybe a few small lies."

She checked for a reaction. "Of course not. It's perfectly safe. Thank you for your concern."

Mr. Brinkley finished his last nugget, sat, and began licking his rear.

"Well now, how should I interpret your sudden desire to clean your bottom? A reflection on me? No, you wouldn't be that rude. How about it's always a good idea to be vigilant for rear attacks?"

The cat stopped licking and stared at her.

She took off her glasses and stared back. The cat was the first to look away. "Ha! I won."

"Murphy, is that you?" Myra called from upstairs. "Is someone there with you? You know you aren't allowed visitors."

"I'm just talking to the cat."

"You're not allowed pets either!"

"Yes, ma'am. It's not mine—"

"Just be sure you remember the agreement you signed. I have others interested in renting your apartment."

"Yes, ma'am." She'd just bet folks were lined up to live under a mobile home.

Let it go. Best not to annoy or upset the woman. This was a perfect place to live.

Moving to the tiny closet, she unwrapped the scarf from around her neck. She kicked off her shoes and finished undressing. She hung up the pants and jacket, then pulled on a pair of black leggings and an oversized T-shirt.

Mr. Brinkley jumped to the ledge above the sink and stared out at the birds swooping over the lake.

After assembling the ingredients for chicken à la Kodiak—anything she could gather from the overpriced and meager offerings at the local grocery store—she placed them in the Crock-Pot and turned it on low.

Her light box was on the closet floor. She'd had it forever, because it was useful for when she needed to copy a drawing onto thick watercolor paper. She placed it on the table, then transferred the rough crime-scene sketch to gridded paper. The location of the table-shaped rock was the first thing she sketched, lining it up with the prone bodies of the dead men. When she finished she placed the drawing in a portfolio, then tucked it into her backpack. She'd take the sketch to the library later in the day to make copies. If she was going out to Ruuwaq Island, she could use the copies for measurements without damaging the original.

The cat jumped onto the table and curled up on the light box.

She scratched him under the chin. She used to have a cat, jointly owned by her sister. They'd each given him a different name. He hadn't cared. He hadn't answered to either name.

What would a super-sleuth forensic artist need on a case? Maybe a clipboard or two? For sure a number of sharp pencils in a holder. In addition to her YouTube research, she'd seen enough composite sketches on television to know to draw the face from the front, not three-quarters as many portraits are rendered. Using the mug photographs Vasily had chosen as a starting point gave her an excellent idea of how the man looked. The photographs had the added bonus of showing the highlights and shadows for shading.

Mr. Brinkley snagged the kneaded rubber eraser and placed it on the light box. She retrieved it and gave him a chamois to play with.

First she mapped out each facial feature with an HB pencil, then adjusted it to match the chosen photograph. The eyes on an average face are halfway between the top of the head and the chin. The width of the eye will generally fit five times across the center of the face. The length of the average nose is one and a half times

21

the width of the eye. The mouth is located one-third of the distance between the bottom of the nose and the chin.

Once the features were in place, she picked up a 6B pencil and darkened the hair. Tilting the paper, she added a few highlights with her portable electric eraser, then blended the strokes around the jaw with a paper stump.

The face didn't look right. She erased and tried again, this time working slower.

A blotch showed up on the cheek where she'd rested her hand and the oils from her skin passed to the face. "Look what you made me do," she said to the cat.

Mr. Brinkley held the chamois in his front paws, rolled onto his back, and kicked the soft leather.

"Thank you for not commenting on oil transfer as an amateur mistake. Yeah, I think I need to start over." She sketched the face again. This time the drawing looked too light against the dark hair, so she added more shading around the side of the face.

A spot of sunlight lit up her drawing pad.

She looked up and checked the time. She'd been working for over two hours. Mr. Brinkley had given up torturing the chamois and was sitting by the door. She stood, stretched, and let the cat out.

The day was becoming overcast and cool, with spats of rain creating a polka-dotted surface on the lake. She was tempted to go for a run, but the composite needed to be finished. She'd go jogging as a reward afterward. The thought made her grin. Years ago, eleven to be exact, she would have scoffed if anyone had predicted she'd enjoy jogging.

Eleven years ago she lived a very different life.

She returned to the table and examined the drawing. If the man was Asian, there wouldn't be a lot of shading around the eyes. She picked up an eraser and shortened the eyebrows, added more shading under the chin, and placed a highlight in the iris. Not great, but done.

After taping a piece of tracing paper over the drawing to protect it, she picked up her cell and called Elin.

The woman answered on the second ring. "Detective Olsson."

"The composite is done, at least as much as it can be without Vasily seeing it."

"Great. I'll pick you up and we'll drive back over there."

Murphy hung up and changed back into her shabby jacket and slacks. If she got any more police work, she'd have to break down and buy something more professional.

The composite sketch went into a file folder, which she added to her art bag along with the rest of her drawing supplies. She placed a green rain slicker next to her shoes by the door.

Elin drove up just as she finished getting ready. Murphy pulled on her shoes and jacket, trotted over, and got into the car. Elin handed her a steaming Starbucks cup. "I didn't ask you what you liked, so I just got you a cappuccino. If you don't want it, I'll drink it."

"Over my dead body." She took a sip. "Ah. Bless your heart and all your vital organs."

Elin grinned. "I called Father Ivanov to let him know we'd be coming. He said he'd meet us there. He's finishing up at the church, but he said Irina is at the house. She'll let us in."

Murphy nodded and cupped the hot drink, unable to remember the last time she'd had enough money to splurge on expensive coffee.

The last time she'd lived without doubt. Or fear.

They parked behind a deep-blue Ford pickup. "Before we go in, could I see the sketch?" Elin asked.

"Sure." She removed the file folder and handed it to the detective.

"Interesting."

Did that translate into "bad sketch"? "Um . . ."

"He looks Filipino." Elin returned the sketch. "As you were drawing this, did you think he looked Filipino?"

"I didn't think about much of anything. I just drew the features Vasily selected."

"We'll post this online immediately, put a bit of a reward with it. That should encourage public-minded citizens. Are you ready?"

"Yep."

At the front door, Elin poised to knock but paused, arm raised.

The door was open an inch.

Elin pulled out the Glock pistol from the holster on her belt. "Hello?" Nudging the door open with her foot, she glanced inside, then around her. "It's Detective Olsson. Anyone here?" Her voice echoed slightly in the empty living room.

Murphy gripped the art bag tighter with her suddenly sweaty hands and hesitated on the stoop.

Elin cocked her head and put her finger to her lips.

The house was silent.

Stay put, she mouthed to Murphy, then crept into the living room, gun extended.

Murphy licked her lips and followed closely behind.

Elin reached for the bedroom doorknob, turned it, and pushed the door open.

Vasily was propped up slightly on the pillows. An old Native woman sat in a chair next to his bed, a Bible in her hands.

Both stared blankly ahead. A stream of blood drifted down their faces from the neat bullet hole in each forehead.

CHAPTER 4

Murphy felt like someone had punched her in the stomach. She staggered backward a step, then spun and checked the room behind her. *Is the killer still here?*

Elin entered the bedroom, took a quick look behind the door and checked the closet, then raced to living room. "Don't move," she ordered Murphy.

She couldn't have moved if she'd wanted to. Her feet seemed attached to the floor.

Elin charged into the kitchen, did a quick turn, then kicked open the bathroom door. She entered, and the rings on a shower curtain rattled. Returning to the living room, she pulled out her cell and handed it to Murphy. "Dial 911, then put it on speaker."

A voice promptly answered. "Nine-one-one, what is the nature of your emergency?"

She moved the phone closer to Elin.

"This is Detective Olsson. I just arrived at 1657 St. Herman Drive. Two people down inside the home. Possible homicide. Adult victims are male and female. Possible gunshot wounds. Send backup and roll medics. Also, get someone over to pick up Bertie Fisher at the airport. She's the state crime-scene technician flying in. Ravn flight 888. Should be touching down around eleven. Bring her straight here. And get hold of the medical examiner in

Anchorage and see if someone can fly over here ASAP. Did you get all that?"

"Ten-four."

"Good."

Murphy disconnected.

"What's going on here?" Father Ivanov stood in the front doorway.

"Bad news I'm afraid, Father. I need both you and Murphy to step outside and wait. We have an active scene and can't have it compromised—"

"Scene?" The priest took a step into the room. "Do you mean crime scene?" He started toward the bedroom.

Elin caught his arm. "You can give everyone last rites, or pray over them, or whatever you need to do soon enough, Padre, but for now I need to preserve the evidence."

His gaze went from her face to the bedroom, then back again. "Are they both dead?"

"Murdered."

"I would like to serve Litia, a special memorial service."

"As soon as we process everything, you can do the service. Now please step outside."

Murphy unstuck her feet from the floor and followed Father Ivanov and Elin to the shaggy front yard. The sun peeked through the clouds, lighting up the landscape with a cheerful glow. That was all wrong. It should be raining. And everything painted in charcoal gray.

The quiet street echoed with approaching wailing sirens. Elin left them to direct the patrol cars.

"What did you see?" the priest asked her.

"I'm so sorry." She wanted to sit down before her legs gave way, but there was nothing to sit on. She leaned against the blue pickup. "Someone shot Vasily and Irina. Right here." She touched her forehead.

That did it. Her knees buckled and she dropped to the ground. *Ground is good.* She could just sit here for a bit and look at the mottled green shag carpet.

No. Not a shag carpet. Grass. Uncut grass.

Father Ivanov knelt beside her. "Are you okay?"

"Yeah, I . . . um . . . needed to tie my shoes." *Idiot. You're wearing slip-ons.*

"I see." He stood. "I thought you were used to this type of thing."

"I'm rusty."

"So they were both dead when you got here?"

She mentally replayed their arrival. Outside of chirping birds, the distant rumble of floatplanes, and a barking dog, there hadn't been any sounds. No traffic had driven past. No cars parked nearby except the blue truck.

She hadn't smelled gunpowder or whatever it was that indicated a gun had been fired. "Yes, they were both dead, and I didn't see or hear anyone running away. What time did you leave this morning?"

"About forty-five minutes after you."

She looked at her watch. "So they were killed sometime between nine and eleven—"

"Ah, so the forensic artist emerges."

Her face grew warm. "I just feel terrible that someone killed that poor man and woman. Why would someone do that?" The thoughts flooded her mind before she could stop them. *Stupid question. You know evil people kill the innocent.* The dizziness passed and she stood. "Sorry. It's been a long time since I worked at the crime lab in Kentucky."

"I thought you said West Virginia. Or was it Virginia?"

"Of course." She folded her arms. "I've worked all over."

Ivanov caught Elin's attention and the detective walked over. "Do you need us both here?" the priest asked. "I can drop Murphy off—"

"Actually"—Elin ran her fingers through her hair—"I was hoping Murphy wouldn't mind helping us out here." The women looked at each other. "We're shorthanded and could use help diagramming the scene."

Murphy hesitated.

"We'll pay you, of course." Elin gave a grim smile. "You did say all your money was in that stolen purse."

"Diagramming. Yes. My specialty." Good thing her pants weren't bursting into flame.

Elin took a deep breath. "Thank you. We won't move the bodies until the coroner arrives from Anchorage. I have a photographer taking pictures now and someone checking for fingerprints. When Bertie gets here, she'll be looking for tool marks, blood spatter, expended cartridges, vacuuming and taping for trace evidence, all the usual scene processing."

"Of course."

"Once they finish, you can go to work. See that big uniformed cop over there?" Elin pointed at a large man holding a clipboard and tape measure. "That's Mike. He'll assist you. When you're done, sign and date it and give it to me."

Murphy gazed at the simple house, then around her at the police vehicles with flashing lights and a small gathering of neighbors. Two officers were unwinding yellow crime-scene tape around the perimeter of the yard. Just outside of the tape, near the crowd of spectators, was a woman with a camera.

The camera was pointed straight at her.

"Who is that woman?" Murphy nodded in the photographer's direction.

"A reporter from the *Kodiak Daily Mirror*," Elin said. "Just ignore the press. I'll let Mike know to help you."

The press. And they'd taken her photograph.

Don't sweat it. No one she knew would be reading a small local newspaper from Alaska. He was in prison, and had been for thirteen years. Her hair was a different color. She'd lost weight. And she was wearing oversized glasses. No one would recognize her. Least of all him.

Maybe. The scar might show in the photo. "Is there something I can do while I'm waiting?" She'd do anything that would take her out of the photographer's sight.

"Sure. We can always use a trained eye." Elin waved a patrol officer over. "Joshua Ward, this is Murphy Andersen. Take her with you when you do the search of the grounds."

Joshua was over six feet tall with umber-brown hair, matching deep-set eyes, and a chiseled jaw. Although the vest and duty belt added twenty pounds of bulk to his upper body, his arms shouted weight training and a gym. He gave her a once-over, gaze lingering on the scar, then nodded briefly. "Sure."

She caught her breath. He was the most strikingly handsome man she had ever seen. The only flaw on him was the wedding ring on his finger.

Not waiting for her to comment, Joshua headed for the street. "Are you with the Explorer Scouts?"

"No." At least he was original about her youthful appearance.

"Oh. We usually use the Explorers when we do a search, especially in thick underbrush or woods."

"I'm a tad old to be an Explorer." She walked faster to keep up.

Joshua glanced at her. "Don't look it. We'll be taking that

alley." He pointed. "And go around to the back of the house. We'll work our way to the front. You'll be an arm's length from me. Pay attention to what you're stepping on. Be looking for footmark impressions, anything that could have been dropped, or really, anything that doesn't look like it's been there awhile."

"I'm a trained forensic artist."

He glanced at her again. "Don't look like that either."

After several hours of using her sleeve to sweep aside the pushki and stare at dirt, clumps of grass, very old, discarded cigarette butts, and beer cans, she was convinced police work was singularly lacking in any appeal, with the possible exception of Joshua. Murphy also believed the killer had simply walked away, out the front door and down the street.

The small crowd of onlookers had grown, and more police vehicles now clogged the street. Her stomach reminded her that all she'd put in it today was a Starbucks coffee.

A plump woman in one-piece navy-blue coveralls stepped out of the house. Her short ginger-colored hair matched the thousands of freckles on her round face. She handed a number of brown paper bags to a patrol officer and pointed toward a van. Elin joined her, spotted Murphy, and waved her over.

"Bertie, this is the artist I told you about, Murphy Andersen," Elin said. "Murphy, meet Bertie Fisher from the state crime lab."

"How do you do, Bertie?" Murphy held out her hand.

"Murphy, did you say?" Bertie stared at her face for a moment, then pumped her hand. "Nice to meetcha, Murph." She let go and slapped Murphy on the back. "Glad to have your help. Ready to do some drawings?"

"Sure." She glanced around, looking for one last glimpse of Joshua.

The man was talking to an Audrey Hepburn–clone female

officer. When he finished, she patted him on the arm and moved to a patrol car. He watched her walk away, then glanced at Murphy.

She averted her eyes to an intriguing section of peeling white paint on the porch, then strolled into the house. With Mike's help, she measured and recorded the living room, kitchen, and bathroom, carefully avoiding the smudges of fingerprint powder. Compared to painting landscapes in acrylics and watercolor, crime-scene diagramming was methodical and tedious. She handed the clipboard with her notes to Mike and turned toward the bedroom.

She slowly approached and hesitated in front of the closed door. *Just don't look at them.*

"Did you forget something?" Mike asked.

"Ah, yeah, my . . . pencil needs sharpening. Go on ahead. I'll be right behind you." She stepped aside.

Mike twisted the knob and entered. Bertie entered the house and went directly to the bedroom.

Taking a deep breath, Murphy counted to ten, then followed. The stench slammed into her nose. Body fluids, coppery blood, sweat from the officers who had gathered evidence earlier, and the sickly smell of death.

She gagged and leaned against the wall. The pale-blue paint color faded to off-white. She blinked rapidly and the color returned. *Mustn't faint. Bad form.*

A hand patted her on the shoulder. "Elin told me you were rusty," Bertie said.

"Yeah."

"If you feel like barfing, go outside." Bertie grinned, revealing a gap between her front teeth and deep dimples in her cheeks.

"I'll be sure to make a run for it." She tried to smile back. "Do you have any idea . . ."

"Too early." Bertie shook her head. "Elin said the door was

unlocked when you came over the first time. No one would have needed to force themselves in. This all went down quickly, so probably he just walked in, pow, pow, and strolled out."

The last thing poor Vasily and the old woman saw would have been the barrel of a gun. She tried to get that image out of her mind. "Anyone have an idea why?"

"I'm a criminalist, working on the evidence, the 'how it happened.'" Bertie rocked back on her heels. "Criminologists work on the 'why it happened,' the thinking of the killer."

"I know that."

Bertie grinned. "I don't care what the killer was thinking. I just want to throw his sorry hide into the slammer."

"Me too. Like on television."

"Yup. It's either *CSI* or *Criminal Minds*. Of course, neither show is accurate."

"Right." Murphy cleared her throat. "But I don't watch much television. I don't even own a TV."

"I do. I'm absolutely addicted to Hallmark movies. And any of those shows about six-hundred-pound people. Makes me feel thin." She patted her ample stomach. "Anyway, making an educated guess about this murder, with these two such low-risk victims, I'd say Mr. Scherbakov set something in motion by revealing what he saw so long ago." She tapped the side of her nose. "And I'm verrrry interested to see what we find when we go to Ruuwaq Island tomorrow."

CHAPTER 5

By the time Murphy finished diagramming, it was raining again, the crowd had thinned to two people, and the bulk of the law-enforcement and emergency vehicles were gone. Bertie offered to drive her home and pick her up the next day for the floatplane trip to Ruuwaq.

"Thank you." Murphy hopped into Bertie's rental car. "The rain's cold and home is a long walk."

"And it's late." Bertie angled to the street.

"I didn't realize the time. It's hard to track with almost twenty hours of daylight." She shrugged. "I wanted to make copies of the sketch I did with Vasily at the library, but it's closed now. Can we stop on the way to the floatplane?"

"The copy shop at the harbor will be open before we have to leave."

"That works."

Bertie was silent for the rest of the drive, apparently as weary from the work as Murphy was. Dampness had seeped into the car, and the heater worked valiantly, but Murphy shivered all the way home. June may be a warm month elsewhere, but on Kodiak it would be a few more weeks before she'd wander outside in shorts.

Mr. Brinkley was pressed against the door of her place, a dour expression on his face for having to wait in the rain.

"Sorry, Mr. B." She unlocked the door, then dashed inside. After kicking off her shoes, she hung her jacket on the hook and shook the rain from her hair. The scent of dinner in the Crock-Pot made her mouth water. The fragrance of cooked food made the one-room apartment feel homey. Murphy's single bed held a potpourri of colorful pillows. Throw rugs covered the yellow-and-white tile floor. Her easel and taboret took advantage of one of the three windows. There was no room for a sofa, and her only chairs were pushed under the kitchen table.

It wasn't as if she had any visitors, and certainly no male callers, so the seating arrangements would be a problem.

She pictured Joshua standing in the center of the room, then shook her head. "Married, remember? That is so not going to happen."

The cat meowed.

"Yes, I could paint him. But how pathetic is that? I'm such a cliché. Living alone, single, mooning over a married man, with a cat—"

The cat yowled.

"Right, I don't own you. But I think I need a dog. A cute little mutt to sit in my lap." She reached for the cat food. Gone. She'd fed Brinkley the end of the bag and hadn't been to the store. "You're getting tuna. Better not complain. That was for my lunch this week." After opening the can, she dumped it into the cat bowl and placed it on the floor. She tossed the can in the trash, then pulled out a plate and served her own dinner.

She sat at the table and stared out the window for a moment. *What a strange day.*

The old house. Green shag carpet. Smell of cordite. Dead—

She jerked, then blinked. The light in the room had brightened.

Focusing on her dinner, she took a bite. The food was cold. "What?" She slammed down her fork. The stupid Crock-Pot must have turned off sometime in the afternoon. Great.

Murphy stood and moved her plate to the counter. She could shred the chicken and give it to the cat tomorrow in case she didn't get to the store.

In a small box by the door, she spotted the mail Myra had left. She froze.

On top of some junk mail was an envelope addressed to Dakota M. Andersen.

Her breath knotted at the back of her throat. The letter had come through a mail-forwarding service she used in Anchorage.

Circling the table, she stared at the brown kraft envelope.

The cat yowled.

She jumped. "Okay, Mr. B., I'll put you out." Her voice shook. She opened the door, but the cat just stared at the rain.

The envelope was torn and smeared with ink from the cheap damp flier underneath. She emptied the contents. A single legal-size letter. She opened it and sat down. The letter was printed on regular copy paper.

Alaska Department of Corrections
Victim/Witness Notification Program

Dear Ms. Andersen,

You are enrolled in the Advanced Notification Program by the Department of Corrections specific to Clinton Lamour Hunter. According to our statutes, upon any escapes from a correctional facility, the Department of Corrections shall immediately notify, by the most reasonable and expedient means available, the chief of police of the city and the sheriff of the county in which the inmate resided immediately before the inmate's arrest . . .

Her head buzzed, and the letter dropped from her numb fingers. After a moment she picked it up again.

. . . We attempted to call you, as prescribed, but found your phone was no longer in service. This is your notification that Clinton Lamour Hunter has escaped custody. His whereabouts are unknown. We strongly urge you to contact your local police or sheriff's department and to update your contact information with our office.

Her stomach constricted, and her hand flew to the scar under her eye. *He can't be loose.* How could Clinton Hunter, the Anchorage serial killer, have escaped?

Would he come looking for her? Again? She hadn't needed any witness protection program after he'd been incarcerated, only a notice if his status changed. The Victim/Witness Notification Program was the only entity that had her old address—indeed, any of her addresses.

The walls closed in on her. Her breathing came in sharp gasps. She stumbled backward, then fell, tipping over the cat food dish. Slowly she reached over and stopped the bowl from clattering.

When she righted herself, she slammed and locked the kitchen door. She raced to each window to pull the blinds, then to the closet. She pulled down her suitcase, placed it on the bed, and started grabbing clothes from the top drawer of her dresser. She could leave her art supplies. Just take her brushes. Enough clothes to fill one suitcase. Catch the flight—no, ferry. She could take her bike on the ferry.

She paused, hands full of T-shirts. How would she pay for it? More importantly, she needed ID. And her driver's license had been stolen. Without a license, she couldn't go on either a plane or a ferry. Not until she got a new one. And applying for a license required a social security number, proof of residency, and date of birth. She was off everyone's radar right now, but she'd show up once she applied. The press had hounded her before. They'd do so again if they found her.

And Clinton Hunter? He'd want to kill her.

She put the shirts back in the drawer. This time things would be different. She wasn't going to be a helpless victim ever again. She touched her scar.

Murphy picked up the framed photo of her twin sister and sat at the table. Mr. Brinkley jumped onto the next chair, curled up, and closed his eyes.

"What should I do, sis?" she whispered.

Her sister stared outward at a point in space.

"Please talk to me. Tell me what happened. Why did you come to Kodiak?"

Her sister didn't reply.

They'd never found her sister's body, only blood. Not even enough blood to make the police check it out. She'd had to tell them about her suspicions, and even then, they were reluctant to follow up.

But eventually they found all the other bodies.

She stroked the carved walrus ivory necklace she'd made from her sister's earring. Her throat closed up thinking about the uncertainty, the waiting, the hoping. Even the prayers. The stupid, useless prayers.

She'd felt so helpless then. So driven now. Her mission.

After returning the photograph to the table, she moved to the suitcase. No rush on packing. No place to run to. No way to get off Kodiak.

Those five dead men on Ruuwaq, her sister finally responded. *They had families, just like you. You can help bring closure to them. Their families have been waiting for years.*

"You always were the smart one, Dallas, the practical one," she said.

And you were always the strong one, Dakota, her sister whispered back.

"I'm not strong. I'm always afraid."

Strength comes from being afraid, facing it, then triumphing over it.

Her eyes burned from unshed tears. "I'm so sorry, sis."

Don't be, she whispered back. *Just get to the truth.*

Mr. Brinkley hopped off the chair and sauntered to the door. She peered through the blinds. Though it was late, the northern sun wasn't ready to set. The rain had stopped. Clouds once again painted the sky in smoky gray. Out in Shahafka Cove, a fishing boat escorted by a seagull caucus headed to port. She let the cat out.

Murphy unpacked the few things she'd thrown into the suitcase and put it away. She placed a blank canvas on her easel. Beside it, tubes of acrylic were lined up on her taboret by color.

Starting a painting now was out of the question.

Concentrate on the ordinary. Focus.

Checking the tray of sea glass, she noted she was getting low. She'd head out to the beach behind Boy Scout Lake to collect

more this week. The beach by the trailer park had better pick-
ings, but now it was in private hands.

Murphy picked up the letter from the Department of
Corrections. Myra would find it if she left it lying around. Murphy
returned it to the envelope and put it into her pencil bag. She
opened a backpack, added a sketchbook and the pencil bag, then
set it by the door.

After dividing and freezing her dinner, reserving some chicken
for Mr. Brinkley, she made a small pot of coffee and prepared for
a long night.

———

She was standing in the center of the living room of the old
house. The coffee table lay on its side, one leg broken off. The
sofa was slashed, with stuffing spilling onto the floor. Graffiti
was spray-painted on the walls. In the center of the room was a
bare mattress leaking filler from its stained and worn ticking. A
filthy sheet covered someone dozing, tangled hair splayed across
the mattress.

Harsh breathing sounded behind her.

She turned in slow motion. The shiny knife slashed down her
face. She tried to scream but no sound came out.

Her body slammed onto the floor.

Heart ramming her ribs, Murphy opened her eyes. The chair
was on its side next to her. The cold yellow-and-white tile of Myra's
basement apartment was beneath her. Early-morning light peeked
through the blinds of one window.

She pushed off the floor, grunting, then checked the time.
She'd fallen asleep at the table and had that dream again. The
dream she thought she'd outgrown or left behind.

Bertie Fisher would be arriving in a few hours to pick her up for the trip to Ruuwaq. Good. She needed to get away from the claustrophobic basement—though flying out to look for five long-dead men on a remote island would hardly get her mind off of murder.

CHAPTER 6

Murphy hadn't asked Bertie what to wear, so she contented herself with the standard Kodiak attire of jeans, hooded sweatshirt, rain jacket, and Xtratuf rubber boots.

Promptly at eight, Bertie drove up. Murphy bolted her last gulp of coffee, grabbed her backpack and jacket, made sure no one else was lurking, and joined Bertie in the car. A cold, wet breeze stirred the trees, and the air smelled of saltwater and fish.

Bertie wore khaki pants, waterproof duck shoes, and a black tactical vest with a variety of pouches and compartments. Her name was embroidered on one pouch and *Crime Scene* on another. A hooded rainproof jacket was in the back seat. She put the sedan into gear. "You need to make copies of the drawing, right?"

"Yes. So we can each have one to write on. I'll transfer all the measurements and information to the original before turning it in to Elin."

"I like that. You're meticulous. I noticed that before."

"Before?"

"When you were measuring the house, of course."

"I'm happy you didn't call it obsessive-compulsive."

"Persnickety came to mind."

Murphy grinned. "Precise?"

"Conscientious."

As they drove, Murphy kept her head down and fiddled with the strap of her art bag. When they reached the harbor printer, she dashed inside and made several copies, then jogged back to the car. Bertie was on her cell when she returned.

"That was Richard Zinkerton, the other technician," Bertie said after hanging up. "He'll arrive later today. He's taking over the double homicide and is in a royal snit that he can't fly out to the island with us, but the weather might not hold."

"Whatever you think is best—"

"What's best is to do whatever we can before he arrives. He's a pain in the patootie." Bertie grimaced and muttered, "I can't believe they're sending him."

"Ah. I see. You're saying you could throw Richard in a lake and skim attitude for a week."

Bertie chuckled as she started the car and pulled out into the street. "Also, because it's in their jurisdiction, as you know, usually an Alaska State Trooper would go with us, but no one is available right now. They said go ahead and start the preliminary investigation and evidence collection."

Murphy nodded and slid down in her seat. The longer she kept up this pretense, the more likely she was to give herself away with a massive blunder.

"Elin told me we have to navigate a small cliff once we get to the island," Bertie said when she stopped for the traffic light. "I borrowed a telescoping ladder. Hopefully the cliff will be under eight feet. We'll be hauling a crime-scene kit, camera, sifting screen, and grid-marking kit in backpacks, assuming you don't have a lot of gear yourself."

"I travel light." Murphy patted her backpack. "Just two clipboards, a sketchpad, and some pencils and markers in a pencil bag."

"Hmm. That backpack won't hold all that we need to take. I've got an extra. Someone from the police department will be meeting us with a metal detector before we fly. We'll drag the detector up the cliff by rope."

Bertie turned on Mill Bay Road and continued to Lily Lake, a long, narrow body of water filled with floatplanes and edged with water lily pads. Houses lined one side of the lake, while commercial buildings bordered the opposite shore. They parked in a dirt lot and strolled to a small dock where the floatplane waited. A man wearing an Alaska Department of Public Safety baseball cap and blue overalls strolled from a nearby metal building. He carried a black-and-gray parka. His resemblance to the actor Sam Elliott was remarkable.

"Thought you'd be here earlier." He headed to the dock. "I don't like the look of the weather."

Murphy gazed up at the cloudless sky. Bertie shrugged. They trailed after him to a parked de Havilland Beaver.

Bertie caught up. "I'm Bertie Fisher, and you are . . . ?"

"Jake. Jake Swayne, Alaska Wildlife Trooper. If you or the kid has to go to the bathroom, do it now. Bathrooms are in that building. If not, bring your gear to the dock and get in. Kid"—he pointed at Murphy—"get in the front." He continued to prepare the plane for takeoff.

He's about as warm and fuzzy as Mr. Brinkley. Murphy returned to the rear of the car to help unload.

Bertie hauled out a pair of oversized backpacks and placed the crime-scene kit in one and the grid-marking kit and sifting screen in the other. "You can put your drawing stuff in this one." She handed a black one to Murphy. "Ya know, Murph, you're easy to work with. And you have good instincts. I take it you're not working right now because . . . ?"

"I'm on sabbatical."

"Well, if you decide to stay here instead of returning to your department, maybe you should consider applying for a job with the Alaska crime lab. We don't have a forensic artist on staff and always seem to need additional personnel." She slung the backpack over her shoulders.

"Do you have enough work for a forensic artist full-time?"

Bertie shrugged. "I think once departments learn all you can do for them, sure. And a lot of the things we do in the crime lab you could learn on the job."

"I'll consider it."

"Of course, I don't usually encourage thin people to apply." She patted her double chin. "Your type makes me feel fat. Fatter."

"If it's any consolation, I used to weigh a great deal more."

"No! I don't believe you."

"Absolutely. My thighs used to applaud my every step."

"How'd ya do it? I've tried everything but having my stomach stapled. And please don't tell me diet and exercise. Those are cuss words."

Murphy's weight-loss plan was equal parts worry, grief, and fear. She almost said so. But a patrol car parked next to them, and Joshua stepped out. He spotted them and waved.

"I brought the metal detector and two probes you asked for, Bertie." He grabbed the items from the trunk, then strolled over with the detector and a pair of T-shaped, four-foot long, yellow metal rods.

"My, oh my," Bertie muttered. "That man is eye candy and I gotta sweet tooth."

"Thank you," Murphy said to Joshua, then adjusted her glasses so her hand covered her scar. "If you, um, could put those on the plane . . . ?"

He sauntered to the dock and handed the tools to Jake, moving with the fluid grace of someone who had earned a black belt.

She expected him to leave as soon as he was done, but after he'd handed over the supplies, he returned to her.

You can't stand here forever with your hand hiding your scar. She picked up the backpack Bertie had given her and slung it over her shoulder. The weight almost tipped her sideways.

Joshua grabbed the backpack before she fell and slipped the other strap over her shoulder. She knew her face would be red but hoped it wasn't obvious.

"Hey, Murphy." He leaned against Bertie's car. "I just wanted to apologize for calling you an Explorer Scout yesterday. I didn't mean to be insulting."

"No offense taken."

"Would you allow me to take you to dinner sometime to make it up to you?"

Her gaze went to the wedding ring on his finger. "No, thank you."

He noted her glance, held up his left hand, and wiggled his fingers. "I'm not married. I wear this to discourage unwanted attention. Not that it works particularly well."

Murphy's mouth dropped open. She made an effort to shut it.

His cheeks reddened slightly. "That sounded bad."

"The answer is still no thank you." Murphy pushed past him, her hand brushing his arm. It was like shoving against a rock.

Bertie stood near the dock, eyes wide as Murphy approached. "Did he just ask you out? And did you honestly turn him down? What's the matter with you, girl?"

"As my mother used to say, he's a self-made man and loves his creator. I don't need that kind of ego."

"Ego-schmego. So what if he has cold lips from kissing mirrors.

He's prettier than you are. Go out with him and enjoy the view." Bertie clicked her tongue and watched Joshua drive off. "But hey, if you're gonna throw him back into the ocean, toss him my way."

"If you two are done ogling," the pilot said, "let's get going." Jake took the backpacks and placed them along with the other gear into the rear of the plane. "Okay now, weight's the thing in flying these planes. They're like a teeter-totter. I have to be sure the weight is balanced. You"—again he pointed at Murphy—"when you get into the front seat, be careful. It's tight, so watch out you don't bump against anything. And whatever you do, don't touch anything." He held out his hand to help her step from the dock to the pontoon. A three-step ladder led to a row of seats.

She crouched and slipped between the seats, then twisted and crawled into the right front seat. It was crowded with instruments but surprisingly roomy once she sat down. Bertie was seated in the rear of the plane.

Jake opened the door next to the pilot's seat and boarded. "Fasten your seat belt. Life vest is under the seat, except yours—"

"My name is Murphy. Not Kid."

"Right. Yours is in the door. Two exit doors in the back. Two up here. Got that?"

"Yes."

Jake pointed to the headphones. "Noisy. You'll need them. Put the microphone next to your mouth and speak loudly, as if you were mad at someone."

The headphones muted the sounds of the engine somewhat, but the roar was still substantial. Jake twisted a knob, flipped switches, and punched in some information on a screen near her. After Jake cleared his takeoff, the engine grew louder as they surged forward. The front of the plane rose. She could no longer see where they were heading. She looked out the side window. They flew past houses, and the pontoon split the water like a boat. The spray disappeared as they lifted off the lake.

They passed over a field, then the roofs of the houses, which shrank as they climbed into the cerulean-blue sky. Land disappeared and the ocean's ultramarine-turquoise shading of the Woody Island Channel gave way to Maya blue. Irregularly shaped islands covered by spruces and grass studded the liquid landscape. In the distance, plumes of water from whale spouts spritzed the ocean surface.

She pressed her hand against the plane's window. The view was breathtaking.

"I flew over the island yesterday for Elin." Jake's voice, clear in the headphones, intruded on her thoughts. Murphy reluctantly looked at him.

"The location is not much more than a speck." He twisted a knob overhead. "And you'll have to go up a cliff. I see you brought a telescoping ladder. I don't think that will be long enough." His gaze lingered on her. "Do either of you know how to climb?"

"I've done some rock climbing."

He studied her for a moment. "You'll need it for the last few feet. I have to stay with the plane. They don't pay me enough to climb cliffs. I'll send you up with a rope ladder that should cover the height of the cliff. Once you reach the top, you can attach it to make it easier to go up and down."

"Easy is good," Bertie said.

"So, just to be on the same page, what are we looking for on the island?" she asked Bertie. "Assuming the bodies are gone."

"Pretty much what you would on any case—look for anything—pieces of metal or bullets, clothing, bones, graves, unusual vegetation—"

"What?"

"Sometimes people are buried with seeds on their clothing. The seeds can sprout."

"Oh!"

"Just look for anything. I'll take photos, you'll hone the sketch, then we'll set up the grid, probe the ground, scan the area with the metal detector, and come back."

"Whoa there," Jake said. "You have about a three-hour window before the weather closes in. Do you think you'll be able to do all that?"

"Hmm. Probably not." Bertie leaned forward. "We'll photograph, measure, grid it out, and do a probe. If we find anything, we'll get the metal detector. If we run out of time, we can do that next time, along with sifting."

Murphy returned her gaze to the view. Kodiak Island was on the right, covered with a jagged, snowcapped mountain range. The land rose from the ocean in azo green broken up by tufts of spruce trees. Dark moving dots appeared on a ridge.

"Buffalo." Jake nodded in that direction. "Can't really have cattle with all the bears. Elin told me you haven't been on Kodiak all that long." Jake took out a CD and placed it into a player, then pushed a button. Music poured into Murphy's earphones, followed by a smooth male voice. "Kodiak Island is the second-largest island in the United States, ninety-nine miles long by ten to sixty miles wide. It was originally inhabited by the Sugpiaq Natives, but in 1784, Russian settlers established a presence . . ."

Bertie touched Jake on the shoulder and shook her head. He clicked off the travelogue.

Murphy glanced back at the technician. "Bertie, if we're tight for time, how about we concentrate on the area near the rockslide and work outward from there." She held up a copy of her sketch of the bodies. "Maybe we can start up here"—she pointed—"and move to here."

Bertie grinned. "All coming back to ya, isn't it? Like riding a bicycle."

Coming back? Murphy frowned. "What do you mean?" Bertie winked at her. She reached into one of the many pockets on her vest, pulled out a small notebook, and handed it to Murphy.

"What's this?" Inside was lined paper divided into two columns. One column was labeled *Facts and evidence*, the other, *Questions*.

Bertie said, "It's modeled after accident reconstruction techniques, you know, the formula S (mph) = $\sqrt{30\,(f)(d)(BE)}$ where you . . . This may not be the way you did it back in . . . ?"

Had she told Bertie Kentucky or West Virginia? "Back east."

"At our crime lab, this is what we use to keep track of the things you need to find out and the things you already know."

"But I never said I was actually looking for a j—"

"Tut, tut, never question a job offer. Now, start by putting your name on the outside of the notebook and the case number, which is 17–6–14384058, and the type of case."

She sighed and did as she was told. She hesitated over the type of case. "What would you call this? A multiple homicide? Murder-suicides? Mass suicides? Mass murder?"

"For now call it unknown deaths."

She jotted the suggestion.

"Now, inside put the date at the top of the page." Bertie pointed. "Then write everything you know about this case on this side. As you write what you know, also note what you don't know, your questions."

"What about poor Vasily's and Irina's murders? Are they connected?"

"That would go in the questions column."

Under *Facts and evidence* Murphy wrote *Five victims, all male, death ten years ago, signs of violent death, no other reports of finding bodies, had to get to island somehow—boat? Bodies removed/ disposed/buried by person or persons unknown.*

Bertie leaned over the seat and read what Murphy had written. "See? Good instincts. A natural. Keep going."

Murphy tapped the last notation. "Jake, do the Kodiak bears ever, um, swim to outlying islands? I mean, they're big enough to carry off a human body."

"Yeah, a Kodiak can weigh upward of twelve hundred pounds. They stand over nine feet tall on their hind legs, but there's no reason for any bears to go out there. It's remote and difficult to get to, and the bears like to stick to areas where they're comfortable and food is plentiful." He frowned as he looked to his right. Indigo clouds peeked up from the horizon.

Murphy returned to her list. Under *Questions* she wrote *Cause of death, what happened to bodies, what happened to transportation, Vasily and caregiver murder connected? Identity—Filipino?* Once again she spoke to Jake. "I've never really paid much attention. Does Kodiak have a large Filipino population?"

"Big enough. They have their own church. The fish canneries hire 'em."

Adding *Cannery workers?* to her questions, she wrote *Why on island?*

"There it is." Jake pointed.

Ruuwaq Island wasn't much more than a pile of rocks, cliffs, and a dot of green. Jake circled once so they could see the land from the air, then brought the plane in for a perfect landing on the water.

Murphy tucked her notebook into the pocket of her jeans.

He taxied to a tumble of boulders next to the cliff. "The rocks are slick, so watch your step. I'll be monitoring the weather. You need to be back here at"—he glanced at his watch—"sixteen hundred hours at the latest. Here." He handed Bertie a two-way radio. "If the storm comes in faster, I'll call, and you run."

Bertie took it and placed it into one of her vest pockets.

He opened his door, slid onto the pontoon, then to a rock. Grabbing a rope dangling from the wing, he maneuvered the plane into position, then helped the women out. "Hold this rope until I get your gear out." Bertie grabbed the tether while he unloaded the backpacks, probes, and metal detector. Murphy hauled them to the bottom of the small cliff.

The sea was clear and calm, gently rolling around the rocks that formed a tiny beach. The water was clear enough to see the steep-sided bottom where translucent, fist-sized jellyfish pulsed.

Murphy took stock of the cliff. A more gradual ascent to the top was to the right, but the cliff was substantially higher at that point. The rocky face in front of her was jagged, with lots of hand- and footholds. She could probably climb up without even using the telescoping ladder, but she hadn't brought enough gear to climb safely. She handed Bertie her glasses so they wouldn't fall off.

"You be careful," Bertie said. "This is an unforgiving place. Don't get so caught up in looking for clues that you lose sight of the big picture."

"I'll be careful." With Jake's and Bertie's help, she secured the ladder and scrambled up. As expected, the short climb to the top of the cliff from the ladder was relatively easy, even with slick rocks. She leaned over the precipice, gave Bertie a thumbs-up, then secured the ends of the rope and rope ladder to a large boulder. She tossed one end of the rope to Bertie, who attached the first backpack. By the time Murphy hauled up both backpacks, the probes, and the metal detector, she was soaked with sweat and the palms of her hands were raw.

Bertie crawled up last, grunting with the effort. "Please tell me my thighs are thinner after this climb." She handed Murphy her glasses.

Murphy put them on, pursed her lips, and checked Bertie from head to foot. "Yes. I'm sure you just dropped two sizes."

"Good girl. Lie to me. You'll nail the job and get a raise."

Murphy blinked at the word *lie*. Bertie didn't seem to notice. After pulling the backpack on, she took a good look at the island. The land rose to a rocky summit on the right and sloped down to a rubble of jagged rocks tumbling out to the sea. A cool, damp breeze chilled her face and whistled around the boulders. Beyond the shore, the vast ocean stretched out to the horizon, undisturbed by any sign of boats or land. Vasily had mentioned hearing gulls, but the only sound she heard was the wind.

Though the day was bright with sunshine, she could understand what Vasily meant by a coldness in the heart. This windswept piece of craggy earth was a tiny, godforsaken dot.

She shivered.

Bertie, backpack in place and metal detector strung over her shoulder, stepped next to her. "You okay?"

"Yeah, I think so. I'm just imagining Vasily finding those bodies."

"We've got work to do." Bertie patted her arm. "It's best to not have too vivid an imagination about now."

CHAPTER 7

They set off toward the rockslide and soon reached a shallow dip in the landscape.

"Elin told me what Vasily said and saw," Bertie said. "But you were there and did the drawing. You need to take the lead."

Murphy nodded and pulled out a copy of the sketch, then compared it to the land. "Okay." Her voice sounded muffled to her own ears. "The bodies would have been over there. Vasily said he didn't notice the bodies at first, so they had to have been in something like this. A slight hollow. And there"—she pointed—"is the table-shaped rock."

Her skin grew clammy. It was one thing to do a drawing of a possible homicide site. This was unmistakably real. *Am I standing on their graves?*

Bertie took off her backpack and unstrapped the metal detector, placing them on the ground. Reaching into the backpack, she pulled out a digital camera. "I'm going to start by taking photos."

"Right. Um . . . what do you want me to do? I'm used to a . . . smaller crime scene. You know, an inside-a-room kinda thing." *Lame.*

"You mentioned the rock. Take a tape measure and get the

dimensions. It's an established point of reference. You'll be using the Cartesian coordinate system. Once you have the rock measurement, starting at that corner"—Bertie pointed—"use a compass and establish a line going north—"

"Line?"

"Just fasten the dumb end of the tape measure to the ground at that corner. Walk straight north, unwinding the tape as you go. When you reach the end, fasten that end of the tape measure to the ground. We now have a north-south line."

"Oh yes, of course."

"That line will help us establish anything we recover based on an x-axis and a y-axis measurement. We'll measure outward from the north-south line at a 90-degree angle. We'll need two sets of measurements for each item we find. For example, if we find a gun over here"—Bertie walked over to a small rock—"it would be 5'6" north and 4'8" east."

She nodded. "Yes. I'm used to lasers and stuff like that."

"We have a few, but mostly we have budget cuts. Alaska doesn't have income tax or sales tax, and the main industry, petroleum, is in the toilet. I have to share with the other crime-scene team members, and old or cold cases get leftovers. You'll find the compass and tape measure in the kit in your backpack."

While Bertie took photographs, Murphy approached the table-shaped rock. The surface was slate gray on three sides with an undercut fourth side that looked black. As she measured the undercut, a smear of black appeared on her hand. Dropping to her knees, she examined the rock's surface, then the moss-covered ground next to it.

"Whatcha got?" Bertie squatted next to her.

She showed her hand. "This came from that surface."

Bertie ran her fingers over the ground in front of them and

came up with a gray-black piece of what looked like bone. "All right, now that's what I'm talking about. Bring me a probe."

She retrieved one of the T-shaped metal rods. By the time she returned, Bertie had poked a small, cadmium-yellow flag into the spot where she'd found the bone, placed a scale next to the bone, and taken photographs. She took the probe from Murphy and shoved it into the ground. It stopped after four inches. "Feels like solid rock." She tried several more spots, all with the same results. "Well, we know they didn't bury the bodies. At least not intact."

Murphy tried to smile. Her mouth felt stiff. Was the remoteness of the island ratcheting up her unease, or the idea of finding body parts?

"Let me fiddle around here for a bit, take more photos." Bertie waved her arms. "Get some earth samples, maybe do a bit of digging. You can work the metal detector." She stood with a grunt, picked up the machine, and showed Murphy how it worked. "Walk in a straight line, as if you were mowing a lawn, moving back and forth slowly." She pointed. "Begin over there. When you reach the end of the depression, move over a few feet and repeat going the other way. Don't just be watching the indicator. Look at the ground. Watch for plastics like buttons, an indication the ground's been disturbed—"

"Bones?"

"Bones. Yell if you find anything, and stay put. We'll mark it, measure, and collect it."

Murphy walked to the starting point, near the end of the tape measure, and started moving forward. She'd only gone a few steps when the metal detector beeped. "Got something!"

Bertie converged on her location, poked a flag into the ground, placed an evidence ruler next to the object, and took a photo. She then held it up. "It looks like a belt buckle."

Murphy took the rusty object from Bertie. "It's really small for a belt. Maybe a small dog's collar?"

"Yeah, good call, Murph." Bertie pulled out an evidence bag from a pocket and handed it to her. "Label it and drop the buckle inside. Note on your chart what you found. When you're done with the metal detector, you can come back and measure the location."

The sun dimmed as a cloud passed in front of it, and a blast of cold wind blew around them.

She zipped up her coat, but the cold stayed inside.

Bertie glanced up and pulled up her collar. "We'd better hurry. I've tagged a few more things by the rock. If you'd go over and measure those flags, I'll take over the metal detector. 'Kay?"

"Sure." Murphy took out a clipboard, attached a piece of gridded paper to it, and sat on the ground near the table rock. Four cheerful yellow flags marked a three-foot-square area.

Clouds continued to build. The temperature dropped. Her ears were getting cold and her nose ran.

The metal detector let out a warbling beep. "Murph?"

Something in Bertie's voice gave her goose pimples. She stood. "What?"

"Listen to this. It's going crazy." Bertie pointed to the meter on the metal detector.

She trotted over. "What does it mean?"

Bertie turned in a small circle. The meter dropped down, then shot back up when she returned to the spot. "I'm going to walk along the rockslide." Bertie started forward and she followed. The meter remained high.

Bertie stopped. "There's a large hunk of metal behind that slide. Large and fairly straight."

"Like a building? Or a boat?"

"If it's a boat," Bertie said, "and metal, it probably isn't a fishing boat, as they tend to be wood. Maybe something from World War II?"

"What?" she asked.

"The Japanese invaded the Aleutian Islands in 1942."

"I think I read something about that, but Kodiak isn't in the Aleutians."

"Have you visited Fort Abercrombie?"

She shrugged. "No."

"That was a military reservation put in to guard the naval installation on Kodiak. They call all this 'the forgotten war.' There's leftover bits and pieces all over." Bertie paused at the end of the slide. "Nothing registering here, so if it is a boat, it's roughly thirty-five to forty feet long."

A drop of rain plopped into Murphy's hair. She pulled up the hood of her waterproof jacket and stared down the length of the rock fall. The section farthest from the water had the larger boulders. The segment nearest the water had smaller rocks but seemed to have piled up higher. It did appear as if the slide was remarkably uniform. "Let's see what we can find in that end." She pointed to the smaller boulders on her left.

The women moved to the end of the slide nearest the water.

Bertie's radio squawked. "Bertie? Jake here. You need to finish up and get moving. Storm's moving in fast. Over."

"Will do. Over." As if to emphasize his words, the sun disappeared completely behind the clouds. "Let's hurry!"

They'd reached the end of the slide, and Murphy trotted ahead so she could see it clearly. Methodically she examined each section. The jagged rocks were slate gray, black, and dark sepia in color, and ranged in size from baseballs to large stability balls. She was about to give up when one shape took form. The stones seemed vaguely rectangular and about five feet up. Gingerly she climbed up the slide.

"Murph, be careful up there. Those rocks are slick."

She climbed farther. What had looked like a couple of very black rocks was an opening. "I think I found something."

"Don't risk it, girl. Come on down."

One by one, Murphy removed some of the loose stones. "Look."

"I don't want to look. I want to get back to the floatplane."

Sticking her head into the opening, she waited until her eyes adjusted. "Pitch black." She looked back down at Bertie. "Do you have a flashlight?"

Bertie glanced toward the cliff, then back at her. "Oh, all right. One quick peek, then we run." Gingerly Bertie clambered up the rocks to her. "Here." She pulled a small flashlight from one of her vest pockets.

Murphy snatched it up and turned it on.

Bertie glanced around again. "Just be sure you—"

She crawled through the opening.

CHAPTER 8

Murphy cleared the opening, then twisted around until her feet were hanging down. She played the flashlight around the space. The ground was about five feet below, accessible by sliding down the rocks.

She clenched her jaw. *There's nothing here to be afraid of.*

The sharp stones ripped her jeans and tore at her raw hands. Reaching the floor, she swung the light around the space. "This is a building," she called to Bertie. "You can come down." *Please come down.*

"I'm not sure I'll fit through the opening."

"Sure you will. Just watch out for sharp stones."

While Bertie wiggled through, Murphy examined the space. The room was square, about fifteen by fifteen feet with curving walls. The opening Bertie was crawling through was a ventilation opening over a door. Opposite was a partial wall destroyed by the slide. The ceiling bowed downward, with rotting wood sagging under rusting corrugated sheets of metal. The space reeked of moldy wood and stagnant water from the leaky roof.

Something rustled in the corner.

Murphy spun her flashlight and illuminated a rat. "Yaaaahhhh!"

"Ugh." Bertie joined her on the ground. "Nasty things, rats."

Reaching into a pocket of her vest, she pulled out a set of nitrile gloves. "Here. Put these on before you touch anything."

Murphy took the gloves and put them on, then threw a rock at the rat.

The stone landed solidly in the rodent's side. It squealed and scurried behind an overturned table.

"Nice shot." Bertie's light followed the rat, then followed the curving walls to the ceiling, eight feet from their heads. "What am I looking at? Submarine . . . ?"

"It's a Quonset hut."

"Quonset hut?" Bertie asked. "As in World War II housing?"

"Housing, hospitals, dining halls, you name it. These were a prefabricated building developed before the start of the war. I bet I could even figure out when." She noted Bertie's expression. "Oh, sorry, when I studied art, I loved art history and architecture. Minored in architecture in my undergraduate degree. Transepts, naves, flying buttresses, all that. And even the lowly Quonset hut."

"And here I thought studying fly larvae was strange." Bertie's light paused at a lockbox on the floor. She bent to examine it.

Murphy's fingers grew cold in the dank interior. She stuffed them in her pocket. "What do you make of finding a building dating from the forties, which had to have been buried for at least ten years or Vasily would have seen it, and five dead men—"

"Maybe cremated." Bertie stood. "The possible bone shard I found could have been burned."

"—possibly cremated, on an island that nobody's heard of?" She glanced at Bertie.

Bertie shrugged. "I have no idea what the story is here, but I'd say there's more than enough going on to warrant a full investigation. The ABI will want to get in on this."

"The Alaska Bureau of Investigation? You think it's that type of crime?"

Bertie didn't answer. She held up the box she'd been inspecting and opened it so Murphy could see. Wet paper pulp. "Well, that's a disappointment. Here, take the camera and get some photos." Bertie handed over the digital camera, then dumped the water from the lockbox. On the bottom, rust enveloped a rectangle of metal. Bertie waited until she took a photo, then pried up the metal and stuck it in an evidence pouch. "Looks like a campaign medal. Your theory of this being from the forties looks good."

A round canister split along the seam was next to the box. Inside, shattered glass gleamed in the light. Murphy took digitals of the canister, then shone the light toward the far wall. Behind an overturned single bedspring, the flashlight lit up a white piece of driftwood. She stepped closer. Not a piece of wood. A bone.

Sweat dampened her back. "Bertie." It came out a whisper. She tried again. "Bertie."

Bertie's flashlight joined hers as the woman came up next to her.

Against the wall, under wisps of decaying fabric, was a body. The cranium and mandible were separate but near each other. Bertie pulled the bed away, then rummaged through her pockets until she pulled out an L-shaped metric scale and placed it next to the cranium. "Murph, get a bunch of photographs of this."

"Is it female?" Murphy's voice trembled. Could it be her sister? "Huh?"

"Is that a female body?"

"Nah. I don't think so. I'm not an anthropologist, but that's a pretty developed ridge brow."

Murphy's hands shook. She tried to hold the camera steady. After several digitals of the skull, Bertie moved the scale to the remains of a shirt. An angular metal object lay on the chest cavity. She aimed the camera, but an error code appeared on the LCD screen.

"Bertie! Come in. Over."

She jumped at the sound of Jake's muffled voice. Bertie removed the two-way radio from her vest. "This is Bertie. Over."

Static followed. Bertie moved closer to the opening. "This is Bertie. Do you read?"

Murphy tried the camera again, then took out her cell phone and snapped a few photos of the skull and metal object.

"Imperative you return to plane immediately! Weather's in the toilet. Over."

"Return to plane. Roger." Bertie threw the radio and scale into her vest pockets. "Let's boogie out of here."

Heart pounding, Murphy returned her cell to her pocket, wrapped the camera strap around her neck, and spun toward the opening. It was almost black.

"Let's go! Let's go!" Bertie scrambled up the tumbled rocks and wiggled through the opening.

Just before Murphy climbed out, she used the light to pan the room one last time, committing the scene to memory. Once outside, freezing wind and stinging rain sprayed her face. The sky was deep gray, and the frothing ocean slammed against the rocks.

They ran.

"The equipment!" Murphy yelled.

"Leave it!"

Frigid blasts flattened the sparse grasses. Her eyes burned, nose ran, and fingers stiffened from the cutting cold. Bertie was ahead, charging across the tiny island as fast as they could run.

Could Jake take off in this weather? She shoved the doubt out of her mind. Her ragged breath was as much fear as exhaustion. They reached the rope ladder. Jake was below, frantically waving them down. She grabbed Bertie's arm and leaned close so Bertie could hear over the wind and rain. "I'll go down first so I can steady the ladder, then you." She didn't wait for Bertie to acknowledge. She grabbed the ladder and swung down. The wind whipped and tugged at her. Her hands could barely feel the rope. She dropped the final few feet, holding on to keep her balance, then clutched the rungs to steady the ladder.

Bertie started climbing down.

One side of the rope snapped.

Oh no! Please . . .

Bertie clung to one rung, legs dangling free. Slowly her white-knuckled grip loosened. Her heavy body swung in the wind.

Murphy gripped her end of the ladder. She tried to steady it. "Hold on, Bertie!"

Bertie's left hand slipped. She swung in a circle, frantically grabbing for the rope.

A gust of wind jerked the ladder from Murphy, smashing it against the cliff.

Bertie plunged backward.

Murphy lurched for her.

Bertie's body crashed to the rocks.

Adrenaline surged through Murphy. Her mouth wouldn't work. She knelt and checked for a pulse. The wind whipped spray across her face. Someone grabbed her and pulled. She screamed and pulled away.

"Easy! It's just me," Jake said. "Is she still alive?"

"I think so." Bertie's unconscious body stretched across the rocks. Murphy whipped off her coat and covered her. "Call for help! We need a rescue—"

"No time and they're too far away." Jake cursed and returned to the plane.

Alive or dead, she can't stay here. My moving her will probably kill her.

Not getting her to the plane will kill her.

Jake returned, bent down, and lifted Bertie's shoulders. "Grab her legs."

She grasped Bertie's legs and struggled to stand. Step by step, they slowly crossed the rain-slicked rocks to the plane.

Jake had flattened two of the seats, forming a bed between the second and third row. They eased Bertie's broken body onto the seats, then Murphy crawled in.

Jake started the engines before she could snap her seat belt. She barely got Bertie strapped in before he yelled, "Hang on. We'll be lucky if we make it."

The sea buckled and surged under the pontoons. He let out full throttle, pulling up and off the waves as fast as he could. An updraft caught the wings and shot them up, leaving her stomach far below. She struggled to keep Bertie's body from moving. Her face was sheet-white, making her freckles stand out like a pointillist painting. Her skin was clammy. Murphy tucked her own coat around her.

The plane bucked like an unbroken horse. She braced Bertie with one arm and clung to the seat with the other. Vomit burned her throat. Her head pounded. Her brain looped the words *pleaseGodpleaseGodpleaseGod.*

Jake radioed their position and requested an ambulance. When he hung up, he crossed himself, using three fingers and moving from right to left shoulder.

She would have felt a whole lot better if he'd started singing "Oh, What a Beautiful Morning."

Jake skimmed across the roofs of houses before landing hard. She bit her tongue and tasted blood.

An ambulance waited near the dock, lights flashing. Next to the ambulance was Detective Olsson, white-blond hair whipping in the wind. She rushed to the plane as soon as it was close enough, helping Murphy through the door and out of the way of the two EMTs poised to help Bertie.

She wanted to help, but Elin pulled her aside. "What happened?"she asked.

"Bertie fell. I need to go with her to the hospital." The wind snatched the words from her mouth.

"Let the EMTs do their job." Elin almost had to shout. "They're superbly trained. I'll drive you over and you can tell me on the way."

She wanted to argue, to be with her newly minted friend, but Elin was right. About all she could do at this point was wring her hands and cry. Spats of icy rain pelted her face. She shivered uncontrollably.

The medical team shifted Bertie to a spinal board. Carefully they maneuvered her from the plane to a waiting gurney, then to the back of the ambulance.

Blinking rapidly, Murphy tried to swallow past the lump in her throat. *I did this. I didn't fasten the rope ladder well enough. It's my fault. And if she dies . . .* She shoved down the thought.

Jake brought her coat over. The lining held a smear of blood. Bertie's blood. Murphy didn't want to put it on, but the rain was steady now and she was freezing.

"Come on." Elin put a hand on Murphy's shoulder and propelled her to the SUV. Once inside, she started the car, turned up the heater, then focused on Murphy. "You said Bertie fell. How?"

"The . . . um . . ." She cleared her throat. "The rope ladder broke. I went first, then Bertie. She fell on the rocks."

Elin put the car into gear, then pulled out, following the ambulance. They'd gone a short distance when she asked, "Did you find anything?"

"Yes. Quite a lot." She told Elin about the burned area, the Quonset hut, and the skeleton.

"So you think there were actually six people on the island?"

The question turned her attention to something besides Bertie's fate. "Um. Well." She thought about the lists Bertie had her write in the small notebook still in her pocket. She pulled it out. "I'll have to add to this, but if we look at what we actually know, we are left with Vasily reporting five bodies. We found a body in the buried structure, and signs that some bodies may have been burned."

Elin bit her lip. "We can speculate that whoever destroyed the bodies may have put one into the Quonset hut."

"But Vasily didn't report the hut, only the rockslide."

"Right. Maybe one hid in the Quonset hut . . . and . . . got stuck?"

She shrugged. "Died at the same time but whoever burned the bodies didn't find his? Who knows?"

Elin drove in silence for a time before saying, "There's no doubt the ABI will want to get involved at this point. The second crime-scene technician arrived, and I have him booked into a motel downtown."

"Bertie didn't seem to like him much."

"He gets the job done."

The ambulance had pulled far ahead of them, lights flashing and siren blaring. Wind and rain gusted against the car.

Opening and closing her hands, Murphy mentally urged Elin to speed up.

Elin glanced over. "Don't worry, we'll get to the hospital in plenty of time." She returned her gaze to the road. "Is that Bertie's camera?"

She'd forgotten she still had it. She pulled the strap over her head. "Sorry, yes. Unfortunately we got off the island so fast we left the backpacks, probes, pretty much everything. There are a few pieces of evidence in Bertie's vest."

"I'll get those from the hospital. We'll pick up everything else when the weather allows."

"Okay."

"I've been thinking about the timing on all this," Elin said. "Vasily found the bodies very soon after death, say within a day or two. According to what you learned, someone else found the bodies and deliberately burned them. All but one, at any rate." She tapped the steering wheel with a manicured nail.

"What if Vasily burned them?"

"We can't rule that out. Someone didn't want them found."

"But short of climbing up that cliff, who would know—"

"Spotters." Elin nodded. "It had to be a spotter."

"What's a spotter?"

"A pilot in a small plane. Jake was a spotter once. It's impossible for skippers to see fish from their boat's wheelhouse, so they hire spotters. In the case of herring, for example, the fishermen form an association, called a combine, to jointly hire the plane and radio the location. These planes are flying up to fifty miles along the coastline, and they're flying quite low. Five bodies on that bare island would be easy for a spotter to see."

"I don't get the connection between the death of five people, a pilot seeing the bodies and burning them, and a skeleton in a Quonset hut."

"Nor do I." A particularly strong gust rocked the car. "And we won't be able to get any answers until this storm passes."

CHAPTER 9

Elin and Murphy parked in front of the salmon-colored hospital, got out, and entered. An older woman manning the information desk wordlessly pointed toward a door marked No Admittance. Beyond that was another small waiting room. They took seats in matching tweed chairs. Shortly a doctor in pale-blue scrubs and wearing a Disney-patterned bandanna on his head entered. "Elin. Good to see you. You're here about the crime-scene technician, I assume."

Elin nodded. Murphy stood, fighting fear.

"She's on her way to surgery." He glanced at his watch. "She had several broken bones and a conk on her head. We'll know more . . ." He tugged a beeping pager out of his pocket. "Okay, gotta run. I'll get back to you."

Elin's cell phone started to ring, and she answered. "Detective Olsson." She listened for a few moments. "Okay, I'll be there in ten." She disconnected and turned to Murphy. "I need to go. Need a ride?"

"No. I'll stay."

"Give me a call when you want to head home. Either I'll pick you up or someone from the department will."

"Thanks."

She couldn't sit still. She paced. Seven steps from the door to the tweed chair. Seven steps back. The clock on the wall seemed to have stopped. Seven steps. Her watch was equally slow. Seven steps. Bertie was the closest thing to a friend she'd had in years, and now she was fighting for her life. And it hurt. A big chunk of clay had lodged in Murphy's chest. Would Bertie be yet another loss?

When a drunk driver killed Murphy's parents, she and her sister were only eighteen. They had each other and that had been enough. At least for Murphy. Dallas had been the outgoing one, the social one, who needed more.

Murphy heard her sister's voice in her head.

Come on, just do this one teeny thing for me . . .

She shook her head, then took off her coat and hung it on a hook. A small bookshelf held coffee in a thermos along with cups, creamer, sugar, and stir sticks. A pen and paper were on the shelf underneath with a package of highlighter pens. Books lined the third shelf. She made a cup of coffee. When she emptied the powdered creamer on the top, it floated in a clump. The coffee was cold. She dumped the cup into the trash and resumed pacing.

An older Native woman wearing a black turtleneck, jeans, and a purple down coat entered with a small girl. The woman's gray hair was pulled back from her round face, and a pair of oversize brown glasses perched on her short nose. The woman sat on the tweed chair as if her legs could no longer hold her weight. She stared blankly at the wall. Her clothing smelled of saltwater and wood smoke.

Her legs took up two of Murphy's steps. Murphy picked up a piece of paper and a pen from the shelf, then sat.

The little girl tugged at the old woman's arm. "Grandma! Grandma! I'm hungry. I want to go home. Grandma, I want my mommy. Grandma!"

The last *grandma* was a shriek.

The woman stared at the child and gently took hold of her arm.

The shrieking continued.

The wail pounded Murphy's ears and ran down her spine. She ground her teeth. She picked up the pen and placed the piece of paper on the table. "I feel like looking at a unicorn," she said over the ruckus.

The child pulled away from her grandmother, preparing for a full-scale meltdown.

Murphy sketched a unicorn and turned it toward the little girl. "How about you? Do you like unicorns?"

The little girl stopped shrieking and peered at the drawing.

"Would you like to color the unicorn?" Murphy stood, retrieved the highlighters, and placed them on the coffee table next to the drawing.

The little girl pounced on the sketch and started coloring.

Swiftly Murphy sketched a princess, chicken, dog, castle, and pony. The child snatched each drawing and continued to color.

"Bless you." The woman held out her hand for Murphy to shake. "My daughter was in a car accident. I just rushed over here with my granddaughter. I didn't think to bring her something to do. I'm Vesper."

"Murphy Andersen." They shook hands.

Vesper pulled out a crumpled piece of paper from her purse, wrote something on it, then handed it to Murphy. Her name and phone number. "I owe you a big favor."

"It was nothing." *Just saving my own sanity.* But Murphy folded the paper into her jeans.

"Ha! That's where you're wrong." Vesper gave her a top-to-bottom once-over. "You're not as young as you look, are you?"

"You're one of the first to figure that out."

"Your face and body are childlike, but you have old eyes. And you are here . . . ?"

"Helping my friend Bertie on a case. She fell." The words *my friend* slipped out. They sounded strange.

"A case? You mean the two people killed yesterday?"

Murphy blinked. "How did you know about that?"

"Kodiak is a small town at heart, and it was all over the news. Wait a minute. Yes, I saw your photo."

"You . . . saw my photograph?"

"In the newspaper." Vesper's face crinkled in a smile.

Her heart raced. There was no way Clinton Hunter could have seen it. Was there? "Ah, well, I'm just helping out."

"Here in Kodiak?"

"On Ruuwaq Island."

The woman straightened. "Where did you say?"

"Ruuwaq Island."

"There's a name I haven't heard in a long time. Uncle's father knew that island." Her gaze drifted toward the ceiling and grew distant. She sighed. "I wish you could have met him. Fascinating life—" Vesper blinked and stared at her. "You're a soul searcher."

"A what?"

A nurse stepped into the room. Both of them turned.

"Vesper Amason?" The nurse looked back and forth between Vesper and Murphy.

"Yes?" the older woman said. Her hand clamped onto her coat, white knuckles showing.

"Mrs. Amason, your daughter will be fine. You can see her now." The nurse opened the door wider and stood to one side.

"Wait." Murphy reached for the other woman. "Before you go, Vesper, what's a soul searcher?"

"We'll talk later. You have my phone number." Vesper took her granddaughter's hand and left.

"Excuse me?" she said to the nurse before the woman could leave. "Do you know anything about Bertie, um, Bertie Fisher?"

"Your mother?"

That's right, stupid HIPAA laws. "Yes." The lie slipped out smoothly.

"I believe she's still in surgery." The nurse quietly closed the door.

The lump in her throat made swallowing impossible. She jumped to her feet and moved to the window, lifting her chin to keep the tears from burning down her cheeks. *Please, God, please spare Bertie. If You need someone, take me.*

God didn't answer. The clock continued to crawl through the seconds, minutes, then hours. She paced and tried to ignore the hollow feeling in her stomach.

Her phone rang. "Hello?"

"Hi, Murphy, it's Elin. Any word?"

"Not yet. I'm staying here until I do hear."

"Give me a call, no matter what time, okay?"

"Yeah. Thanks." She disconnected. More pacing. Maybe she should go outside? Get fresh air. No. What if the doctor came?

The doctor did finally arrive, still wearing the Disney bandanna, at 4:42 a.m. His eyes were red-rimmed and surrounded in purple, his skin pale. He stared at her.

Now her legs couldn't support her weight. She dropped to the chair. "Is she . . ."

"The nurse said Bertie is your mother. I'm sorry. I didn't realize. She's in intensive care. It was touch-and-go there for a bit. Once she's stabilized, we'll transport her to Anchorage. Is there someone we can call for you? Your dad?"

"No. I'll go—"

"I'm sorry. You won't be able to travel with her. You'll have to book a commercial flight or private plane."

"Can . . . can I see her?"

"Just for a few moments."

She followed the doctor to the ICU, a two-bed facility. Bertie was hardly recognizable under the bandages, tubes, and wires. She touched Bertie's hand. "Ah, Bertie, you can't leave me. You're the first friend I've had in a long, long time." *When are you going to learn not to let people get close? There's so much less pain when you keep life simple.*

A nurse moved next to her, checked Bertie's IV, and said, "Get some sleep. Leave your number at the nurses' station and we'll call you if there are any changes."

Nodding, she did as the nurse said, then returned to the small lobby and picked up her coat. Before putting it on, she took out the notebook Bertie had given her and opened it. Finding a clean page, she transferred Vesper Amason's name and phone number from the slip of paper. Underneath she wrote *Soul searcher?*

Elin had told her to call when she needed a ride home, but somehow calling before 5:30 in the morning seemed rude. She didn't live that far away. And it would already be light out. She could walk. After putting on her coat, she paused.

Her house keys were with her art bag in Bertie's rental car on Lily Lake. She'd have to wake Myra and endure a lecture.

She headed outside.

The raging storm from the day before had passed, replaced now with a gray-white fog bank that cloaked the landscape. Five steps from the medical center's front door, she couldn't see the building or the cars parked in front of her. Her footsteps were muffled in the foggy stillness. The air was clammy and penetrated her clothing. She shivered.

Clack, clack, clack.

She stopped.

Clack. The footsteps also ceased. Someone wearing hard-soled shoes was on her right. Someone who paused when she did.

Again she moved forward, this time as silently as she could.

Clack, clack, clack. The steps grew closer.

She ran back to the hospital, backing away from the door once inside. No one followed her in.

She dialed Elin's number.

"Elin Olsson." The woman's voice held no sign of being awakened.

"Murphy here. I'm sorry to disturb you, but could I get a ride? There's . . . it's foggy."

"Someone will be there soon."

She took a seat where she could see all the doors.

A rusted truck, windows shattered, sat up on blocks on an overgrown lawn. The house was barely discernible in the overgrown trees surrounding it. Evil hissed from the door . . .

She jerked her head up. The hissing came from the hospital doors. She'd drifted off to sleep.

Joshua, dressed now in civilian clothing, glanced around the room and spotted her. He strolled over. "Need a ride?"

"I think Elin is arranging—"

"Yep. I'm it. Shall we go?"

She reluctantly untangled her legs, stood, and immediately sat back down. Her foot had gone to sleep. "Sorry."

He held out his hand.

She stared at it for a moment before taking it. At his touch, a ripple ran up her spine. She let go as soon as her feet could hold her weight. "Thank you," she said stiffly.

They left the hospital, moving through the dense fog to an older silver Toyota pickup. The only footsteps she heard were theirs. Whoever had been outside, he wasn't following her now.

He unlocked the passenger side door and held it open for her. "Thank you," she said again, this time without the frosty overtones.

"You live on Mission Lake?" He started the truck.

"Yes."

"One of those big houses facing the sound?"

"Hardly. One of those rusty trailer houses facing the lake."

He pulled out of the lot, his truck crawling through the fog. The early-morning air smelled of campfire and salt. The odor of burning wood grew stronger. An officer materialized on the side of the road, waving a light. Joshua rolled down the window. "Hey, Steve, what's up?"

"House fire. Gotta turn around. Road's blocked."

Her stomach clenched. She grabbed the door and jumped out. Steve called to her, but she raced ahead.

Pungent smoke filled the air. Flashing lights tinted the fog with yellow, red, and white. A crackling roar, punctuated by men yelling, split the normally peaceful morning air.

She jerked to a stop beside a firetruck.

Myra's house was a raging inferno.

CHAPTER 10

A fireman grabbed Murphy's arm and propelled her away. "You need to stay back!"

"I live there."

He let go of her arm. "Come with me." He led her over to a fireman directing the action. "Chief. This kid says she lives there."

The chief turned to her. "Who else lives there?"

"Myra Hampton. She lives upstairs."

"Your mom?"

"My landlady."

He took a closer look at her face. "Okay. I'll need to talk to you. Tom, put her in my SUV."

"Wait!" She took a deep breath of smoky air. "Where's Myra?"

The chief wouldn't meet her gaze. "We're not sure. Fire's too hot. Please wait for me in my rig."

"There was a cat. A yellow cat named Mr. Brinkley—"

The fireman jerked his thumb. A neighbor sat in her car parked on the street, holding Mr. Brinkley.

Something crashed.

Murphy flinched and looked at the inferno. The roof had caved in. Firefighters had been training their hoses on the houses on either side of the blaze. They now directed the sprays of water on the gutted shell of Myra's trailer. The stench of burned plastic, wood, and fabric filled the air.

Without knowing how, she found herself in the back seat of an SUV. All her painting and jewelry-making supplies were gone, along with the only photograph of her sister. She literally had only the clothes on her back. She wrapped her arms around her shoulders.

Selfish thinking. Myra could very well have lost her life, and you're fussing about a few brushes and beads.

Had her landlady fallen asleep with a cigarette?

Or had Hunter seen the photo in the paper and found her?

A shudder ripped through her. She slid down in the seat, then peered around at the activity.

Don't be silly. How would he have found her so fast?

Easy. He had family. They believed he was innocent, framed by the police and her. He'd head straight to their house, ask for money, probably borrow his brother's driver's license.

I have no place to go. No money. No identity. She pictured Joshua's strong arm around her, protecting her.

No. She had to be her own strength, tend to her own life and lies. Forming bonds with people like Bertie and Joshua would only keep her from what she was here to do.

More people arrived to watch the fire. They drifted in and out of the swirling fog like apparitions. She recognized a few. The woman who lived next door. An older man who walked his basset hound past the house every day. She spotted Joshua looking around, probably for her. There was Elin.

Murphy jumped from the car and raced to the detective. "Elin!"

"Murphy! You're safe! When the call went out on the fire, I recognized your address. How about your landlord?"

"I don't know."

Elin folded her arms and stared at the fire. "Any ideas on how the fire started?"

"Ah, well, Myra was a chain smoker."

Elin nodded. "Be sure you tell the investigator that. And I still need to sit down with you and get everything that happened on Ruuwaq." Her phone rang. "Detective Olsson. Yeah, I'm at the fire now. How did you hear about it?" She listened for a moment, her gaze moving toward the Russian Orthodox cross on the house across the street. "I suspect she will. Let me ask." She looked at Murphy. "Where will you be staying?"

"I don't know. I'll find someplace."

Elin spoke into the phone. "No. She could use your help."

"I'll be fine." Murphy swallowed hard. "Really."

Elin raised her eyebrows at Murphy but spoke into the phone. "Salmon Run Lodge? Of course I know it. I go there often, but that's way out of our budget—" She listened another moment. "Can you get hold of him ASAP and get back to me? It needs to be a live-in position. Oh, that's good. Thanks." She disconnected. "I know you mentioned you're 'on sabbatical.'" Her fingers made air quotes. "But I suspect you're not independently wealthy or you wouldn't be living under a trailer, riding a bike, or wearing the wrong size clothes."

Murphy winced. "Maybe 'between jobs' would have been a better choice of words."

"And Kodiak isn't the cheapest place to live—" Elin's phone rang and she answered it. "Yeah. Okay. I'll ask." Elin looked at her. "I'm sorry I can't offer you a position on the force, but can you wait tables, clean, and mix drinks?"

What choice do I have? At least I'd be out of sight. "Where is this lodge?"

"What lodge?" Joshua stepped next to Elin.

"Salmon Run Resort," Elin said. "Murphy needs a place to stay and a temporary job."

He turned to her. "It's not a remote resort. Big place northeast of town. You can actually drive there."

"In that case . . ." She nodded at Elin. "Yes on tables and cleaning. As for bartending, I can open a bottle of wine and pour a beer."

Elin returned to her cell. "Yes. We'll be there in a little bit." She waved her hand at the fire chief. He raced over. "Chief, Detective Wright will be working with you on this. I'm taking Murphy here out to Salmon Run Lodge. She'll be staying there should anyone need to get any information from her."

"Gotcha. Thanks." He turned back to the fire.

"I can drive her over," Joshua said.

Her heart sped up slightly. She tried not to look at him.

"Bad idea," Elin said sharply, then smiled at him. "It's almost time for breakfast. Have you ever had one of their cinnamon rolls?" Elin left Joshua behind and led Murphy through the tangle of emergency vehicles that loomed out of the fog.

"Elin, um, Joshua claims he isn't married, but he wears a ring . . ."

"So you noticed. And he's noticed you." Elin's gaze slid down Murphy's body. "Yes, he would notice." Her voice was barely above a whisper. She cleared her throat. "You'd bring out the white knight in him. He is a twelve on the one-to-ten hunky scale. And he's a widower." Elin didn't speak for a few moments, then nodded her head as if agreeing on something. "He thinks it's the ring that keeps women at bay, but they run like jackrabbits when they find out part two."

"What's part two?"

"Baggage."

"Baggage?"

"He comes with four boys."

Elin grinned wickedly. "Still interested?"

"I never said I was interested—"

"Right." Elin stopped in front of her SUV. "Hop in."

Salmon Run Lodge, as it turned out, wasn't that far from downtown Kodiak, but it took almost an hour to drive there. They pulled up to what looked like a giant log house, surrounded in white cotton-candy fog, with a spacious porch spanning the front. The entrance featured a pair of oversized carved doors. Above, on the second floor, eight dormers punctuated the log siding.

"It's smaller than I expected," Murphy confessed.

"This is just the family home. The main lodge is behind those trees."

They parked on the side of the building and walked to the front door, which opened into a well-appointed living room with a log bar at the end. An extra-wide staircase leading to the second floor partially separated the living area from the spacious dining area on the right. The air was fragrant with the smell of cinnamon and baking bread.

A craggy-faced man somewhere on the far side of sixty sat in a wheelchair by the window, reading a book. He'd parted his silver hair on the side and combed it backward off his face. His jaw was wide, with a firm chin. A light-blue button-down collar peeked from the neck of his cream-colored fisherman sweater. A red-plaid blanket covered his legs. Lying next to him, a large black Labrador raised his head, thumped his tail a few times on the floor, then went back to sleep.

The man closed the book at their appearance, marking his place with a bookmark. "Good to see you again, Elin." He looked at Murphy. "Welcome to Salmon Run Lodge." His deep voice was well modulated. "I'm Denali Stewart, the owner. You must be the new help. We seldom have openings for staff. Working here is quite an honor."

"Yes. Thank you for the job. I'm Murphy Andersen."

"Murphy, first things first. You're not in any trouble, are you? We have an unstained history and a reputation to uphold."

"No, sir. I just need a job and a place to stay." She tucked her hand behind her back and crossed her fingers.

Denali stared at her for a moment, then looked at Elin. "The cinnamon rolls are out of the oven and Olga has coffee made." His eyes crinkled in humor. "You don't have to be polite. Go on in and help yourself. I'll talk a bit more to Murphy here."

Elin didn't wait for more encouragement. She headed toward the dining room.

Denali waited until she disappeared behind a door. "How old are you, Murphy? If you're not old enough to serve drinks, I may have to rethink my offer."

"I'm thirty-one."

He snorted. "That's the problem with getting old. Everyone looks like a kid."

"You're not the first to think I'm younger than I am." She removed her glasses so he could see her face.

"My mother looked young. That's her in the photos in the dining room." He rolled across the floor, then nodded toward the rear wall.

She moved to where she could see the collection of old photos of Alaskan scenes printed on canvas and framed images of family members. A beautifully mounted Distinguished Service Medal rested in the center of the display. The array had an intimate feel to it. Nearby was an intricate stained glass door leading to an office.

Denali rolled closer and pointed to a photograph of a handsome man. "That's the only picture I have of my dad, Paul Stewart." The photograph was oddly formatted, with his father almost on the edge and a wide space beside him. He had light-colored hair with wide shoulders and slender hips. Before she could ask, he said, "Apparently part of the photograph was mildewed, according to my mother, and had to be cut away."

Another photograph showed a much younger, black-haired Denali in front of a floatplane, grinning at the camera. He'd been extremely good looking. "Those two were Elsa and Shawn, my daughter and son-in-law." He indicated an image of a man and woman on a fishing trawler with a brown tabby cat perched on the railing. "I blame myself that they're gone. They had fine careers ahead, and this whole estate they would have inherited." The family resemblance between his daughter and the younger Denali was unmistakable.

"Sounds like you were very proud of them."

"I was. They are Lucas's parents. My grandson. Lucas is twelve. He lives here. That's his photo—" He abruptly stopped talking.

She looked at him.

He shook his head. "I don't know why I'm telling you about my family." His voice was gruff. He indicated the door through which Elin had gone. "Olga's in there. She runs the household. She'll be your boss. Go in and see what she wants you to do."

She trudged toward the kitchen. Before she could enter, a plump blond woman came out. "Ah, you must be the girl Elin was telling me about. Terrible about your home." She looked closer at Murphy's face. "And you look exhausted. Tell you what. I have breakfast covered here at the family home. We still haven't hit the high season for tourists at the main lodge, which for us is mid-July to late September. Best bear viewing and great fishing. No one's exactly overworked right now. Go up and take a nap. Room 4, upstairs at the end of the hall on your left. Door's open, key on the desk. When you get up, you'll see a few uniforms in the closet. Find one that fits. You'll find a three-ring binder with employee information. Before you come back down, read over it and let me know if you have any questions. Okay?"

"Yes. And thank you."

The second floor had more photographs mounted on canvas with the overall theme of fishing. She found room 4 and entered. The small room held a double bed with a white chenille bedspread, battered chest of drawers, desk, and tiny bathroom. Unlike the wilderness-themed lodge, this room was spartan and plainly decorated. The window overlooked the dense woods behind the house. Kicking off her shoes, she pulled out the notebook Bertie had given her and placed it on the chest of drawers, then opened the employee binder.

Salmon Run Lodge is rich in Kodiak history and heritage. The family has owned this land for four generations, and everyone, from governors to movie stars, from the heads of Forbes 500 companies to Pulitzer Prize–winning authors, has been welcomed through these doors. The staff is charged with keeping and maintaining the high standards that have made Salmon Run famous.

The main guest buildings were on your left as you drove onto the grounds. You will be primarily working here at the family quarters. You must wear your uniform at all times while working at the lodge. The uniform is denim jeans and a red-plaid flannel shirt with the lodge's logo on a patch over the pocket.

We leave the front door of the lodge unlocked during the

day, but after 10:00 p.m. all doors are locked. If you're planning on going out again, please take your room key, which works on the front door. The wet bar is in the living room. Guests of the owners are not to serve themselves, so you will be expected to take care of drink orders before, during, and after dinner.

The office, located behind the dining room, has a copy machine, computer, and printer for family members only. Employees may not use this service.

Individual guest schedules for fishing, bear watching, and other events are posted on the whiteboard behind the kitchen door.

Although your principal duties are to serve the family, you may, on occasion, be asked to help out elsewhere on the resort grounds or in the main lodge.

Be ready at 5:00 a.m. for breakfast service at 7:00 a.m., and dinner service at 4:00 p.m. with dinner at 6:00 . . .

She flopped onto the bed and fell asleep as soon as her head hit the pillow.

She was closer to the old house, now level with the jacked-up, rusted truck. She wanted to run, but her legs were made of cement . . .

She awoke with a jerk. The dream was back with a vengeance. After checking her watch, she pulled out her notes and glanced through them. *Quonset hut.* She should refresh her memory of the history of that structure.

Using her cell, she accessed the resort's internet. She was deep into the background of the Quonset hut when her cell phone rang. "Hello?" she croaked. Her throat was raw.

It was Elin. "The medical center called. Bertie is awake. They'll be sending her to Anchorage in the next few hours, but if you'd like to see her—"

She checked her watch. "Yes, but I need to clear it with Olga."

"Already did. I'll come by and pick you up."

She charged into the bathroom. Mercifully the medicine cabinet held deodorant, a new toothbrush, and toothpaste. She took time to slather on deodorant and brush her teeth before racing downstairs.

A boy with thick, dark umber hair, an oval face, and even features was behind the bar popping the tab on a Coke. He was dressed in a long-sleeved Seattle Seahawks T-shirt. He ducked his head when he spotted her and dashed for a back room. She recognized Lucas, Denali's grandson, from his photograph on the wall.

Elin pulled up as Murphy stepped from the lodge. The fog had lifted somewhat, leaving gauzy wisps around the dense spruce that crowded the building. The slap and hiss of water and the smell of sea life told her the ocean was nearby. She jumped into the car with Elin. "Thank you."

"I should be thanking you." Elin put the SUV into gear. "We may have a lead on that drawing you did with Vasily. I wasn't sure it would work as the drawing was pretty . . . loose, but Bertie said that's how composites are supposed to look."

"I'm glad it helped."

"That's the good news."

She swallowed. "And the bad news?"

"I'm afraid they found a body in the mobile home."

Poor Myra. Murphy slumped in her seat. "Do they know how the fire started?"

"Not yet."

When they pulled into the parking lot of the salmon-pink hospital, Elin said, "Richard Zinkerton wants to talk to you.

85

Denali has agreed to let him come to Salmon Run Lodge for dinner tonight. Killing two birds and all that."

"He's not staying at the main lodge?"

Elin got out of the car and locked it. "Hardly. That place charges over a thousand dollars a night."

They hurried inside. The overflowing waiting room smelled of wet clothing and rubber boots. People leaned against the wall or spoke quietly. The nurse at the entrance to the intensive care unit would only allow one at a time to visit Bertie. Elin insisted Murphy go first.

Bertie looked so fragile amid the beeping machines. A large bandage circled her head, and her face was the same color as the sheets.

"Murph," she murmured.

She took Bertie's hand. "How are you feeling?"

"Like I fell off a cliff."

"I'm so sorry. It was all my fault—"

"Murph, Murph, Murph." Her words were little more than a sigh. "The wind caught the ladder and I slipped. It was an accident. Don't beat yourself up."

"They told me they're sending you to Anchorage. I guess I won't be seeing you again."

Bertie stared at the ceiling for so long that Murphy reached for the call button.

"No." Bertie now looked at her. "Don't call anyone. I have a favor to ask."

"Sure. Anything."

"Don't agree until you hear the favor." She took a breath and winced. "Ouch. So, Murphy Andersen, I know who you are."

CHAPTER 11

Murphy took a half step backward. "What do you mean?" Her voice came out high and squeaky.

"You're not a forensic artist." Bertie grinned wickedly. "Though I covered for you with Elin. You're Dakota Murphy Andersen, twin sister to Dallas Andersen, who was the last victim of Clinton Lamour Hunter, the Anchorage serial killer."

"*Believed* to be the last victim. They never found her body."

Bertie was silent.

"How did you guess?" she finally asked.

"I followed the case, of course. And . . . well, even thinner and with those fake glasses, you have a distinctive look."

Murphy ducked her head and touched her scar.

"After . . . that happened," Bertie said softly, "did you—"

"Get advice? Reconstruction? Yes. The best plastic surgeons. There's only so much they could do."

"I'm sorry . . ."

Clutching the walrus-bone necklace made from her sister's earring, Murphy inhaled sharply. "So you know who I am. No big deal. All that is ancient history. I've moved on."

Bertie squinted at her. "Sure. Right. Whatever you say."

"It's true."

"And that's why you're in Kodiak?"

"I like it here."

"And it's just coincidence that your sister was in Kodiak before she . . . disappeared."

"Everyone believes she's dead. They believe she was dating Hunter, came here on vacation with him, returned to Anchorage, and he killed her there. But I don't. Hunter never confessed to her murder. So I'll continue to look. If only I hadn't taken that trip, I would have been home when he first started dating her, taking her places. Maybe I could have stopped everything from happening."

"Well then. Given that, I think we could still have an . . . arrangement."

"Arrangement?" Murphy leaned against the wall.

"I don't want to leave this case in the hands of Richard Zinkerton. Every time he's stepped in on any of my cases, he's blown it. I think it's deliberate. He's trying to head up the crime lab, and to do so he's got to make me look bad."

"But—"

"In return for helping me, I'll help you get information on your sister. What do the police know? What happened to her body? And I'd bet no one's in any great hurry to solve that mystery with Hunter safely—"

"He's escaped."

Bertie again went silent.

"They don't know where he is. I got a letter . . ." Murphy shifted her weight.

"A letter?"

"From the witness people."

"Oh, Murph, that must be terrifying for you. Are you afraid he might track you down here in Kodiak?"

"I don't know. After all this time, I wouldn't think he'd be after me." *But someone burned down my house.* "I do want to find out what happened to Dallas. What do you need me to do?"

Bertie took a cautious breath. "Right. I want you to stay close to this investigation. Report what you hear to me. If I'm lucky, you'll be able to give me something on that Stinkerton skunk."

"What do you specifically want to know about . . . ah . . . Stinkerton?"

"Everything."

"If he's really that bad a crime-scene technician, how does he still have a job?"

Bertie's face wrinkled up as if she smelled something bad. "He's really not such a bad criminalist. He's just ambitious, bent on mucking up my cases. He's trying to destroy my reputation. I want to catch the rat red-handed."

"How can I find out about Stinkerton? My role in this investigation is at an end."

"They still think you're a forensic artist. Use your abilities."

"Art?"

Bertie shifted and winced. "Yes, art. And your ability to get people to talk to you."

She shook her head. "I don't know."

"Think about it. Call me." Bertie closed her eyes as if exhausted.

"But—"

The nurse from the night before entered and pointed at her watch. "Time's up."

Murphy gently squeezed Bertie's hand, then followed the nurse as she made her way to the smaller waiting area. The nurse handed her a card. "Here's the number where your mom is being transferred. You can call later today to see how she's doing."

"Thank you."

Elin was waiting for her in the larger waiting room. "What do you think?"

"I think she's looking pretty good, but in a fair amount of pain."

Elin grimaced. "This whole thing just stinks. Let me get you back to Salmon Run before you lose your new job. I'll come back and pay a quick visit before she leaves."

The fog still hung like cotton batting around the hospital. They got in Elin's car and headed toward the lodge. Murphy licked her lips. "You, um, mentioned you may have a lead on my composite drawing."

"I got a call from one of the managers at a seafood processing plant. I'll be heading over there tomorrow."

"It's my custom to follow up on any leads my sketches bring. Do you think I could go with you?" She slipped off her glasses and looked at Elin. "I might think of something to ask."

Elin glanced at her, then did a double take. "I've never noticed your eyes. They're an unusual color."

"Gray blue. What do you think of my suggestion?"

"It makes sense. The appointment's at ten. I'll pick you up before that. We'll get to the bottom of this case yet and bring whoever is responsible to justice." She nodded as if agreeing with herself, then concentrated on the road for a few moments. "I've looked further into the timing of Vasily's visit to Ruuwaq. I couldn't pin down the exact date he went there, but around that time period, several boats were stolen. As none of the boats were large, and none recovered, it's possible the five bodies he discovered were the thieves. They may have taken refuge on the island from a storm, or met there for some reason." She shrugged. "I'll be following up on that more."

"Is Stink—uh, Richard, taking over the case?"

"No. But when I picked him up from the airport, he told me he wanted all my case notes and everything Bertie had collected. I said I'd give him copies of the notes and bring him the camera tonight. He made me drive straight to the hospital to get the evidence from Bertie's vest." She snorted. "She was barely out of surgery."

"Mmm."

"He was incensed that you, a civilian, were allowed to go out on the island to collect evidence, even when I told him your background. He said he would be writing Bertie up for compromising the scene."

Instead of dropping Murphy at the front door of the lodge, Elin drove around to the side and put the car into park. "They'll want you to use the kitchen door."

"Thanks." She got out of the car.

"Oh, and, Murphy, I apologize for rattling on and on about my cases. I don't usually do that, at least not with someone outside of the department. Thank you."

She shrugged. "Sure. I'll see you tomorrow."

"Actually, I'm coming back here for dinner. I'm bringing Richard. Remember?"

"Oh. Right." Murphy shut the door, then watched Elin drive off into the fog.

In the kitchen Olga was slicing asparagus, with a row of pies on one counter. The fragrance of baking salmon came from the ovens. "There you are." She pointed with a paring knife. "Write your cell number on the whiteboard over there in case I need to get hold of you. Then go change into your uniform and come back down. Set the table for seven. Denali will be at the far end away from the kitchen, so no chair at that spot. Silverware and napkins are on the sideboard."

Murphy wrote her number under the few events scheduled for the guests at the resort's main lodge, then raced to her room and found a reasonably well-fitting pair of jeans and shirt in her closet. No time for a shower. She refreshed her deodorant and hoped it would be enough.

When she returned to the main floor, Denali, Lab by his side, was holding court with Jake, the pilot, now dressed in jeans and a sweatshirt. Father Ivanov, still in the black cassock and green tennis shoes, sat in an easy chair by the window. A middle-aged man wearing dark tortoiseshell glasses sat on the sofa in front of a crackling fireplace. Lucas, Denali's grandson, leaned against the wall near the bar. The room smelled of burning pine and baking salmon.

No one paid any attention to her as she headed to the dining room. As she set the table, she listened to the conversation.

"So here's the funny thing," Denali was saying. "I told Bill Gates that I liked his wife's answer better than his."

Everyone chuckled.

"Tell us more about your trip," Father Ivanov said to Jake.

"They climbed that cliff and were gone for several hours," Jake said. "The storm blew in even faster than I thought. It's a miracle that lady survived the fall and we made it out."

"I told Elin to just let well enough alone on that island." Denali slapped the armrest of his wheelchair. "What's the toll now? Six dead and one seriously injured? If your plane had gone down, it would have been nine dead."

"If you count the murder of Vasily and Irina, there are eight dead people," Lucas said.

Father Ivanov shook his head. "There's no reason to put that double homicide in with the bodies on Ruuwaq, is there?"

"You don't think they're connected?" Denali asked. "Seems

quite the coincidence that they should be gunned down before Vasily could say anything else. What did that crime-scene lady come up with before she was hurt?"

Jake leaned forward. "Not much on the flight out. She was having Murphy write stuff down. Right, Murphy?"

Everyone turned and looked at her. She busied herself with placing bread plates. The clatter of the dishes on the table seemed overly loud.

"Bertie, um, she was just brainstorming possibilities."

Olga poked her head out of the kitchen. "Go serve some drinks." She glanced at the table and grunted. "Good. You know how to set a table. Last one didn't know a bread knife from a salad fork."

Murphy moved to the wet bar in the corner of the living room. Shelves displayed various glasses and liquors, while the small refrigerator under the counter held beer and white wine. A small round serving tray sat on the counter. She noted the brands and approached the men. "May I get anyone something to drink?"

"Coke," Lucas said.

"Do you have a cabernet sauvignon?" the priest asked.

"Yes."

"I'll have a small glass."

Jake caught her attention, pointed to the priest, and held his fingers apart, indicting the other man needed a large glass. "And I'll have a Scotch with water."

"Make that two," Denali said.

The newcomer reached over and offered her his hand. "I'm Ryan." The man appeared to be in his forties, with an open, likable face and lopsided grin. His sepia-brown hair receded from a high forehead. The combination of heavy, square glasses and hunter-green corduroy jacket gave him a scholarly look. He reminded her vaguely of Tom Hanks. "Just flew in from Anchorage. They were telling me about this case of yours. Six dead bodies discovered over ten years ago on a remote island, bodies burned, all but a skeleton in a Quonset hut?"

She shook his hand. "Nice to meet you, Ryan. I'm Murphy. Technically it's Detective Olsson's case. I'm just doing some sketches." She retrieved her hand from his grip. "May I get you something to drink?"

"I'll have a glass of that cab."

She nodded and retreated to the bar. She returned shortly with the drink order.

Gravel crunched as several cars pulled up in front of the lodge. Elin got out of the first one. Murphy gave her a quick wave out the window, then handed Ryan his wine. "You seem to be pretty up-to-date on our progress."

"It's not as if it's a secret, is it?" Jake shrugged, then drained his glass of amber liquid. "I mean, those guys have been dead for a long time."

"Bertie mentioned the ABI would probably step in—" Murphy started.

"Not until I give them my report." A short, ginger-haired man in his late forties, with a neatly trimmed goatee and beard, and sour expression, stood at the open front door. "I'm Richard Zinkerton, like Pinkerton with a Z, CSCSA, CCI, ICSIA." Richard held up a badge, then took off his jacket and tossed it on a chair. "Nice digs." He looked around. "Really nice. Sure beats the fleabag Economy Inn. That place reeks of fish."

"Someone must hate him," Lucas muttered.

Elin entered after him carrying a paper bag.

Denali turned his chair toward Zinkerton. "I'm glad you and Elin could join us for dinner. Welcome to Salmon Run Lodge. I'm the owner, Denali Stewart." He introduced everyone, including Ryan Wallace, who was a journalist writing a piece about the history of the lodge. "And that's Murphy Andersen, the artist who went out to Ruuwaq with Bertie."

She crossed to Elin. "May I get you something to drink—"

"You're a bartender?" Zinkerton's gaze drifted down her body, coming to rest on her chest. "And a kid to boot. Bertie actually took an underaged bartender along on an investigation?" He smirked. "Internal affairs will love to hear this one." He took a seat near the fireplace. "At any rate, I'll need to talk to you. Sounds like Bertie will be out for a while."

She made an effort to unclench her hands. "Elin, may I bring—"

"You can bring me a Chivas Regal, neat," Zinkerton said. "If ya got it. If not, Glenlivet." He jerked his thumb at Murphy and said to Denali, "Is she legal?"

Murphy made a point of not looking at him. "Elin?"

"Club soda." Elin made a face at the back of Zinkerton's head, then handed Murphy her jacket and held up the paper bag. "And I brought you some clothes."

"Thank you." A sudden lump of gratitude filled her throat. She took the coat and bag, returned to the bar, and stored them on a chair.

She poured a highball glass of Jim Beam and ice for the technician.

"I guess you didn't hear me," Zinkerton said peevishly. "I said—"

She held up the bottle. "We're just out of Chivas and Glenlivet. Will Jim Beam do?"

Zinkerton shrugged. Denali shot her an appreciative look.

Taking a chilled glass from the refrigerator, she added ice and a slice of lime, then poured the club soda. She brought both drinks into the living room.

Elin took her soda and winked at her.

She winked back, then handed Zinkerton his whiskey. He downed it in one gulp, then thumped the glass back on the tray. "Bring me another. Rough day and rough flight over." Once more behind the bar, she found and filled a clean glass.

Elin handed Bertie's digital camera to Zinkerton. Without speaking, he signed the chain-of-custody form she handed to him, then turned on the camera.

Murphy brought his second drink, lingering behind him as he scanned the photos. He grunted when he came to the photographs from the inside of the Quonset hut, then paused when he came to the skeleton. "When did you say I can get out there?"

Elin said, "Depends on the weather."

Murphy leaned closer. "Watch out for the rats. The skeleton—"

He held up his hand. "No. I'll come to my own conclusions. You're not a certified crime-scene technician, let alone a trained laboratory analyst." He took a long gulp of the whiskey and once again placed it on her tray. "You're lucky to have been asked to go along."

She straightened and strolled to the bar.

"So what's your first move?" Ryan asked Zinkerton.

"And you are?" Zinkerton asked.

"Ryan Wallace. I'm here—"

"Right, the journalist. I don't discuss my cases with the press."

Grabbing the whiskey bottle, Murphy dumped a hefty amount into the glass, debated on spitting in it, opted not to, then brought it to Zinkerton.

"But maybe you have information I need to know," Zinkerton said. He took the full glass from Murphy and bolted half of it down.

She should have spit in it.

"And what might that be?" Ryan asked with that enigmatic half smile.

Olga entered. "Dinner is served." She gave a brief jerk of her head to indicate Murphy should follow her into the kitchen.

She went reluctantly. *I'd love to hear his answer.*

CHAPTER 12

"The first course is coconut shrimp with spicy orange dipping sauce." Olga handed Murphy several plates. "Be sure you serve from—"

"The guest's left and remove from the guest's right. Yes, ma'am." She took the three appetizer plates and rushed back to the dining room.

Everyone was seated and Father Ivanov was offering a short prayer in Russian.

She stopped, bowed her head, and breathed a sigh of relief. She hadn't missed anything.

When he'd finished the prayer, she started serving the meal.

"So I usually get sent to the highest-profile cases." Zinkerton stuffed a shrimp into his mouth. "This one on that island—"

"Ruuwaq," Father Ivanov said.

"Yeah, whatever." Zinkerton waved his fork and stabbed another shrimp. "Was a cold case, so I sent a less experienced investigator."

Murphy placed the last appetizer in front of Lucas, then said quietly to Zinkerton, "I thought Bertie was a senior investigator."

Zinkerton placed his fork on the plate with a clank. "Look, girl." He spoke just above a whisper. "You're nothing more than a waitress and bartender. I don't know why Bertie dragged you along on this case, but you need to keep your trap shut until I interview you, which I've decided I'll do tomorrow instead of tonight. Understand?"

"Yes, sir," she said through tight lips. Tomorrow when he wasn't as sloshed.

"Now bring me another drink."

No one at the table noticed the exchange. She walked stiff-legged to the bar and poured Zinkerton yet another generous drink. It took all her willpower not to dump it on his head when she returned with it.

By the time the main course was served, Zinkerton had downed two more drinks and was slurring his words. "Sho, the real reason Bertie went on thiz case is my wife's sick. Been sick. 'Bout a year now. Gotta wait until someone's available. But I been thinkin' 'bout it. The way I figure, this island place was where they were hiding drugs or schomething." He took another drink.

She paused in picking up a dirty dish. "Don't you think the Quonset hut was important?"

He pointed a finger at her. "You're suffering from *CSI* syndrome. Too mush television. You don't know what's importan' and what's not. That"—he looked around the table—"takes years of work and training."

Enough. She carefully placed the dirty dish on the sideboard with a shaking hand, then turned to Zinkerton. "The Quonset hut on Ruuwaq was a T-rib design and had rusty steel."

All the table conversation ceased, and everyone's attention focused on her.

Ryan cleared his throat. "Um . . . aren't all Quonset huts made of steel and therefore prone to rust?"

"Yes, but the original huts, made in 1941, were made of light-weight corrugated sheets that would rust comparatively easily. They were later replaced with more rust-resistant steel."

Denali nodded. "That's right. They would have used non-strategic steel because of the war."

"So you're dating that hut to sometime between 1941 and 1945?" Elin asked.

"I think it could be dated tighter than that." She stared at Zinkerton. "When we measured the building, we found it to be thirty-five to forty feet long. The original 1941 structures were sixteen feet by thirty-six feet. And the T-rib design was phased out around 1942."

"That's excellent, Murphy!" The priest beamed at her.

"What makes you such an expert?" Zinkerton's face flushed.

She opened her mouth to answer, *A master's degree in fine arts with an undergraduate minor in architecture*. Then she paused and looked at Elin. "There's more. Starting in 1942, Frank Hobbs, an engineer in Seattle, developed Pacific Huts. They were shaped like the Quonset huts but were made of wood. They were cheaper, easier to ship, and stayed warmer. They were used extensively in Alaska."

"So all indicators suggest the Quonset hut you found," Elin said, "may have been one of the original ones from 1941 to early 1942."

"Fascinating," Ryan said. "So now you need to figure out when the slide buried it."

"I'll do the figurin'," Zinkerton said. "And any research needed." He tried to draw her attention to his nearly empty glass.

She ignored him and continued to clear the table.

"Speaking of research," Denali said to Zinkerton, "weather permitting, are you going to Ruuwaq Island tomorrow?"

"Yeah." Jake spoke from the bar where he'd just filled his glass with bourbon.

She winced at the amount of alcohol in his glass, thinking about his piloting the next day. Elin caught her expression and mouthed, *He'll be fine.*

Jake sauntered to his seat. "The fog's supposed to lift before morning. If it does, we'll fly out tomorrow about ten, with Richard here and an Alaska State Trooper."

Zinkerton turned to Father Ivanov. "Hey, I have to ask. Are you a Ruskie?"

"I was born in Russia. I came to Kodiak to attend the St. Herman Theological Seminary about six years ago and stayed."

"Why?" Zinkerton didn't wait for an answer. He downed the last of his drink, then stood, swaying slightly.

Elin also stood. "If you're done eating, I'll drive you back to your motel."

Zinkerton glanced at his watch, a gold Rolex. "Gotta call home, but a bit early to call it a night, don't you sink? I'm okay. Thansh for the offer."

"It wasn't an offer." Elin strolled to his jacket, still thrown over a chair, and retrieved his car keys. "It was a directive." She looked at Denali. "I'll send someone over tomorrow to pick up my SUV." She pulled a clunky key ring from her purse and peeled off a single key. "Spare in case you have to move my rig."

"Well, hey." Zinkerton stumbled toward her. "I don't mind being taken home by a pretty girl." He pulled out a keycard. "Room 32. Come in and check out the decor."

Elin's eyes narrowed.

Murphy made a point to turn her back and stack dirty dishes, hiding her grin. She'd give her left arm to see Elin rearrange Stinkerton's face.

After they left, the group moved to the living room and settled into the comfortable chairs and sofa around the crackling fireplace. She finished clearing the dishes.

Olga brought a coffee service set into the dining room and handed it to her. "Cognac in the bar. Big pot is regular, small is decaf."

The tray was heavy. She lowered it to the coffee table and turned. Before she could take drink orders, Denali said, "You have an impressive knowledge of Quonset huts, Murphy. There seems to be a lot more to you than a barmaid and waitress. What's your story?"

"Just like reading a lot," she muttered. *Fool.* She had put herself into the limelight by showing off. She kept her head down as she headed to the bar.

She stopped abruptly at the bar. Elin had left her jacket. Glancing out the window, Murphy saw no sign of Zinkerton's car. Once she was done serving and cleaning, she would put the coat in Elin's SUV.

The conversation moved from crime to politics. By the time the evening wound down, Murphy was dropping on her feet. Denali was the last to retire down the hall, dog padding softly behind.

She still had the cognac glasses and coffee service to wash, and the living room to straighten. It was close to one in the morning and finally dark before she finished.

Picking up Elin's jacket, she strolled to the table where Elin had left the single key. Murphy grabbed it and stuffed it in her pocket. She walked outside to place the jacket in Elin's car.

A phone rang.

She checked Elin's coat. Her cell was in the left side pocket. The number was blocked. She was about to ignore it, but what if this call was from Elin?

"Murphy Andersen."

A female voice answered, "This is Detective Buchanan of the Kodiak Police Department. Who did you say you were?"

She clutched the phone. "Murphy Andersen. Are you calling for Detective Olsson?"

Silence. "Ah . . . no, Ms. Andersen. I'm calling from a phone found on an unidentified man. This number was the last one dialed."

"Oh no." It came out as escaping air.

"Would you tell me who called you earlier?"

"You said he's unidentified. Is he dead?"

"I'm afraid so."

"How? Why?"

"Um . . . you mentioned Detective Olsson. How do you know—"

"I'm a forensic artist working with Detective Olsson."

"I see. Could you give me his name?"

"What does he look like?"

"Red hair. Mustache and goatee. Name?"

Murphy slowly sank to the porch. "Not until you tell me what happened."

The woman let out a sigh. "It appears someone robbed, then murdered him."

"Where are you? Or should I ask, where is he?"

"Ms. Andersen, you said you'd give me his name if I told you what happened."

"I lied. It's becoming a habit. Where is he?"

"In the harbor. Beside a Dumpster outside the Shady Lady Saloon."

Murphy tried to work up some spit in her suddenly dry mouth. "His name is . . . was . . . Richard Zinkerton."

CHAPTER 13

Would you be willing to come down and identify him?" Detective Buchanan asked Murphy.

"Yes. I'm on my way." After Detective Buchanan gave her directions, Murphy hung up, pulled Elin's key from her pocket, and raced to the SUV. The fog had started to lift, but it still looked like a layer of gauze covered the surroundings.

She pulled from the driveway and turned toward downtown Kodiak. She was driving without a license.

Even without directions she could have located the crime scene. Red, white, and blue strobe lights blazed like a carnival midway. An officer stationed on the street impatiently waved away the few cars and onlookers.

The saloon was three buildings away from Zinkerton's motel.

Murphy parked in the motel lot, then checked to see if anyone was paying attention to her. If Hunter had flown to Kodiak to find her, he wouldn't be staying at a place like this. At least before he was arrested, he'd preferred the fancy hotels. She'd tracked her sister and Hunter to the nicest hotel in town, but not before they'd both dropped off the map.

Dallas's name had been on the room registration.

Murphy stroked the necklace. "I'll have a lot to share with Bertie," she whispered. "I just hope she keeps her side of the bargain." She got out of the car and walked to a patrolman un-rolling cadmium-yellow crime-scene tape. Before he could prevent her approach, she asked, "Where's Detective Buchanan?"

He jerked a thumb in the direction of an attractive woman whose auburn hair was held back by a black headband. She wore navy slacks, a beige blouse, and a black windbreaker, with a gold badge and a pistol at her waist. When she spotted Murphy, she stopped talking to a uniformed officer and moved in her direction. "Ms. Andersen?"

"Yes." They shook hands.

"Let's get this over with." Detective Buchanan motioned her to follow, then strolled toward an alley. "The bartender said the man was already three sheets to the wind when he came in about 10:30. He demanded a drink but was refused. He threw a hissy fit and left shortly after." They approached a black Dumpster beside a door marked No Entrance. A few flies buzzed nearby. The acrid odor of urine burned her nose.

Murphy's stomach tightened and footsteps slowed as she drew near. Counting the skeleton on Ruuwaq and the double homicide, this would be the fourth dead person she'd seen in less than two days. She'd known two of the victims, albeit for a short amount of time. Earlier this evening Zinkerton was calmly eating dinner, enjoying himself, oblivious to the feelings of any other person—except maybe his wife. She could under-stand someone throttling him. Shoving down the uncharitable thought, she focused on the scene.

Zinkerton lay on his back, sightless eyes open and pointed at the gray sky. A bloody gash on his temple had leaked down the side of his face. A dark crimson puddle pooled beside him.

She sucked in a deep breath of air, then instantly regretted it. The stench of the Dumpster and reek of body fluids filled her nose. Moving away, she took several breaths to clear her lungs.

"Yes. That's Richard Stink . . . Zinkerton."

"I'm sorry about your friend."

"He wasn't my friend. He was the crime-scene technician here from Anchorage. I met him last night."

"*He's* the technician? Oh great. I guess I didn't need to call him in. He's already here." She snorted at her gallows humor. "Didn't I hear that the other technician was also hurt?"

"She's been transferred to a hospital in Anchorage."

"So Zinkerton called your phone because . . . ?"

"It's actually Detective Olsson's phone. She forgot it in the pocket of a coat she left at Salmon Run Lodge. I would imagine Zinkerton was calling about the arrangements for tomorrow's— make that today's work." *See how far you can push your luck in getting information for Bertie.* "I've, um, as I said on the phone, I'm the forensic artist working with Detective Olsson. You know that double homicide?" Lying was becoming a habit.

"Yeah. We must be running a murder special this week."

"Um, what do you think happened here with Zinkerton?"

"We think he stepped into the alley to relieve himself," Buchanan said. "His pants were unzipped, and it smells. Someone came up behind him and smashed him in the head, then stabbed him. His pockets were inside out, no wallet or jewelry, so we're looking at a robbery-homicide."

"He was wearing a gold Rolex. He made a big deal about it at dinner. I'd imagine he flashed it around the bar as well."

Detective Buchanan pulled out a small notepad and pen, then jotted a note. "What else can you tell me about Mr. Zinkerton?"

Murphy recounted the evening. Buchanan's eyebrows rose

when she heard Detective Olsson had been the one to drop him off at the motel, but she continued to write.

Glancing around the narrow alley, Murphy asked, "Why'd they leave his cell on him?"

"They didn't." Detective Buchanan moved around the Dumpster, pulled out her flashlight, and aimed it at the ground. "It was there, near the wall. We think it fell out of his pocket when he was attacked, and it slid."

"You said no wallet or jewelry. I take it there wasn't a keycard for a motel?" She folded her arms. "He was staying just up the street at the Economy Inn."

The detective raised her eyebrows. "On purpose?"

"I think your department put him up there."

Buchanan put her notebook away. "Someone sure didn't like him."

"Mmm."

"They sometimes rent rooms by the hour."

"Really."

Buchanan gave a brisk nod, then turned and moved toward the motel. "I don't suppose you know what room he was in?"

"Thirty-two."

Buchanan glanced over her shoulder at Murphy.

"He mentioned it before he left the lodge."

"I didn't say anything," she said.

"You didn't have to. Just for the record, I met him today. He wasn't the most . . . likable of people."

Buchanan held up her hands. "Okay. Okay. It's none of my business. You don't have to convince me."

Murphy bit her lip. *Why is it so important for me to convince her that he was someone I just met?*

She followed the detective to the Economy Inn's office, a small space with fake wood paneling, old posters, and hand-lettered warning signs. No Smoking! No Pets! No Noise after 10:00 p.m.!

The clerk needed a shave, shower, and clean change of clothing. "Now what?"

"I need you to let me into room 32." Detective Buchanan tapped a nail on the counter.

"Got a warrant?"

"He's dead."

The clerk turned a shade paler. "Someone didn't just croak in one of the rooms, did they?"

Detective Buchanan just held out her hand. "Key."

The clerk pushed a few buttons on a machine, swiped the plastic keycard, and handed it to her. "Let me know when you're done."

Buchanan snorted, grabbed the key, and headed toward Zinkerton's room.

The door to number 32 was open a crack.

Buchanan grabbed Murphy's arm and pulled her away. "You packing?"

Packing? "Oh, a gun. No."

Slipping her cell from her pocket, Buchanan dialed. "Yeah. I'm at the motel, outside room 32," she whispered. "Door's open. Send backup." She hung up and pulled the Glock from her holster.

They didn't have to wait long. Two beefy uniformed officers soon arrived and took positions on either side of the door. "Police," one of them said. "Come out with your hands up!"

Curtains twitched in the rooms around them, but no one emerged from number 32.

Bang. The same officer slammed open the door.

Murphy jumped.

Light spilled out of the room. Both men rushed in, guns drawn. After a moment, a voice said, "Clear!"

Buchanan reholstered her pistol, then pulled on a pair of blue nitrile gloves. "Don't touch anything." She waited for the officers to exit, then entered the room with Murphy.

Zinkerton's open suitcase rested on a stand, with the contents spread across the room. Someone had pulled out and discarded the dresser drawers, tossed the mattress, and overturned a chair. A lamp lay on its side on the battered bedside table.

A small folded piece of paper sat just inside the door. Buchanan took out a pencil and nudged it open. It was the keycard envelope with the room number penciled on the corner of the paper. "Made it pretty easy for the killer to know which room would be empty." She tilted the envelope and the plastic card slipped out. "And to get in the room."

Murphy slowly looked around, peered into the trash can, then pointed to a carry-on roller bag in the corner. "Would you open that?"

Detective Buchanan picked up the bag and lifted the lid. Empty. "He probably had a laptop in here."

"Maybe a laptop. Probably a digital camera and several bags of evidence he got from Bertie. They're all missing." She looked at Detective Buchanan. "I don't think this was a random homicide and robbery. I think Zinkerton was murdered for evidence."

"From that double homicide you were working with Detective Olsson?"

She blinked at the lie she'd told earlier. "Um . . . no. From what I saw, Detective Olsson put all that into bags and had them loaded in a van. I'd bet they're at your department. Um . . . in evidence."

"So what are we talking about here?" Buchanan asked.

"Another case. Bertie, that's the crime-scene technician who was hurt, and I flew out to Ruuwaq Island on a cold case." She explained the details of the past two days. "Zinkerton took the stuff we gathered . . . the evidence . . . from Bertie's vest at the hospital. And I saw Elin give Zinkerton the camera. He had it when he left the lodge."

"When you say 'stuff' and 'evidence,' what are we talking about?"

"Some dirt. Part of a dog collar. Maybe a bone."

Buchanan folded her arms. "Ms. Andersen, I can't say I knew the Kodiak Police Department had a forensic artist."

"I'm on loan."

"I see. Do you have your credentials with you?"

"Not exactly."

"Well, what exactly do you do when you're not working with us?"

"I work at Salmon Run Lodge."

"So you're a civilian. And your job at the lodge is what? Housekeeping?"

"Waitress."

"You've made my point. Without credentials, as far as I'm concerned, you're an amateur when it comes to crime."

Murphy's face grew warm. Considering the five bodies she'd sketched, the skeleton, two deaths yesterday, and Zinkerton, she'd probably been involved in more murders in the past two days than Detective Buchanan had in her career.

"Just look at this place." Buchanan waved her arm around the room. "It's clear someone used this opportunity to toss the room looking for money or things to sell, probably for drugs."

"I just don't think so. Someone took a great deal of trouble to make it look like a robbery. But why would someone toss all the clothes out of a suitcase, then take the trouble to close up and replace a roller bag? Why would they take bagged evidence—dirt, a buckle, a bone? Worthless items for a crook. The lampshade isn't damaged, which it should be if it were knocked over. It was placed on its side. And that keycard was left so you'd be sure to find it."

Buchanan frowned and slowly turned in a circle, staring at each item Murphy had pointed out. "Maybe."

A man in blue coveralls appeared at the door. "Got something for me?"

Buchanan nodded and said to Murphy, "I'll have more questions for you, so don't leave town."

Murphy trudged to Elin's SUV, got in, and locked the doors. If what she believed happened to Zinkerton was true, someone was going to great lengths to prevent whatever happened on Ruuwaq Island from being unearthed.

CHAPTER 14

Murphy barely closed her eyes before the alarm sounded at five that morning. *At least I didn't dream.* She rushed showering and dressing, then raced to the kitchen to help Olga.

"Goodness, child, you look like you were up all night!" Olga clicked her tongue. "What's the matter?"

She'll find out soon enough about Zinkerton. "Nothing. Um, strange bed . . ."

"Well then, go set the tables. The one by the window will be for Mr. Stewart and his grandson, Lucas. The second table, the one on the side, will be for Mr. Wallace."

"Yes, ma'am. Why is Mr. Wallace here rather than the guest lodge?"

"He's writing an article about Salmon Run. He has more access to Denali this way."

It didn't take long to set the three place settings. Olga checked her work, smiled in satisfaction, then had her cut fresh fruit into a big bowl.

Murphy's stomach growled.

"When's the last time you ate?" Olga asked.

"I don't remember."

"I can't have my staff fainting from lack of food now, can I?"

Murphy soon found herself at a table in the corner of the kitchen with a mound of pancakes in front of her. "Thank you."

"Pffff." Olga waved a spatula. "Eat. I can take care of three men for breakfast."

She dug into the stack of pancakes, not stopping until her plate was clean. "That was the best breakfast I've ever eaten." She wiped her mouth with a napkin.

"I sure don't know where you put all that food," Olga said. "I don't expect anyone here for lunch, so I'll leave a sandwich in the refrigerator with your name on it. I have a gal that comes in to clean. If Mr. Stewart invites more guests here at the family home, you'll be helping her. I'll need you back here to prep for dinner at four. Did you have any plans for the day?"

"I'm going to a cannery with Elin."

Olga paused in rolling out dough. "Really?"

"Something to do with the sketch I did."

"Are you or that awful man—"

"Richard Zinkerton."

"That's him. Are you going back out to the island?"

"No, ah, Mr. Zinkerton's . . . no."

Olga seemed satisfied with her answer.

Murphy put her dishes in the dishwasher and headed to her room. Once there, she locked the door and found the small card she'd been given at the hospital. After talking to a few people, she finally got Bertie's room number. Bertie answered on the first ring.

"Hey, Murph, 'bout time you called. I'm going stir-crazy here. What's happening?"

She caught Bertie up on her impending visit to the cannery and Zinkerton's demise.

"Well. I'm not sure what to say. I couldn't stand the man. If I weren't here in this hospital bed, I could be a suspect. I wanted to kill him often enough." She sighed. "He was good to his wife, I will say that. As obnoxious as he was, and as drunk, he easily could have started something in that bar with a local. You said his Rolex was taken. Well, there's some justice in that. It was a knock-off."

"I think whoever killed him took the photos and evidence from Ruuwaq." She explained the appearance of the motel room.

"I don't know, Murph. We didn't collect enough evidence to do diddly-poo." She was silent for a few moments. "With Zinkerton dead and me laid up, I'm not sure how soon another technician will be sent over to work on Ruuwaq. Older and cold cases are low priority." She was silent again. "I don't mind telling you, this whole thing reeks. I think you need to get out there as soon as possible." Another pause. "Tell ya what. I know this retired pilot, Butch Patterson—"

"Elin mentioned him. He was the one who told her about Ruuwaq. But why not use Jake?"

"Right now there's not a lot of people I trust. Butch was the eye in the sky who was working on the Terror Lake dam project. You know the story."

"I don't know the story."

"Really? It was the oldest missing plane crash in Alaska and one of the oldest in US history. He was the guy who flew over the tundra in a fixed-wing plane and identified the bears they needed to dart, age, take blood from, and collar."

"For tourists—"

"Nah. One of those environmental studies on the impact of a dam on the Kodiak bears. Once he spotted one, he'd radio to a helicopter waiting in a staging area. The helicopter would swoop in and the biologists would shoot the bear with a dart, then land and tag it. They lost their dart kit at one point, and when they went looking for it, they stumbled on a forty-year-old plane crash, bodies still in it."

Murphy gripped the phone tighter at the mention of bodies.

"Anyway, he's the best pilot out there and he owes me a favor. I'll call him and ask him if he'd fly you out to Ruuwaq. If he can't land, at least he's super at aerial reconnaissance. If he can put down, you can get the stuff we left behind. In fact, since Elin probably hasn't officially turned the case over to the troopers, see if she'll go with you. If she's along, you can finish gridding the area. Do the same in the Quonset hut. Get more photos."

"I don't know—"

"Come on, Murph! Think of it as on-the-job training. You'll have an actual case under your belt for when you apply at the crime lab."

"But—"

"And above all else, update your notebook on facts and questions."

"I'll try. Now it's your turn. What did you find out about my sister?" She sat on her bed, grabbed a pillow, and hugged it to her stomach.

"Give me a minute." Paper rustled and something clattered. "Just got started, so not much yet. I noticed the necklace you wear and grab on to when you're stressed."

"I do?"

"Yep. Figured it had something to do with your sister."

"I found it in her things at the hotel where she'd been staying. It was an earring. I only found the one. I took it to all the jewelry stores in Kodiak, then to the Alutiiq Museum. No one recognized it."

"Take a photo of it with your phone and send it to me."

"Okay."

"I'm having the Anchorage police send me a copy of your sister's file."

"Okay." This time it came out a squeak.

"Hey, and listen. Be careful. Three people connected to this case are dead."

"I will. Bertie, now that Zinkerton is dead, do you still want me to report everything to you? You're no longer needing to watch over your shoulder."

"I do. I want to stay in even closer touch with you. I'm really worried about you. And now it's you who has to look over your shoulder. Be safe." She disconnected.

"Safe," Murphy whispered. She stayed on the bed hugging the pillow for a few moments, then jumped up. Elin would be arriving soon to pick her up for the cannery visit. She needed to change out of the jeans-and-flannel-shirt uniform into something Elin had brought her, still downstairs in the paper sack behind the bar. She slipped from the room and tiptoed down the stairs.

Denali and Ryan were in the dining room.

"So," Ryan said, "I couldn't help noticing the Distinguished Service Medal on the wall around the corner. That was given to your dad?"

"Yes." Denali's voice was low. "He was a war hero. Built the lodge here but never lived in it."

"World War II?"

"Yes."

She pressed against the wall and listened.

"What did he do to earn the award?"

"Long story, and some of it is still classified, but it was awarded by express approval of the president."

"Is he buried around here?"

Silence grew until she thought they'd moved away.

"There's a family cemetery. If you'll excuse me, I have some business to attend to." His wheelchair squeaked, growing closer.

She dashed up the stairs before Denali came around the corner and could see her eavesdropping. She stayed out of sight in the hall until he passed, with Lucas following. Why did he end the discussion?

Once again she trotted downstairs and grabbed her sack of clothes. The morning air still smelled of freshly brewing coffee, pancakes, and maple syrup.

Ryan was standing in front of the wall of photographs. He spotted her. "Good morning."

"Good morning."

"I was just asking Denali about these photographs. Didn't get very far. Do you know who they are?"

She fetched the paper bag holding her clothes and joined him. "Denali said that's the only known photograph of his dad." She pointed. "That's his daughter and son-in-law, the parents of Lucas."

"How did you find that out? I couldn't get Denali to say ten words about his family."

"I guess he was in a talkative mood." She ducked her head and ran back up the stairs before he could ask any more questions.

Elin had brought her everything from clean underwear to a zip-up brown hooded sweatshirt with a Kodiak logo on the front. "Thank you, m'friend," she whispered around the tightening of her throat. She found a pair of jeans and an off-white sweater that looked like they'd fit. As Murphy took off her uniform jeans, the key to Elin's SUV dropped from the pocket. She placed it on her dresser. She'd return it today.

Taking off her necklace, she placed it on the bed to take a photo. She snapped several, then scrolled back to be sure the images were clear. She stopped. Three photographs before the necklace were images of the skull and the round metal object from the Quonset hut.

I need to tell Bertie I have these. And Elin.

Safe, her sister whispered in her mind. *Think about this for a moment. Everyone connected to that island is showing up dead.*

"You're right," Murphy said aloud. "Bertie doesn't even trust Jake now."

You need to be cautious. You're dodging whoever killed Vasily and Irina. You know Zinkerton was murdered for the evidence he had. And Clinton could be out there as well. He may even be the person who killed your landlady.

She lifted her necklace and put it on. "I'm not running from Clinton. I'm ready to defend myself. Kill him if I have to."

You can't exact revenge on Clinton if you're dead yourself. No one knows you took these images, Dallas whispered.

"So you think I shouldn't tell anyone? Even Bertie?"

I think you need to be careful. You don't know who your enemies are.

Murphy forwarded the photos of the necklace to Bertie. Someone softly tapped on her door.

She spun, almost dropping her phone, then checked her watch. Where had the time gone? She unlocked the door.

"Ready to go interview the guy at the cannery?" Elin said. "Hey, are you all right? You're as white as a ghost."

"Yeah, sure. You startled me. Did you hear the news?"

"About Zinkerton. Yeah. Couldn't have happened to a nicer person." She clapped her hand over her mouth. "That wasn't nice." She headed down the hall without waiting.

Murphy grabbed her jacket and trotted after Elin's retreating back.

"Joshua drove me over to get my car," Elin said over her shoulder. "He told me about it."

"Is he still here? I mean . . ."

Elin stopped. "No. He left to take care of his boys."

"Okay."

Elin stared at her for a moment, then started walking again. "Anyway, I guess I left my cell in my car. No one could call me."

"I have a confession to make." She caught up with Elin as they reached the front door. She told Elin about taking the call, driving her car, and identifying the body. "I still have your spare key. Do you want me to get it now?"

Elin paused at the door and put her hands on her hips. "No. We'll be late. But I have to say, you're starting to worry me. As of now you're on the witness list for the murders of Vasily and Irina, the arson—"

"Arson!"

"It's official. I guess you hadn't been told yet. The fire marshal found an accelerant in the rubble. Now you've identified Zinkerton and were at that crime scene. You're a one-woman crime wave."

"You don't think I had anything to do with any of those events!" Murphy grasped the doorframe to keep from falling.

"I don't. But a lot of folks just might."

CHAPTER 15

Murphy and Elin got into Elin's SUV. "Tell me about the witness at the cannery." Murphy snapped her seat belt.

"Technically, it's called a processing plant. Carl Alavaren is the man we'll be interviewing. He's the office manager." Elin maneuvered out of the parking area and headed downtown along Spruce Cape Road. The fog had lifted, though in places it was still snagged by the velvety olive-green hillsides. Clouds were rolling in, casting the day into dappled shades of silvery gray. "He's worked at several onshore facilities for over seventeen years. He thinks he recognizes the composite you did."

They reached the center of town and turned toward the marina, home of one of Alaska's largest and most productive fishing fleets. From there they turned onto Shelikof Street, driving past the bar where Zinkerton had been murdered. Yellow crime-scene tape blocked the alley.

"I told Detective Buchanan that I didn't think Zinkerton's murder was random," Murphy said as they passed. She continued to stare at the cheerful yellow tape.

"His personality would certainly bring out homicidal instincts in others."

"I didn't mean that. I think he was murdered for the evidence from Ruuwaq Island."

Elin signaled a turn just up the street from the Shady Lady and pulled into the parking lot of a seafood store. She didn't speak until she'd put the SUV into park and turned off the engine.

"Have you ever heard the saying, 'When you hear hoofbeats, think of horses, not zebras'?"

"Of course. It means look for the simplest explanation of events. It's often used in the medical field."

"It's also useful in law enforcement. Leave the investigation on this case to Detective Buchanan. She's thorough, tough, and persistent. She'll get answers." She got out of the car.

Yeah. And I'm just a kid, a civilian, an amateur, a waitress, and a bartender.

Oh, and don't forget: a Rhodes Scholar with a master's degree.

Murphy had seldom thought of her education before all the murders started. She'd been content to work on her mission to find her sister, paint and sell small acrylics, and make sea glass jewelry. Maybe all Bertie's comments on joining the crime lab had triggered her thinking of what she'd put on a résumé.

The odor of fish was almost palatable. Seagulls or bald eagles perched on every streetlight or squawked overhead. Around them, men and a few women bustled about dressed in waders or coveralls, Xtratuf boots, and hooded sweatshirts. The seafood store was a one-room attachment to a larger metal building painted a flat azure blue. Inside were large refrigeration and freezer units holding stacks of king or Dungeness crabs, cod, salmon, and halibut. Two young men were behind a tiny counter.

"Help you?" the older one asked.

"Carl Alavaren?" Elin asked.

"Go outside, around the corner, up the stairs."

Like the seafood store, the stairs seemed to be an afterthought attached to the side of the building. At the top was a door leading to an open warehouse filled with bales of cardboard boxes with lockers lining one side. The women followed the yellow and black markings painted on the cement floor to a glassed-in office in the rear. A long counter separated Elin and Murphy from the two women working at computers. Before they could ask for Carl, a short, black-haired man approached the counter. "Detective Olsson, good to see you. Come on into my office."

They strolled around the counter, past a wall of file cabinets under statistical fish-and-game charts and colorful seafood posters, into a small room overlooking a rooftop. In the distance, the ocean sparkled under the breaks in the clouds, and the islands rose like emerald gems from the water's surface.

After Elin introduced her and they took their seats, Carl said, "My memory is hazy, but when you mentioned the timing and that there were as many as six men involved, I thought I'd give you a call." He licked his lips. "The article I read mentioned a reward?"

Elin glanced at Murphy. "Yes, if this leads to an identification."

He nodded, then opened a drawer, pulled out a file, and opened it. "Eddie Pelino." He handed Elin a photograph. She held it so Murphy could see. The image was startlingly close to the composite. "Age twenty-two. From Manila. Philippines. He wasn't a greenhorn." He looked at Murphy. "A first-timer. He'd worked at the facility on Akutan."

"I'm sorry," she said, "I'm not familiar with—"

"An island in the Aleutian chain, about 750 miles southwest of Anchorage," Elin said.

"The largest seafood production facility in North America," Carl added. "It employs over fourteen hundred employees during peak season. Eddie transferred from there to work here."

"Why would he do that?" Murphy asked.

Carl grinned. "Let's just say Akutan is . . . remote."

"How many employees do you have here?" Elin asked.

"We're pretty small. About sixty-five day workers. Roughly half that at night. But we're still the third-largest processing plant in the US."

Elin straightened. "Can you make copies of all the employee records between—"

"Nope." Carl shook his head. "We destroy records older than seven years."

"Then why did you still have material on Eddie?" she asked.

Carl shifted in his chair, hummed a moment, then licked his lips. "I knew him. Sort of. We were both from Manila."

Carl's answer set off warning bells in Murphy. Carl sounded like her—when she lied.

"But Eddie was a get-rich-quick kinda guy." Carl finally looked back at her. "And you don't get rich processing seafood."

"I see." Elin gave him an encouraging nod.

"You're on your feet for long hours, all day or all night. It's noisy, smelly, cold, and wet. You clean, trim, cull, and grade fish. Nope. No real money in that."

"So how was Eddie going to get rich?" Elin prodded.

"He got it in his head to become a fisherman."

"Fisherman?" Elin shoved a lock of hair from her face. "But he'd need a boat and permits and—"

"Details, legalities." Carl waved his hand. "He didn't care about such things. For all practical purposes he could just as easily have panned for gold or bought a lottery ticket."

"But he was going to fish . . . how?" Elin asked.

Again Carl broke eye contact. "Um . . . get a group together and . . . um . . . steal a boat."

"And he did." Murphy took off her glasses and stared at Carl.

Carl blinked and tried to look away. "Um. Well. Yes. Even

then, instead of stealing something like a Chignik seiner, he took a sport fishing boat."

No one spoke for a few moments. The bang and grind of machinery filled the air. Finally, Elin said, "That's the dumbest harebrained scheme I've ever heard."

"You didn't know Eddie. He was always full of plans. He had this dog—"

"Tell me about the dog," Murphy said.

Carl glanced out the window. "I don't know, kind of a terrier. About this big." He held his hands a foot apart. "He was gonna get a female, breed these dogs, start a new line of super rat killers, and make a fortune." The phone rang and Carl answered.

She gave Elin a questioning look. "Rat killers?"

"Rat terriers, probably. Rats can be a huge problem in Alaska," Elin said. "They can totally change an entire ecosystem. They eat birds, eggs, seeds, contaminate everything they come into contact with, damage buildings and wires . . . and cost billions of dollars in damage. Not just here, but around the world."

"I found what I think was part of a small dog collar on Ruuwaq Island, and I saw a rat in the buried Quonset hut."

"I'm not surprised. A number of islands have been infested with the rodents since before World War II."

Carl hung up after muttering a few words. "I gotta get back to work." He slid Eddie's file across the desk to Elin.

Elin and Carl stood, but Murphy stayed seated. "Tell me, Carl, when you told Eddie about a boat he could steal, why didn't you go with him that day?"

CHAPTER 16

arl dropped to his chair. "How did you know?"
"I didn't, but there had to be some reason you kept his file,"
Murphy said.

Elin sat down and leaned forward, her gaze going from his
face to Murphy's.

"I didn't tell him to steal it." Carl's voice went up a notch. "He
just asked if I knew of a boat that wouldn't be missed right away."
The phone rang again. Carl ignored it. "I guess he couldn't get the
seiner, so he took the sport boat."

Elin pointed at him. "But you knew his plans."

Carl wouldn't meet her gaze. "I might have suspected."

Murphy figured he knew more than that but couldn't prove
anything at this point. "When was this, the date he stole the boat?"

Carl licked his lips again. "I don't know exactly. He quit in
May of that year, but I saw him around for a while afterward."

"Who were the other five men?"

"I don't know. There's a fair-sized Filipino community in
Kodiak. He may have asked some of them. Maybe he played cards
with them or something."

"Cards?" Murphy asked. "Is that how you knew Eddie so well?"

Carl's tongue snaked out and wet his lips. "Nothing wrong
with a game or two of poker."

"As long as you win?" Elin asked. "Is that why you called this in? Needed some reward money?"

Carl threw up his hands. "I just know he took a boat and was never heard from again."

"And even though you knew who had stolen that boat, you never reported it?" Elin asked.

"No." He looked at her, then out the window. "I never planned on telling anyone anything. Ever," he muttered.

This time Murphy stood when Elin did. "I may have more questions later," Elin said. "So don't plan on taking any trips."

Carl leaned back in his chair and wiped his face. "You'll let me know about that reward, right?"

"Yeah, I'll let you know."

They didn't speak until they'd reached Elin's car. "You interview people very well. I'm impressed. What do you think?" Elin asked after sliding behind the wheel.

"You seem to know at least one person who died on Ruuwaq Island ten years ago. I'd say you need to know why. And how." She thought for a moment. "You know it was after May, the year, and the type of boat stolen. You could find the date it was reported missing, which would narrow down the timeline—"

"Not as narrow as you'd think." Elin started the car. "A lot of big sport boats are owned by rich people who seldom take them out. It could have been missing for some time before it was reported. I'll look into it, of course."

"Maybe you'll get lucky," she said.

They pulled out of the parking lot. "Maybe." Elin turned toward the lodge. "This case could have a simple explanation. Six inexperienced men get into a small boat and run into trouble. They land on Ruuwaq Island with no food or water. Not even wood to start a fire. They become desperate, fight, but one of them finds and hides in the Quonset hut. Maybe the rest of them resort to attempted cannibalism like the Donner party or the Andes flight disaster."

Murphy grimaced. "Nasty, but possible. But I don't think they were on that island that long."

"But . . ."

"But?" she asked.

"If they were simply victims of stupidity and an accident, why were their bodies burned? Who burned them? Why did the guy in the Quonset hut not try to get out? And why were Zinkerton and Vasily murdered?" Elin sighed. "This whole thing is like an onion. I just keep finding more layers." She glanced at Murphy. "Hey, I'm sorry. It's not your problem."

"I don't mind helping you." And she needed to stay close to the case or Bertie wouldn't get her the information she needed on her sister. "Um, keep me in mind if you need any more drawings or anything."

"Be careful what you ask for." Elin smiled.

They arrived at the lodge, but Elin kept the SUV running. "I've got a million things to do today. I'm still working on Vasily's and Irina's murders, so I'll say good-bye."

"The spare key?"

"Next time."

"Okay then, bye. And thanks for the clothes." She jumped from the SUV and ambled into the lodge.

Denali was on the phone at the wet bar. When he spotted her, he put his hand over the receiver. "Olga left you a sandwich. It's in the fridge with your name on it." He pointed to the kitchen. "This call's going to take some time."

She nodded. Entering the kitchen, she found everything spotless and smelling faintly of bacon. The sandwich, wrapped in clear plastic, sat next to an apple. She grabbed both and returned to the main room of the lodge. Denali's black Lab sat by the front door, staring intently at the wood as if he could mind-meld the door open. She pointed to the dog, then shrugged her shoulders to Denali.

Denali waved that she could let the Labrador out.

As if sprung from prison, the canine sprinted down a path toward a line of trees. She followed slowly, eating the apple. Through the pines on her right was the main guest lodge, a three-story log structure with masses of glass windows. She pushed through the branches to the parking area. A Porsche Cayenne, two Cadillac Escalades, and a Mercedes SUV were parked in a row. A group of guests were waiting to load into the Salmon Run van. All wore waist-high waders, expensive cameras, and designer travel attire. One guest, an older woman, waved to her.

"Going bear watching with us?"

"No." Murphy smiled. "Looks like you're going fishing." She nodded at the waders.

The woman laughed. "Apparently the best bear viewing this time of year is Katmai National Park, on the mainland. We'll fly in on a floatplane, land in the bay, and have to wade in about half a mile. Quite the adventure."

The van driver strolled from the lodge and gave the signal to load.

The black Lab nuzzled Murphy's hand and headed back toward the residence. "I get you, dog," she whispered. "Staff and other riff-raff stay on the other side of the trees."

Before entering the woods the path meandered past a storage barn with four-wheelers, a truck with a snowplow, and mainte-nance equipment. Birds chirruped, whistled, warbled, and called from the trees. The sun made a brief appearance before clouds engulfed it. The trail ended at a split. The dog was waiting for her, tail whipping the air, feet dancing.

"Do you have a preference?" she asked.

His gaze drifted to her sandwich.

"I see. I was thinking more directional."

He may have been a retriever, but at the moment he was impersonating a pointer. His liquid-brown eyes studied the food in her hand with intense interest.

"If I give you a bite of my sandwich, will you suggest which path I should take?"

He answered with a loud licking of his chops.

She opened the wrapper. Before she could remove one side of the sandwich, the dog snatched all of it. One gulp and lunch was gone.

"Okay then. Have a sandwich."

Unfazed by her sarcasm, he held up his side of the bargain and turned to the trail on the left. Patches of fog shrouded some of the trees, and the air was tangy with pine. The forest ended in a small clearing. A black iron fence enclosed a small cemetery punctuated with jagged gray headstones. The fog was heavier here, curling around the edges of the glade. The birds were silent.

Denali's grandson was inside the fence, staring at a headstone. His shaggy brown hair tumbled over his brow. His long, thin arms poked from his hooded sweatshirt as if he'd just had another growth spurt. His face was losing its childish roundness, stretching into adult proportions.

She started to turn around. Cemeteries were creepy, and way outside her comfort zone. And she never knew what to say to someone standing at a grave. The Lab raced up and bumped into the young man. Lucas patted the dog's head. "Hello, Quinn." He turned and spotted her. "Oh, hi, Ms. Andersen."

"Hi there, Lucas. I didn't mean to interrupt."

"S'okay," he muttered.

Taking a few steps nearer, Murphy caught sight of the largest headstone, an obelisk mounted in the center of a square granite slab. Near the bottom of the obelisk was a metal plaque engraved with *Paul Stewart, 1918–1946*. So. This was the family cemetery that Denali had referred to.

The young man turned his back to her, picked up a rock, and chucked it at a tree. He missed. Folding his arms, he looked down.

She selected a stone and tossed it at the same tree. She hit it.

Lucas looked at her out of the corner of his eye, bent down, and chose another pebble. He took aim, then threw it at a sapling. *Thwap!*

Murphy moved closer, found a small rock, zeroed in on the same tree, and let fly. *Whack!*

His mouth twitched in a tiny smile. "Not bad."

After finding a perfectly round pebble, she sidled next to him, bent forward a bit, and hurtled it at a stump. It bounced off, flew up, and smacked the sapling.

"That's awesome. I bet you're fantastic at skipping rocks." He looked at her directly for the first time and relaxed his stance. "Have you ever used a slingshot?"

"Yup. Both kinds."

"Both kinds? I didn't know there were two."

"The standard Y-shaped slingshot and the shepherd's sling."

He furrowed his brow.

"Think Daniel and Goliath."

"I think it's David and Goliath."

"Just seeing if you were paying attention." She casually nodded toward the large obelisk. "Paul Stewart. Is that your great-grandfather?"

"Yeah. Grandpa's dad. He was a war hero, you know. He won a Distinguished Service Medal."

"I saw that in the lobby. Very impressive."

"He was a doctor."

"I see. Medical or PhD?"

"Medical. Like a scientist. Come here and see." He moved to the other side of the obelisk and pointed. Recessed into one side was a rectangular metal plaque divided into six squares with cast images on each one—an ant, a bird, some kind of amphibian, a shaggy cow, a turtle, and a shark. Carved above into the granite were the words *All creatures great and small.* "He studied stuff. I figured out those are invertebrates, birds, amphibians, mammals, reptiles, and fish."

"Very clever of you." She squatted in front of the plaque. "All the granite here looks the same. So does the lettering and even the plaques. I wonder why."

"Ask Olga. I don't know."

She stood and waved her arm at the forest. "I didn't realize your family owned this place for so long."

"Grandpa Denali was born here. Great-Grandpa Stewart built it but never lived in it because he died in the war." He pointed to a smaller headstone. "That's Great-Grandma's grave." The dates indicated she'd died in her midforties. A small sculptured angel was on one side. "And that's Grandma Stewart." JoAnne Stewart had been only fifty when she died. Her tombstone had Proverbs 31:6 and a plaque with praying hands.

"I wonder why Denali's parents weren't buried next to each other."

"I asked Grandpa about it once. He said she was mad at him. Probably because he died so young." Murphy sidled over to a marker nestled on one side of the small family plot. Two names were carved into the surface—*Shawn Taylor* and *Elsa Stewart Taylor*. Above the names was a bas-relief of a fisherman holding on to the wheel of a boat. Murphy had seen this image once before—she cast her memory about until she could recall. Yes, it was the same likeness as the bronze sculpture from the Gloucester Fisherman's Memorial in Massachusetts. She'd visited Gloucester when finishing her degree in Rhode Island. Carved into the granite above were the words *They that go down to the sea in ships*.

She thought about the photograph she'd seen in the lobby of the young couple.

"Shawn Taylor was my father," Lucas offered. "Elsa was my mom."

Both had died the same year. Before she could ask, the young man guessed her question. "I was almost two when they died. They were fishermen. Their boat was eventually found, but . . ."

She reached over and touched his arm. "I'm so sorry."

He shrugged. "It's been a long time." He stared at the ground and whispered, "Such a long time." Shaking his head, he said, "Even though I never really knew them, I still come here almost every day and talk to them. And to find it."

"Find it?"

"Yeah. I overheard Grandpa say he'd find it here, but when I asked, he only said 'something from the past.'"

"The past. I suppose past memories are here."

He nodded. "Grandpa's pretty much raised me. And Olga. Sometimes Uncle Jake."

"Jake Swayne is your uncle?"

"Yeah. Grandpa's half brother. They had the same mother."

"And that's why he eats at the lodge so much. He's part of the family."

"Sure, but he lives right over there." He pointed toward the woods.

"I see."

Lucas bent down to scratch the dog's ear. "There's pictures of my folks at the lodge."

"I saw them as well. You look like your mother." She checked her watch, then looked around. The fog had grown thicker, swirling over the gravestones. "I hope I don't get lost out here in this fog."

He pointed. "Stay on that trail and keep to the right when it branches. You know you're on the right path when you reach the equipment shed. The other path will take you to the hangar, the private landing field, and eventually the road."

"Hangar? Private landing field?"

"Uncle Jake has an apartment in the hangar. And a lot of our guests are stinking rich and fly in on their own planes."

"I saw the main lodge on the way over here. How big is this place?"

"Big. And this year we'll be getting bigger. Grandpa's putting in another lodge building. It'll double our size."

"So your grandpa and Jake will run—"

"Not Uncle Jake. He told me he doesn't want to be tied down. That's why he's a pilot."

"He's sure picked a beautiful place to fly around. I've got to go. Come on, Quinn."

The Labrador jumped to his feet, staggered a few steps, and vomited.

CHAPTER 17

Lucas knelt beside the dog. "What's wrong with him?"

"I don't know." Murphy joined him. "He seemed fine when we left."

The vomiting grew more violent. "Not good," she said. "Help me get him back to the lodge." They pushed, pulled, and urged the dog up the trail. The Lab alternately staggered, vomited, and lay down as if exhausted. She took off her jacket, passed it under the dog, and handed one side to the boy, creating a sling. They got as far as the storage barn before the dog could no longer stand at all.

"I'll get help," Lucas said. "You stay with Quinn." The young man took off.

She sat beside the dog on the wet ground and cradled his head. "Quinn. Poor puppy. You'll feel better soon. The vet will know what to do." The damp coldness seeped into her. She shivered.

Shortly Lucas appeared. "I told Grandpa. He called the vet, then told me to watch for his truck and point out where you are." His lower lip quivered. "Is Quinn going to die?"

"I hope not."

He touched the dog, then ran back up the trail.

"Good Quinn. Don't die . . ." She stroked the dog's head. *The dog acts like he was poisoned,* Dallas whispered in her mind.

"But—" She pictured Quinn snatching her lunch.

That's right. You *were supposed to have eaten that sandwich.* Dallas's voice faded.

It seemed like hours but was probably less than twenty minutes before Ryan arrived. "I just heard." He bent down and lifted the dog. "Come on, big guy, let's get you some help."

She trotted behind, trying to keep up with his long strides. As they reached the lodge, a truck pulled up and a large man with an impressive black beard, green flannel shirt, jeans, and rubber boots jumped out. Lucas grabbed his arm and pointed at us.

Ryan placed the dog on the ground as the man charged over, knelt, and pulled a stethoscope from his rear pocket. He listened to the dog's heart and lungs, checked his gums and eyes, then, still without speaking, effortlessly scooped him up.

Murphy followed him, her arm around Lucas. The vet loaded Quinn into his truck. "I'll call when I have something, son." He ruffled Lucas's hair, jumped in his pickup, and sped off.

Lucas wrapped his arms around her shoulders and sobbed. "Don't let him die! Please don't let him die!"

It had been so long since anyone had hugged her, leaned on her like that. She stood arms akimbo for a few moments before she awkwardly patted him on the back. In spite of herself, her vision blurred. When she could speak around the brick in her throat, she said, "I'm sure the vet will do everything he can. Let's get you inside and get you a tissue."

He let go.

Touching his narrow shoulders, she gently nudged him toward the residence.

Ryan held the door for them. She mouthed, *Thank you* to him. Denali was in the living room as they entered. He reached

135

under the blanket covering his legs, pulled out a starched white handkerchief, and held it out for Lucas.

The boy took it and blew his nose, then hugged his grandfather.

Denali slowly rubbed the boy's back and murmured in his ear. When Lucas finally stood, Denali said, "Go wash your face, son."

Lucas trudged toward his room.

Denali's intense gaze followed him. When the door closed behind Lucas, Denali looked at her. "Someone will pay for making my grandson cry. Now, what happened to my dog?"

"I don't know. He seemed fine, full of energy, then he started to throw up."

"Did he eat anything?"

The little hairs on her arms stood on end. "He ate . . . my sandwich."

Denali waved away her answer. "That wouldn't have hurt him. Did you see him eat anything else?"

"No. Do you think someone . . . tampered with my food?"

"Don't be ridiculous. Olga made that lunch for you. Are you accusing her of trying to kill you?" His face was now flushed.

"Of course not." She backed away. "I'm sorry. I . . . I think I'll go for a walk." She brushed past Ryan and headed outside before she could say anything else that would anger Denali.

She couldn't blame him. Someone poisoned his dog.

No. Someone tried to poison you.

She jogged toward the cemetery. It was far more comforting to believe Quinn had grabbed a piece of rotting animal that made him sick. Slowing as she approached the family plot, she picked up a stick and used it to peer between the clumps of salmonberry brambles and pushki.

She'd made it all the way to the grave site without finding

anything and was returning to the lodge when she ran into Ryan, standing at the fork in the trail.

"Ah, Murphy, are you all right? I don't think Denali is mad at you."

"No. He's worried. I'm fine. I was just retracing our path, looking for something Quinn could have eaten."

"Any luck?"

"No."

"Well then, maybe you could direct me? Which way to the cemetery?"

"Go down this way."

She was about to brush by him but stopped. "So why are you wanting to see the family graves?" She took off her glasses and stared into his eyes. Removing the lenses seemed to help people trust her.

Ryan blinked a few times, then folded his arms. "I thought you knew I'm a journalist doing a story on Salmon Run Lodge." He started walking toward the graveyard.

"But you're not?" She joined him.

"That's partly true. I'm an investigative journalist following up on a story. An old story, or so I thought. It brought me here."

A cool breeze slithered up the back of her sweater. She rubbed her arms.

He didn't say anything until they reached the graves. Slowly he walked around Paul Stewart's obelisk, then he moved to Lucas's parents' grave. "What happened to them?"

"I understand it was a fishing accident."

"Who told you that?"

"Lucas."

His eyes narrowed. "Seems the whole family is willing to talk to you."

She shrugged. "You just have to know how to throw rocks."

"What?"

"What old story brought you here?" Again she stared into his eyes.

He seemed to be unable to look away, then he laughed. "Wow. I just remembered a dog I had when I was a kid. He had the same kind of look in his eyes." Turning completely around, Ryan surveyed the surroundings, sniffed, and rubbed his neck. "I haven't thought of that dog in years."

"What happened to him?"

He shrugged. "We lived on a farm. When my dog couldn't work anymore, my dad shot him. He said when something's no longer useful, it's time to get rid of it."

"I'm sorry." She continued to stare at him, but he no longer looked at her face. "Tell me what brought you here."

"To the lodge?"

"The cemetery."

He lowered his voice. "What do you know about Operation Fair Cyan?"

"Cyan?" she asked. "Like the color?"

"Yes."

"And fair? Like pleasant looking, or like f-a-r-e?"

"F-a-i-r. I found it on a heavily redacted letter in a dusty file. Someone had inked over much of the material, but in a few places, the ink wasn't opaque. I was able to get a document examiner to help me decipher the writing."

"And that led you here?"

Ryan nodded to the gravestone. "As a matter of fact, yes. The name was in Paul Stewart's file."

"So the old story you were researching had something to do with Paul Stewart?"

"No." He folded his arms. "I was originally researching the death of Reinhard Heydrich."

"Heydrich? Why does that name ring a bell?"

"It should. He was one of the main architects of the Holocaust, the Final Solution to the Jewish people."

A small shiver went through her.

"Heydrich was head of the Sicherheitsdienst, the Nazi security service." Ryan stared off into the distance. "He was an organizer for Kristallnacht—"

"Night of broken glass."

"Yes. The pogrom in 1938 where hundreds of Jewish buildings, businesses, and synagogues were destroyed. In spite of Heydrich's prominence, the decision was made to assassinate him. Operation Anthropoid was launched. Several men were airlifted into Czechoslovakia, where Heydrich lived, with orders to kill him. They ambushed him and threw a grenade into his convertible, which wounded him. He died several days later in the hospital." Ryan looked at her. "Now, here's the interesting thing—a number of people believe the grenade lobbed into the car contained botulism, which got into his wounds."

"Sounds like an interesting story, but—"

"But what's the connection between Paul Stewart and Reinhard Heydrich? Between Operation Fair Cyan and Operation Anthropoid? Even the events of seven thirty-one?"

"Seven thirty-one, as in July thirty-first?"

Ryan shrugged. "The simple answer is I don't know. The official files on Heydrich are still closed. I was able to get a report from the British Secret Intelligence Service, which suggests the botulism that killed Heydrich might have been acquired from Paul Stewart."

"Paul Stewart is a common name. Are you sure it's this Paul Stewart?" Murphy nodded toward the gravestone.

"The report was dated 1941. It named a Paul Stewart at this address."

"That's pretty specific. Have you asked Denali about it?"

Ryan shook his head. "Denali once sued an author for a book that mentioned Paul in a negative light. Seems like Denali is protective of the family name." Ryan chewed his lip for a moment, then looked her in the eyes. "Maybe you could get him to open up. See if you can find out what links Heydrich and Stewart. Or what Operation Fair Cyan was all about. Actually, any information will be useful."

First Bertie wanted her to find out about Zinkerton. Now this. "I don't know, Ryan."

"Aren't you working that case on Ruuwaq Island? And a Quonset hut from 1941?"

"Well . . ."

"I pay my informants very well."

With some money and Bertie's help, she could do a lot more to find her sister. "No promises, but a quick question. Do you think Paul Stewart was a German spy or—"

"No. He was doing something for the US government. I want to know what." He stuck out his hand. "Deal?"

"Deal."

Turning, she strolled toward the lodge. She glanced back just before she left the clearing.

Ryan hadn't moved. He was staring at her.

CHAPTER 18

Denali was in the lobby when Murphy returned. "Where have you been?" he asked.

"Looking for a source of the poison."

He softened a little. "Any luck?"

"No. I went all the way to the family plot."

"I saw Ryan go in that direction."

She decided not to share their strange conversation. "Yes. He was interested in the graves. For the article he's writing."

He stiffened, then shook his head. "A rip-off of a sculpture from the Gloucester Fisherman's Memorial? Stupid sayings about animals featuring a shark, a yak, and a turtle? A proverb about drinking too much? Our little cemetery is certainly interesting."

"But it brings you peace?"

"I see you've been speaking to my grandson as well."

She nodded. "This sounds morbid, but the headstones all look like they came from the same block of granite."

"They did. A friend . . . um . . . someone had all the headstones redone for the family."

"An interesting gift." Murphy waited but Denali said nothing more. He picked up the book in his lap. "Can I bring you something before dinner?"

"No. You go ahead. You have some time before Olga will need you."

She was suddenly starving. Throwing a quick wave at Denali, she entered the kitchen, raided the pantry, and found some crackers. She leaned against the counter while she ate.

Slowly she approached the house, passing a rusty truck on blocks. Reeking garbage burned her nose . . .

Murphy flinched. She'd been standing over the garbage in the kitchen, staring at the contents. Daydreaming? But that was a nightmare. Why couldn't she daydream about Joshua? "Hey, Bertie," she whispered. "I think I'm developing a sweet tooth."

She turned to leave, glancing at the whiteboard behind the kitchen door.

In crude handwriting, scrawled in red marker across the bottom, were the words *I've found you.*

Adrenaline rocketed through her body. Her hand flew to her mouth to cover the scream. She shot from the kitchen, scrambled up the stairs, and slipped into her room. After locking the door, she raced to the window and pulled the curtains, then peeked out.

Clinton Hunter had found her. He could have been the one to poison the sandwich. He had to be watching, waiting for Olga to leave. The doors were unlocked. Easy to sneak in. No one would see the whiteboard from any place but inside the kitchen.

She crouched on her bed holding a pillow, shaking.

Fraidy-cat.

"What?"

You're a fraidy-cat. Her sister's voice echoed in her head.

"Did you just miss what happened? Clinton found me. He

poisoned my sandwich. He tried to kill me!" She hugged the pillow tighter.

So that's what you're going to do about it? Hide in your bed? Why not put that pillow over your head?

"What am I supposed to do?" Murphy pushed the pillow aside and stood. "He's an escaped convict with lots of family money and support—"

You know what you have to do.

She walked to the dresser and looked in the mirror. Dallas's face stared back at her. "I can't tell Denali. He'd fire me on the spot. I'll erase the message . . ."

Before you do anything, remember Denali has a grandson. He'd move mountains to keep that boy safe—especially from a serial killer who's wandering around his home looking for you.

"Then I'll need a gun to protect the child. And myself."

You'll need money to buy that gun, and to get away. Ryan is going to pay you.

"How about you, Dallas? How can I find you?"

You'll find the answers. They're already in your hands . . . Her voice faded away.

"Wait!"

Go now. Erase . . .

Murphy crossed the room, opened the door, and crept down the stairs. The house was silent.

She entered the kitchen and erased the threat from the whiteboard with a shaking hand. Red marker clung to her fingers like blood. She returned to her room and scrubbed the marker from her fingers.

Clinton had failed to poison her. He was a sneak and a coward, so he'd take advantage of times when she was alone. She'd need to be vigilant and make sure she stayed around people. She also needed to get away from the lodge, but first she had to get the information from Bertie to find her sister, and get the money from Ryan.

She clenched her teeth. She'd start by updating that notebook Bertie gave her.

She found the small notebook where she'd left it. Taking it to her bed, she sat cross-legged and leaned up against the wall. Under *Facts and evidence* she'd written *Five victims, all male, death ten years ago, signs of violent death, no other reports of finding bodies, had to get to island somehow—boat? Bodies removed/disposed/ buried by person or persons unknown.*

She crossed out *had to get to island somehow—boat?* and wrote *boat stolen, Eddie Pelino? 1941 Quonset hut, body in hut, skull photo and metal object in phone camera, all evidence to date given to Richard Zinkerton. Zinkerton murdered. Vasily and caretaker Irina murdered.*

Under *Questions* she'd written *Cause of death, what happened to bodies, what happened to transportation, Vasily and caregiver murder connected? Identity—Filipino? Cannery workers? Why on island?*

She couldn't really cross out *Identity—Filipino?* or *cannery workers* yet as she didn't have solid proof.

Closing her eyes, she pictured the inside of the Quonset hut the last time she'd looked around. "Rocks," she whispered.

"Rocks," she said again, louder. How did that building get covered in rocks? She tapped the tablet, then wrote *Earthquake?*

After picking up her phone, she logged on to the internet, then typed in *earthquake, Alaska.* Her search took her to the Alaska Earthquake Center webpage. A map looking like a colorful grouping of bubbles showed earthquake activities over the last two weeks. It noted that earthquakes occurred in Alaska every fifteen minutes on average. In 2014, over forty thousand earth-quakes were detected.

"Of course," she murmured. "The Pacific Ring of Fire. Some of the largest earthquakes ever recorded."

Typing in the year Vasily found the bodies, she discovered three notable quakes—two in the Andreanof Islands and one in Kasatochi. The strongest was a magnitude of 6.6. That would be enough to shake loose a landslide, but on an island almost a thousand miles away?

"Think, Murphy. If the man died when the slide occurred . . ."

She stood and strolled to the window. "That skull was intact, but I couldn't see if there were any injuries to the body, as it was hidden by the rotten clothing." The skin between her shoulder blades prickled at the thought. "Bertie and I were able to get into the building without much effort. What kept him from escaping?"

Returning to the bed, she sat, grabbed the pillow, and wrapped her arms around it. The log walls creaked as they settled. In the distance, the muffled roar of a floatplane came through the window. "Then again," she whispered, "what are the odds that six people became shipwrecked on an obscure island, and five of them killed each other? One fellow hid from the carnage, only to be trapped by a quake that occurred almost a thousand miles away at the same time? That kind of coincidence stretches the imagination too far."

What if the body in the hut wasn't related to the other five? Who knew how long that skeleton had lain in the Quonset hut before she and Bertie found it? Or maybe he was the one who killed everybody. Or found them and burned the bodies. Or they found him and it made them go crazy—

Useless, simply useless speculation.

Starting a new page, she wrote *Paul Stewart, Reinhard Heydrich,*

Operation Anthropoid, Distinguished Service Medal. Lucas said his great-grandfather was a doctor, so she added that. Under *Questions,* she jotted *Connections? Operation Fair Cyan.*

After thinking for a moment she started a third page, heading this one with *Timeline.*

1941—Quonset hut
1946—Paul Stewart died
Ten years ago—five? six? men dead
Two days ago—Vasily and Irina murdered
Yesterday—Zinkerton murdered, Myra in house fire

She slammed down her pencil. The Quonset hut dated to World War II, as did Paul Stewart and Reinhard Heydrich. But there was an almost-seventy-year gap between the war and the bodies on the island, and another ten years between those bodies and the current murders.

"And none of the events may even be related," she whispered.

The next page held the name and phone number of Vesper Amason, the Native woman with the screaming granddaughter from the hospital. Below that were the words *soul searcher?* Murphy circled the words, then memorized the phone number.

She gave up. For now, answers eluded her.

After changing into her uniform and pulling up her hair, she paused. In spite of Detective Buchanan's doubt, Murphy still believed Zinkerton was murdered for the evidence he had. And Vasily could have been murdered for what he knew about Ruuwaq.

Her gaze drifted to her notebook. It contained information someone might want. She looked around the room for a hiding place. Everything seemed obvious.

Stepping into the hall, she once again noticed the Alaskan

regional photographs mounted on canvas. If they weren't screwed to the wall . . .

They were hung by a wire on the back, leaving a hollow made by the stretcher bars. She tucked the notebook behind a photograph of a grinning fisherman holding up a huge fish, making sure the cover of the notebook was slightly wedged between the stretcher bars and canvas. If someone were to run a hand over the canvas, they'd feel the small raised area, but she'd bet no one even looked at the photos.

———

Olga soon had her peeling potatoes.

"Denali told me about Quinn," the housekeeper said. "Said the vet sent the blood and urine contents for testing. He thinks the dog got arsenic poisoning."

A cold sweat dampened Murphy's back. Obviously Denali hadn't told Olga about her poisoned-sandwich comment. "Where could Quinn have gotten into arsenic?"

"He's having Lucas go through everything in the equipment shed tomorrow."

"I see." She concentrated on the potatoes for a few minutes. "How long . . . how long have you worked for Denali?"

"Oh my, ever since his accident."

"Accident? The one that . . ."

"Put him in that wheelchair, yes. Car accident. Icy roads. His wife, JoAnne, perished."

"How sad."

"It was terribly sad. Bad times. Really bad. He'd just lost his daughter and son-in-law and was flooded with grief. JoAnne was a mess herself, tipping the bottle all the time. He had some kind of split or altercation with a man who'd become like a father to him. I think the only thing that kept him sane was that medal of his dad's. I think he was focusing on how brave his dad was during the war, and that he needed to be . . . Look at me! Gossiping like an old woman." She picked up a pot holder. "Why don't you talk about you?"

"There's not much to talk about. I'm on my own. The apartment I rented burned down. My landlady died. I got this job."

Olga pulled a pan out of a cupboard and placed tinfoil on it. "How long have you lived on Kodiak?"

"About a year."

"What brought you here?"

"Did you want me to slice the potatoes or leave them whole?"

Olga paused with a stick of butter. "Don't want to talk? That's okay with me. I can tell you're educated, well brought up, polite, a good worker, and in a heap of trouble."

She stopped peeling. "Why do you say that?"

"Because a lot of people around you are turning up dead."

———

Dinner that night was quiet and somber. Father Ivanov joined them—apparently a common occurrence—as did Ryan, Elin, and Jake.

As Murphy served the first course, Elin was speaking. "Of course, the good news is that Bertie is on the mend."

Lucas was somber with red-rimmed eyes. She rubbed his shoulder slightly when placing his plate, and the young man gave her a weak smile.

"The ABI decided to send someone over to look into our crime wave." Elin put her napkin in her lap.

"What is that, three murders in two days?" Father Ivanov asked. "Don't you usually have less than three murders in a year?"

"Way less, and if we count Murphy's landlady, it's four. The fire was arson."

"What about Ruuwaq Island?" Denali asked. "You're done with that place, aren't you?"

"It's a bit on the back burner," Elin said. "But we still have supplies out there—a metal detector and so on. Jake, maybe you could fly—"

"No," Jake said. He and Denali exchanged glances. "I'm . . . spotting bears for the next few days."

"Well then, we'll get Butch Patterson. Maybe Murphy could even finish diagramming the scene and take some more photos of the Quonset hut and the body." An uneasy silence fell on the diners until Father Ivanov started talking about Alaskan politics.

After everyone finished eating, Lucas yawned and stood.

"Night, son," Denali said. Elin, Jake, and the priest added their good nights.

Lucas went to Murphy and gave her a hug. This time she returned it. "Good night, Lucas," she whispered.

He left.

When she glanced up, all eyes were on her. "Does someone need something?"

"Well, well, well." Jake raised his eyebrows at Denali, then took a sip of his drink.

After a moment, Denali cleared his throat. "What are the Seahawks' prospects this year?"

"Not a chance," the priest said.

"You a betting man?" Jake asked.

Murphy crossed the living room and stepped outside to get some fresh air. The front of the house gently sloped to the rocky beach and ocean beyond. Another storm loomed on the horizon. Leaning against a log rail, she tugged out the clip holding her hair and let the weight of it settle across her shoulders. A bald eagle and a pair of crows were having a disagreement over something. When a magpie joined in, the eagle decided to leave. She watched him fly across the treetops and out of sight.

Movement under the pines drew her attention. A man sitting in a silver pickup parked under the trees was watching her.

CHAPTER 19

Murphy was about to turn and run when the man got out of the pickup. Joshua Ward. In uniform.

When he came close enough so she didn't have to shout, she said, "I hope you're not here to arrest me."

"Should I arrest you?" He smiled, displaying perfect teeth. The sleeves of his black uniform stretched across his well-muscled arms.

Four kids. Life could be so unfair. "I don't think so. I'm not a black widow or anything like that."

"I see. You're more like Jessica Fletcher on *Murder, She Wrote*. You show up and people drop like flies."

"I hope not." Her hair blew across her face. It probably looked like a rat's nest. She put it back into the clip.

"How can I help you, Officer Ward?"

"Officer Ward, is it now? What happened to Joshua?"

"Joshua."

"Better. I came out to see how you were doing."

She rubbed her sweaty hands on her jeans. "Doing? I'm doing fine."

"I got a call from Bertie—"

"Bertie!" She turned toward the front door. Before she could take a step, Joshua was next to her on the porch.

"Please don't be angry." He was near enough to touch. "She got hold of me and told me about you—"

"What do you mean, 'about me'?"

"She told me Clinton Lamour Hunter had escaped prison. She explained that you were . . . not comfortable with telling police your real identity and therefore wouldn't have police protection. She wanted me to keep an eye on you."

Murphy glanced at the lodge.

"Don't worry. I can keep your secret."

The urge to touch him, to have him hold her, was almost overwhelming. "I . . . I would appreciate that."

"And Bertie said she's going to help you find out about your sister."

"Yes." She brushed a stray hair from her face and looked away. When she found Dallas she could relax. Find peace. Stop lying. Start loving.

"The way I look at it"—he edged closer—"the best way to keep an eye on you is to take you to dinner."

She could feel his nearness, the heat from his body. Better just end this before it went any further. She stepped away and studied the top of her shoe. "Elin tells me you're a widower. I'm sorry."

"Thank you. Cancer. She went quickly."

"And that you have four boys."

He was silent so long she looked up.

He was grinning at her. "Sounds like Elin is a tad bit jealous."

"It's none of my business."

"For the record, there's no longer anything between us. And as for my boys, well, at least it's out in the open. No surprises. Travis, Max, Cody, and little Sammy. Did—"

The door opened. Father Ivanov stepped out. "Oh, hello. I

don't believe we've met. I'm Father Antoniy Ivanov." He held out his hand.

Joshua took it. "Patrol Officer Joshua Ward. I work with Detective Olsson. Just touching base here with Murphy."

"Nice to meet you. I was just leaving." He walked halfway down the stairs, then turned back. "You are welcome to worship with us at our church anytime."

He smiled. "Thanks."

"I should be going back to work," Murphy said.

Joshua grabbed her hand. "Think about dinner. And you'll call me if you have any problems or if you notice anyone hanging around."

The touch of his hand made her legs rubbery. "Yeah, sure. Call." She extracted her hand from his grip. *How stupid can you sound?*

Elin was just inside the door pulling on her jacket. "Was that Joshua?"

"Yes. He was just . . . asking how Bertie was doing."

Elin's eyebrows rose. "Uh-huh. Surrrre he was. You don't look like the mommy type. Don't forget those four boys."

"Elin, really, I—"

Elin placed her hand on Murphy's arm. "I like you, Murphy. I want to stay friends, so let me be clear about this. Joshua's off-limits. Understand?" She squeezed Murphy's arm, then left without looking back.

———

Murphy was exhausted after finally cleaning up. The twilight darkness that passed for night allowed her to look out each window and check around the lodge for unwanted visitors before closing the blinds. The building creaked and moaned around her as the logs settled. As she headed through the dining room to go to bed, she glanced toward the stained glass door of the office tucked into the corner. She paused.

The employee notebook explicitly stated the office was off-limits.

But everyone was asleep.

No one would know if she downloaded the photos from the Quonset hut. She could make a copy, then delete them from her phone. Should it be stolen, no one would know she'd even taken the pictures.

"Don't you think you're being a bit paranoid?" she whispered. Who'd take her phone? And so what if they did? The Alaska State Troopers or the Alaska Bureau of Investigation would soon be taking over the case. They'd return to the island and take their own photos.

The lodge shifted and sighed around her. Sibilant rain pattered on the metal porch roof.

Tomorrow she'd probably return to the island with Elin and Butch anyway.

She found herself staring at the wall of family photographs. Moving closer, she examined each one. Denali as a young man. His daughter and son-in-law on their boat. His beautiful but, according to Olga, drunken wife. Such sadness through the generations reached back to Denali's father, Paul.

Why was there only one photograph of his father? She moved closer to the old print. Time had lightened the black-and-white image to shades of pale gray. The oddly framed man faced the camera, smiling, arms folded. The edge of a flat surface was just behind him.

She sucked in a quick breath. Could it be? Was that the

table-shaped rock from Ruuwaq? And could the tiny, faint lines be the corrugated wall of a Quonset hut?

A floor squeaked somewhere in the house.

She froze. The sound didn't reoccur.

Do it now. After a swift check around her, she pulled the framed photograph from the wall. She thought for a moment, then grabbed the photo of Denali's daughter and son-in-law and scurried to the office. She opened the door.

Creeeak!

She winced, left the door open, and switched on the light. Inside the small room was a desk holding a computer, an all-in-one printer-copier, and a chair. With trembling fingers, she opened the top of the printer, placed the framed photograph of the man facedown, and pushed the copy button.

Click, click, buzzzzzz, clack.

The copy slowly printed. It was almost white, all the details washed out. She'd have to take the photos out of the frames. Her hands were now shaking so hard she could barely remove the back of the frame.

The pattering rain had grown to a drumming roar. The sound would hide any approaching footsteps.

She pulled out the image. It had been torn rather than cut, explaining the odd placement. A hint of an arm, originally hidden by the frame, was beside the man. She placed it facedown on the copier.

Click, click, buzzzzzz, clack.

After snatching the printout, she prepared the second photo to copy.

Click, click, buzzzzzz, clack.

While the second photo reproduced, she returned the first to the frame.

Thump, thump, thump. Footsteps overhead.

Grabbing the second photo, she jammed it into the frame. She took the copies, folded them, and stuffed them into her back pocket.

Thump, thump, thump. Someone had reached the top of the stairs.

Sweat broke out on her brow. She clicked off the light, stepped out, and shut the door.

Creeeak!

The sound was like fingernails on a blackboard. The footsteps paused.

She hung the photos on the wall, then raced to the kitchen. She just had time to open the refrigerator and grab a container of creamer when Ryan stepped in.

"Oh. It's you." He glanced around the room. "I thought I heard a door opening or closing."

"Really?" She returned the creamer. "I didn't hear anything. I was just finishing up." She closed the refrigerator. "May I get you anything, Ryan?"

"No, no." He shook his head. "When I can't sleep I rummage around in the kitchen. Denali gave me his blessing as long as I don't eat anything scheduled for tomorrow." He picked up the next day's menu from the counter. "How about you, Murphy? Can I fix anything for you?"

"Thank you, no. I'm bushed."

"By any chance did you find out anything since our little agreement?" He reached into his pocket, pulled out his wallet, and extracted several bills.

"I'm following up on the rockslide that covered the Quonset hut." Should she tell him about the torn photograph? No. Not until she had time to study it.

"Good start." He grabbed her hand and stuffed the money into it.

"I haven't given you anything—"

"Think of it as a down payment." He smiled.

"I'm heading for bed." She turned and left the kitchen. She glanced at the office. Through the glass she could see the printer's power light.

She hesitated. Did he see that?

Ryan's measured steps moved behind her toward the dining room.

She raced toward the stairs. Once in her room with the door locked, she opened her hand and counted the money. Five hundred dollars.

She paced. That was a hefty down payment for virtually no information. Even though she needed the cash, was there a chance that Ryan might think it was buying more than information?

She should just return his money and tell him no in the morning.

Smoothing out the bills carefully on her dresser, she sighed. He was right. He did pay well.

But if that was just a down payment, how valuable was the information she was supposed to discover?

CHAPTER 20

She was in front of the house. Beside her, a rusted truck, windows shattered, sat up on blocks on the overgrown lawn. The yard was strewn with garbage. The house was barely discernible in the overgrown trees surrounding it. A weak light shone through the foliage from a window.

Closer now, her legs moving as if through sludge, heart pounding, breath coming in harsh gasps. Her hand reached for the rotting door.

Her hand covered in blood.

She screamed, but only air came out. She tried again, forcing a guttural cry.

Murphy woke bathed in sweat. The dream lingered in her brain like a dim photograph. A prayer formed unbidden in her mind. *Oh, Lord, oh, sweet Jesus, release me from this punishment.*

"Enough." She pushed from the bed. The clock said 3:30 a.m. There'd be no way she could go back to sleep now. She picked up her work jeans lying across the dresser and pulled out the two copies of the photographs. After turning on the desk lamp, she sat and studied them. The flat shape behind Denali's father did look like the table-shaped rock, and the lines could be a Quonset hut. She wished she had the ability to scan the images and run them through a photo editor.

Ha! Who was she kidding? She'd be lucky if she wasn't discovered for making copies.

She moved the light closer to the copy, staring at Paul, Denali's father. *I'm supposed to be a forensic artist. Just what can the artistic version of Sherlock Holmes do with an old photograph?*

She pulled out her phone and Googled *forensic art*. She found a website by an artist in Montana.

Forensic art is any art pertaining to law enforcement or legal proceedings. Types of forensic art are composite drawings, facial reconstruction, unknown remains, image modification or enhancement, courtroom drawings, demonstrative evidence, photographic superimposition . . .

Photographic superimposition. She clicked on that link.

Photographic superimposition is a technique where the photograph of a missing or wanted person is overlaid over the skull of an unknown person. The skull is rotated to create a positional relationship to the facial features until an orientation is achieved. Developed in the 1930s, the original technique used transparent film . . .

She scanned farther down the page.

Josef Mengele, the Angel of Death of the Auschwitz concentration camp, escaped after World War II to South America. Although relentlessly pursued, he was never caught but eventually drowned while swimming in the ocean. He was buried under an assumed name. His body was exhumed, and he was tentatively identified through photographic superimposition. Investigators placed an image of the skull they dug up over Mengele's photograph. The teeth are the only exposed bones in the body, which proved, in the Mengele case, to be a near optimal fit.

Maybe she could try the same technique. In the photo, Denali's dad was smiling.

She found the photograph she'd taken of the skull in the Quonset hut. The light from the cell phone screen might be enough to work as a light table. Placing the photograph over her cell, she manipulated the size of the phone image until they lined up.

The eyes of Paul stared out through the eye sockets of the skull; the nose appeared in the nasal aperture. Paul's lips stretched across the skull's teeth.

She shivered. This was creepy in the extreme. Assuming she had done this right, there seemed to be a match.

The next thought made her lurch to her feet. *If the body on Ruuwaq is Paul Stewart, who is buried in the grave here on Kodiak . . . if anyone?*

She paced across the small room before sitting at the desk. Clicking on her cell's internet icon, she typed in *Paul Stewart, Kodiak,* and *1946,* the year of his death according to the monument.

A short article came up. "The body of Paul James Stewart, formerly of Kodiak, was found today on Afognak Island. He was reported missing two months ago and presumed drowned. He will be buried in the family cemetery. No services are planned."

She leaned back in her chair and did a little more research. Afognak Island lay slightly over three miles north of Kodiak

Island. The tsunami from the 1964 Good Friday earthquake, the most powerful earthquake in North American history, caused the residents of the island to be permanently relocated to Kodiak. In 1946, however, Paul could have been working there.

But if Paul Stewart's body was found on Afognak, why did the skull in the Quonset hut match the photo of Paul Stewart?

Nothing made any sense.

She went to the door and peeked down the hall. The lodge was silent. Olga would be arriving soon to start breakfast. Murphy tiptoed over to the mounted print and retrieved her notebook. Opening the page to where she'd written *Paul Stewart, Reinhard Heydrich, Operation Anthropoid, Distinguished Service Medal, doctor/scientist,* she added *possible skull match between photo of Paul and Quonset hut body. Paul's body found on Afognak.*

Maybe Olga would have more information. Or even Denali.

Had she and Bertie found the body of the real Paul Stewart, entombed in that Quonset hut since 1946?

She reread the article. The date was June 9. Missing for two months meant that he'd disappeared in April. Were there any large earthquakes in April of 1946?

The internet provided a likely candidate. An earthquake occurred April 1, 1946, launching a massive tsunami that reached Hawaii, wiped out a lighthouse in Unimak Island in the Aleutians, killed over 165 people, and caused millions of dollars in damage. Such a quake would certainly be enough to bring the rocks down on the Quonset hut, and a tsunami would explain why the man died.

She jotted the date of the earthquake with a question mark.

That left the body found on Afognak. It would have been badly decomposed.

She grimaced at the thought.

What would have been available to investigators at the time for identification? Dental records and possibly X-rays. The discovery of DNA wouldn't be for another eight years or so. Maybe they thought it was Paul Stewart because Stewart had gone missing around that time and place.

If it was Paul Stewart in that Quonset hut, the troopers or crime lab or some other official law-enforcement entity would be able to recover the skeleton and determine a definitive answer.

Certainly a lowly barmaid, as Richard had put it, shouldn't be the one to question who was buried in the grave on the family property.

She folded the copied images into the notebook, made sure the hallway was clear, and placed it into its hiding place behind the canvas.

She'd update Ryan on her work. Maybe he'd slip her another five hundred dollars. The faster she had funds, the faster she could get a gun and make a run for it. After brushing her teeth, she ran a brush through her hair and clipped it up, then headed downstairs to prepare for breakfast. She couldn't help glancing at the whiteboard.

Olga was already busy mixing some kind of coffee cake. "I had a note that Father Ivanov is joining us, and Elin is coming to pick you up. Knowing her, she'll probably arrive in time for breakfast." Olga beamed. "Figure we'll have five. Put everyone at the big table."

Murphy went out into the dining room. Through the office's glass door, she could see the copier's light was off. Had the machine gone into hibernation, or had someone noticed it and turned it off? She tried not to stare at the wall with all the photographs.

How much more information could she get from Olga? And would any of it be useful?

Olga was humming to herself as Murphy returned to the kitchen.

She casually removed her glasses and cleaned them with a paper towel. "Olga?"

The other woman looked up from her cooking.

"You mentioned someone who was like a father figure to Denali, a man who Denali had a falling-out with a number of years ago. What was his name?"

"Oh my, it's been a long time. I'm not sure I remember." She pursed her lips. "Lonnie? Larry? Leif? I think that's it. Leif something. Last name started with a *B*." She tapped a wooden spoon on the edge of the pot. "A distinguished-looking man. I had a bit of a crush on him at the time, even though he was quite a bit older. He didn't seem to even notice me." She shook her head as if waking. "He was obsessed with security, I remember that. Put in the security system, which was a problem when they had the falling-out. Denali finally had someone dismantle it. How strange that I remembered that now." She picked up the spoon again and continued cooking.

Leif B. Not a promising lead, but something.

"I almost forgot." Olga pulled out some serving plates. "A letter or something was left for you. It's in the living room on the small table by the door."

A letter? A wave of dizziness came over her and she clutched the counter. She left the kitchen on unsteady legs and made her way to the living room. The white, legal-size envelope was propped against a candy dish. It didn't have a postmark. With shaking hands, she opened it.

It wasn't a letter. It was a computer printout of the front page of the Anchorage newspaper from eleven years ago. The headline screamed "Anchorage Serial Killer Caught!"

The room receded around her. A buzzing started in her head. Blackness lapped at her brain. No! She tore the printout and envelope into tiny pieces and dumped them into the trash.

Clinton had been called a thrill-seeker serial killer, one who enjoyed outsmarting the police. He toyed with his victims. Like he was currently playing with her. He wanted to frighten her even more.

This time he'd made a mistake. She was older now, and stronger. And she'd soon be armed.

In fact, once she had that gun, maybe she shouldn't wait for his next move.

Elin drove up, followed by the priest. Murphy raced back into the kitchen. She knew her face would be pale, but Olga didn't seem to notice. She was soon serving the meal.

"How goes the investigation on Vasily and poor Irina?" Father Ivanov asked Elin.

"Irina?" Denali asked.

"His caretaker." Elin took a bite of sausage.

Murphy rearranged some dishes on the sideboard so she could stay and listen.

Elin finally swallowed. "Good news and bad news. The bad news is someone took the time to wipe down all the surfaces in Vasily's home. The good news is he or she missed one spot and we have a set of prints. We've submitted them through IAFIS—"

"What's that?" Lucas asked.

"Integrated Automated Fingerprint Identification System." Elin picked up her fork, speared another piece of sausage, and began chewing.

"Could I have some more coffee?" Ryan asked.

Rats! Murphy wanted to hear more. She scurried into the kitchen, returning with the coffeepot as Elin was speaking.

". . . criminals and terrorists. We'll need to take fingerprints of you, Murphy, and of course Father Ivanov, to eliminate both of you along with others. In fact, Murphy"—Elin turned to see her— "we can do that later today. We'll drop by the station on the way back from the island."

"Okay." Murphy knew she shouldn't worry about her fingerprints. It wasn't as if she'd broken any laws. It wasn't illegal for a law-abiding citizen to drop out of sight.

"I have some news on the identification of the bodies on Ruuwaq." Father Ivanov beamed at the diners. "A woman at the local Filipino church has come forward with a possible identification."

"That's outstanding, Father." Elin smiled. "But I spoke to their pastor and no one brought any details."

"I'm afraid she's what you would call a reluctant witness. I'll need to be with you when you talk to her. Could the two of you"—he nodded at Murphy and Elin—"meet me at Christ's Table, our interfaith soup kitchen, this morning?"

"Not this morning," Elin said. "I arranged to fly out to Ruuwaq Island with a friend of Bertie's. We're going to recover the supplies and tools and possibly do some work there. Maybe later this afternoon?"

"Sure, call me after you land. You know my number."

"Perfect. And that's wonderful news about the new information," Elin said. "I'd love to make some progress identifying those bodies."

The lodge phone rang and Denali picked it up. "Yes. That's fantastic. When? You're kidding. No, nothing turned up. I'll send someone." He disconnected. "That was the vet. He's releasing my dog today."

"I'm waiting for Murphy to finish up," Elin said. "In the

meantime, why don't I go pick him up? What was the final diagnosis?"

"It was as he suspected. Poison. Arsenic."

Elin tugged at her hair. "Denali, that doesn't make sense. He's a trained therapy dog. He wouldn't take food from strangers or anything left on the ground."

Denali's face hardened. "We didn't find a source of the poison in the equipment shed. That means someone put poison in his food."

Murphy kept her face down as she collected dirty dishes. She entered the kitchen and focused on scraping the dishes and loading the dishwasher, but thoughts kept poking into her brain. That stupid newspaper article where they took her photo at Vasily's house must have led Clinton to Kodiak. How he found where she lived below Myra was a mystery, but she would bet he'd burned the trailer, hoping she was sleeping inside. He easily could have followed her to Salmon Run Lodge when Elin drove her here. The poisoned sandwich was evidence of that, and the message on the whiteboard, and the letter.

Maybe he was worried she was getting close to the truth of her sister. He knew she could get anyone to talk. He knew because she got him to talk.

Her sister, Dallas, disappeared while Murphy was traveling on her summer vacation. She grew concerned when Dallas stopped returning her calls. When she'd arrived at the condo they shared, she found blood. Not a lot, but combined with Dallas's disappearance, enough to prompt her to contact the police. The police were not interested. After all, they reasoned, her sister was an adult. Even the earring she'd found at the hotel in Kodiak didn't faze the police.

Murphy dropped soap into the dishwasher and turned it on, then grabbed the necklace hanging around her neck.

She and Dallas had seen Hunter around their condo development in the spring, showing the various properties to prospective tenants. They'd even discussed how good-looking he was.

He'd asked Murphy out on a date three weeks after Dallas went missing. Murphy had already tracked her sister's trip with Hunter to Kodiak and needed to find out more. She agreed.

The kitchen was clean. She headed up to her room to change into clothes suitable for Ruuwaq Island. She still clutched the necklace.

Over dinner with Hunter, she'd asked him about her sister, but he said they broke up in Kodiak. She'd removed her glasses and stared at him. He seemed startled but mentioned he'd been reading about all the missing women, wondered if her sister could now be one of them, then casually commented on all the properties he'd managed. It was a long shot, but something about the combination of names and his work as a rental agent just struck her wrong. She excused herself and made a phone call to the police. They arrested him before he had a chance to run.

And they'd found the bodies.

CHAPTER 21

After pulling on the same clothes from her last visit to the island, Murphy debated on adding the name Olga had given her, Leif B., to her list hidden behind the canvas.

No. She'd do it later. After pocketing the spare key to Elin's car, she grabbed her coat.

Hunter had buried the women, or in some cases just left them as rotting corpses, at different houses he'd managed outside of town. The police found all but her sister. Before they could take him to trial, he escaped and came for her. With a knife. The Lord only knew how she'd survived. They promised her he would never get out again.

Now he was loose.

A gentle tap on Murphy's door was followed by Elin's voice. "Ready to fly out?"

She was more than ready to leave her thoughts behind and work on another puzzle. She handed over Elin's spare key.

"Thanks." Elin dropped it into the purse she had over her shoulder, then headed for the stairs.

Lucas sat on the floor of the living room hugging Quinn. The Lab seemed content to lap up the attention, not even giving his tail a thump as they passed.

They got into Elin's SUV and she drove toward town.

"Are we heading to Lily Lake?" she asked.

"Butch Patterson operates out of Near Island."

Murphy slid down in her seat even farther as they passed through the center of town, a movement Elin didn't seem to notice. Near Island was accessible by a bridge, and the floatplane business was on the side of the island opposite downtown Kodiak.

A tall, lean, mustached man waited by the floatplanes tied up at the dock. His smile lit his face, making his startlingly blue eyes almost disappear. "Any friend of Elin is a friend of mine," he offered after introductions.

Once again Murphy was placed in the front seat, this time looking up the Trident Basin where seaplanes regularly took off and landed. After putting on the headphones, she relaxed and watched as they taxied past the cobalt-green Crooked and Holiday Islands. Sunlight dappled the teal-blue ocean. The scene made her wish all her art supplies hadn't gone up in smoke.

Turning south, they paralleled the breathtaking snowcapped peaks of Kodiak's mountain range, which rivaled the Canadian Rockies.

"How hard is it to fly a plane?" she asked to keep her thoughts at bay.

Butch grinned. "Once you learn how, it's like walking or breathing. You're up here, just you and God, looking at the most beautiful landscape He ever created." He pointed to the different dials and switches, explaining each one. She listened, asked questions, and relaxed slightly. No unpleasant memories demanded her attention.

Butch finally nodded straight ahead. "The island's just ahead." He was silent for a few moments. "I was surprised when Elin told me she was interested in finding an island named Ruuwaq. A friend of mine wrote a book about Kodiak legends. I called him up and asked about the name. He said the word meant 'arrow' and was in his book."

"Do you think I could get a copy of this book?"

"I'm pretty sure it's out of print, but you could try the library."

"What's the title?"

"I don't know, but his name is Jonathan Wilson. Just look for a skinny little book no wider than this." He held his fingers about five inches apart.

"I'll check into it," she said.

"Yeah, do that. I'll circle around the island first before landing."

The tiny speck of brown-black cliffs grew. Butch turned the plane to the left, then banked it in a circle so they could survey the island.

It took a moment for what she saw to register in her brain.

The mountain that had risen behind the Quonset hut was gone. Only a massive pile of boulders remained.

Elin's voice came through the headphones. "Where did you say the Quonset hut was buried?"

Wordlessly she pointed.

"But I don't see anything. Are you talking about that rock pile?" she asked. "How did you get inside?"

She cleared her throat. "Someone blew it up. The whole mountain. Without heavy equipment, you'll never be able to recover anything from the Quonset hut." She glanced at Butch. "Do you have any binoculars?"

"Under your seat."

She pulled the case free and took them out.

"What are you looking for?" Elin asked.

"Just confirming what I suspected. The metal detector we left behind is gone, as are the crime-scene kits, probes, all of it. And

I don't see any sign of the rope ladder. In fact, all the vegetation looks dead." She put down the glasses. "Every scrap of evidence has been stolen or destroyed. The island's been wiped clean."

"Do you want me to land anyway?" Butch asked.

"No," Elin said. "Whatever is going on here, it's bigger than the case I started with. Head back to Kodiak."

After returning the binoculars to the case, Murphy straightened and licked her dry lips. "It seems that someone is going to a great deal of trouble to make sure we don't find out the secrets of Ruuwaq Island."

"That it does," Elin said.

The flight home seemed to take an eternity. As they landed, Elin called the priest. "We just landed."

A half hour later the women pulled into a small, older strip mall with Father Ivanov's soup kitchen at one end and a thrift shop at the other, near the Walmart shopping center. A few battered and rusty cars and trucks were parked across the cracked asphalt parking lot. They parked near the thrift shop. Elin opened the rear of the SUV, put her Glock into her purse, then placed her purse next to a blanket, Kevlar vest, raincoat, and emergency go-to bag. She made sure the doors all locked. "Father Ivanov doesn't allow guns inside Christ's Table. Says it disturbs the diners."

"Diners?"

"The homeless who eat here."

They walked to the soup kitchen. The door was locked, but Father Ivanov spotted them through the front window and let them in. Red-checked tablecloths covered the long tables neatly lined up around the spacious room. At the far end was the serving counter, and behind that a few individuals were preparing the meal. Soft voices, an occasional *clang* of a cooking pot, and the mouthwatering scent of baking bread drifted to their part of the room. Windows on the front and side allowed plenty of sunlight through the partially open blinds. Father Ivanov indicated a table, then asked, "Coffee?"

"Absolutely." Elin nodded and took a seat.

"Sure. Let me help you." Murphy followed the priest to a large urn surrounded by thick, cream-colored coffee mugs. He poured three cups. Murphy knew he took his coffee black, and she prepared hers and Elin's the way they both liked. She brought them to the table and took a seat next to Elin.

"Before we start"—Father Ivanov took a sip—"how did it go on your excursion to the island?"

"A disaster. Nothing is recoverable." Elin played with the mug's handle.

"What do you mean?"

"Someone made sure the rest of the mountain covered that Quonset hut. Only airlifting major heavy equipment would help. Maybe not even then." She shoved some of her white-blond hair off her face, then drummed her fingers on the table. "And I have to say I don't like this. I don't like this at all." She looked at Ivanov. "You mentioned a lady who had some knowledge . . . ?"

"I asked the pastor of the Filipino church if he knew of anyone who disappeared around ten years ago—"

"He said no when I talked to him," Elin said.

Ivanov held up a finger. "Yes, but I asked him about relatives."

"Same difference."

"No. He said when you inquired, he'd been thinking about whether any members of his congregation were missing. I figured anyone hanging around Eddie Pelino probably didn't spend a lot of time in church, so I asked him again, this time about any missing relatives. He has a Friday night service, and he brought it up during the sermon."

"And?" she asked.

Ivanov pulled out a piece of paper and slid it over to her. "Ten years ago, three brothers and their cousin came to visit their aunt here in Kodiak. They were on their way to the processing plant in Akutan. They were here only a few days, and the aunt believed they made it to their job safely. But many months later she learned from relatives that they had disappeared."

Elin took the paper with four names neatly printed in a column.

"Only four?" she asked. "Not five?"

"Four plus Eddie," Ivanov said. "Vasily said he found five bodies. It appears that the skeleton you discovered in the Quonset hut is unrelated."

Murphy studied her mug of coffee so he couldn't read anything on her face. If she hoped to get more money from Ryan, she'd need to protect information before it became common knowledge.

"I'd like to speak to the aunt," Elin said.

Now it was Ivanov's turn to drum his fingers on the table. "She's not exactly hot on the police, if you catch my drift." He thought for another moment. "Tell you what. Let me call her and see if she'll agree to a meeting. If she will, we can go over and talk to her. We can take my car so she doesn't panic when she sees a police vehicle. She lives very close to here. Will that work?"

"Sounds like a great plan."

He stood and moved to the other side of the room, retrieved a cell from behind the counter, and made a call.

The women workers continued to bustle around the kitchen, now adding the scent of melting butter and hamburger to the air.

Murphy was starving. She drank half her coffee and wished for a doughnut. Or a hamburger. Or both.

Elin took a sip of her coffee. "Mmm, you must have made this, Murphy."

"Watch out, Starbucks. I'm on my way up."

Elin picked up the paper with the names. "With this connection that Father Ivanov made, we might just make some progress in spite of the sabotage."

"I hope so." Murphy's phone rang. Bertie. "Hang in there." She signaled Elin that she needed to take the call, then stepped outside. Traffic noise was horrible. She had to raise her voice and push the phone to her ear to hear. "Yeah, Bertie, you've been on my mind. I have a lot to share."

Elin stuck her head out the door. "We got the go-ahead. I'm riding over with Father Ivanov to meet the aunt. I shouldn't be long. Wait here?"

"Sure." She waited until Elin shut the door. "Our trip to the island was a disaster—"

A motorcycle, minus any indication of a muffler, drove by.

"Just a minute, Bertie, let me go back inside. I can't hear you." Father Ivanov and Elin were just leaving by a side door. She waited until the door shut, then continued updating Bertie on their trip.

Bertie listened without interruption.

Still talking, Murphy wandered to the table they'd been sitting at and automatically gathered up the used mugs. Next to the coffee urn was a brown tub that held dirty dishes. She strolled over and placed the cups inside.

Boom!

The side windows exploded inward, spraying the room with shards of glass.

CHAPTER 22

Floor? What was she doing on the floor?

Murphy blinked at the smoke around her. An acrid odor burned her nostrils. Glass shards sparkled like orange mica chips around her.

No sound.

Raising her arm, she saw red freckles . . . no. Blood. Bloody cuts. Her head hurt. Why couldn't she hear anything?

A woman wearing an apron and a hairnet knelt beside her, mouth moving.

What was she saying? Why didn't she speak up?

The woman reached for Murphy's bloody arm, pulling her to her feet.

She snatched up her phone from the rubble and stuffed it into her pocket.

The wall on the side of the building was missing. Beyond that was a raging fireball of a car. And two bodies inside.

Adrenaline flooded her system. Vomit burned the back of her throat. Father Ivanov. Elin.

The woman—Murphy recognized her now as one of the kitchen workers—tugged her away from the inferno.

She shook off the woman's hand and crept toward the destroyed car. Heat lapped at her face. The fire extended outside the car in an oval with a strong odor of gasoline. It was plainly evident the occupants were beyond saving.

Smoke billowed through the shattered glass. A smoke alarm started shrieking, then another.

A second woman, also wearing an apron and a hairnet, grabbed Murphy's hand and led her to the kitchen. Vaguely she could hear a siren in the distance.

The women's faces were the color of parchment. Tears streaked their faces.

The vomit returned to Murphy's throat. She swallowed hard. Two more dead. The bomb had been placed in Ivanov's car. He had to be the target. Poor, poor Elin.

Crackling and popping from the fire, plus the approaching sirens, confirmed her hearing was returning. The police would arrive soon.

The police. How would she explain how everyone around her kept dying? Vasily, Irina, her landlady, Zinkerton, and now Elin and Ivanov? She couldn't. They'd probably take her into custody. And Clinton Hunter would find her neatly cornered and ready for the taking. He'd escaped twice. If he could break out of jail, why couldn't he break into jail to get to her?

She needed to hide, lay low, and figure out her next move.

And do it quickly. Maybe Joshua could help.

A second explosion rocked the building. The two women screamed and fled through a rear door. Police and fire engine sirens wailed in unison with the smoke detectors.

She glanced around the kitchen, then raced to a coat tree where several sweaters, sweatshirts, and aprons hung. Grabbing an apron, she tied it on, then yanked on a torn gray sweater to hide the cuts on her arms. Several hairnets were in a box. She snatched one and stuffed her hair inside.

The sprinkler system kicked in. Black smoke burned her eyes. She pushed through the kitchen door just as a third explosion slammed into the building.

She kept her head down and raced toward the Walmart.

Two fire trucks and several police cars rocketed into the parking lot. An ambulance followed. Several EMTs jumped from the ambulance and raced to the fire.

Small groups of shoppers gathered, watching the excitement. She joined them. "What's going on?" she asked a man in a yellow slicker.

"Don't know. Looks like a fire, something blew up. Probably one of them terrorist things."

Firefighters surrounded Christ's Table, now partially engulfed in flames. She worked her way to the side of the strip mall away from the fire and where the thrift store was located.

Elin's SUV was still parked there.

An officer corralled the small crowd gathering at that end of the lot, moving them away from the action or getting them to move their vehicles away from the building.

The crowd grew around her, many with grocery carts loaded with food. The women guarded their purses but tended to ignore jackets or scarves draped over the carts. She snagged a pale-blue scarf, then a dark-green jacket.

The purses gave her an idea.

It was crazy-bold and stupid. And it just might work. She casually wandered through the throng of people, occasionally pausing to ask a question or listen to someone. Removing the apron, she dropped it next to a car and kicked it under the wheel. The sweater was next, ending up in an empty cart. She twisted the scarf around her neck. Pulling the hairnet off, she ran her hands through her thick hair to make sure it would partially cover her face, then raced to the SUV, waving her arms. "Oh no! Someone help me!"

A firefighter grabbed her arm. "No closer, young lady."

"That's my SUV! It's going to burn up! I have to move it!"

"Okay then, pull out and park over there." He jerked his thumb at the corner of the lot.

"I can't. I locked my purse in the back with the keys. I was waiting for the locksmith. Please help me." Her heart pounded so loud she was afraid the firefighter would hear it.

The firefighter waved over a patrol officer. She was relieved it wasn't Joshua. "Lady here says her purse is locked in her SUV. We need to move her rig."

The officer, a young woman with black hair and a round face, immediately walked away, returning with a slim jim. She took only a moment to spring the door.

When Murphy moved toward the back of the SUV, the officer held up her hand. "Wait." She popped the gate, then looked at her. "Describe your purse."

"Brown, light-brown leather, shoulder strap, gold clasp—"

"Okay, okay, let's get it moved. Did you see anything suspicious when you parked?"

Still keeping her face somewhat averted, Murphy snagged Elin's purse. "No. Like I said, I locked my purse in the back accidentally—"

"Yeah, yeah. Let me see your driver's license. Potential witness—"

The mic on the officer's shoulder squawked. The officer listened for a moment, then looked around. "I see ya. Ten-four." She glanced at Murphy. "Wait here. I'll be right back."

Murphy didn't wait. She fished the single key out of the bottom of Elin's purse, jumped in the SUV, and drove away, not looking back. She was halfway to the lodge before she found a small pullout and stopped. Resting her head on the steering wheel, she let the tears come. *Oh, Lord, what will happen now? Elin is dead. Father Ivanov is dead. Bertie is hurt. I've stolen an SUV and am fleeing both the police and a killer.*

A killer who knew where she lived and worked.

She couldn't return to the lodge as if nothing had happened.

Lord, please send a plan.

A fog was sliding around the trees, growing noticeably thicker. *Fog. Hide. Invisible.*

With her facial scar, she could hardly be invisible.

Maybe she could live in the woods . . . yeah, right. Just her and a few Kodiak brown bears, the largest bears on earth. Experts said they were not particularly aggressive, but they were the same species as a grizzly. Grizzlies were not opposed to eating humanburgers.

Soon enough that patrol officer would start looking for her. The longer she sat here, the more likely a casual observer might notice.

Where might she go?

She opened Elin's purse, looking for ideas. Inside was Elin's Glock. Great. If they put out an APB on her, they could add armed and dangerous. Elin's wallet had forty-seven dollars. Armed, dangerous, and pathetically short on funds. The cash Ryan gave her was stashed in a sock in her room at the lodge.

Vesper Amason. The woman at the hospital with the screaming child. The woman had said she owed her a favor.

It was worth a try. No one knew they'd met. There'd be nothing to link them.

Murphy's cell phone was nearly dead. This call had to go through. She slid down in her seat until she could barely see over the dashboard and dialed. The older woman answered on the second ring.

"Hi." Murphy cleared her throat. "You probably don't remember me, but we met the other day at the hospital—"

"Murphy. Murphy Andersen. How could I forget? How good to hear from you."

"And it's nice to speak to you again under less . . . trying circumstances. How's your daughter doing?"

"She's recovering just fine. The doctor said she was lucky, but I'd say blessed. Lord knows getting her car totaled like that, and with her insurance . . . goodness me. I'm just rambling on and on. From the sound of your voice, I don't think that's why you called. How can I help you, Ms. Andersen?"

"Call me Murphy. I need a place to stay, at least for a few days until . . . well, for a few days. Do you know of any rooms available to rent for a day or two?" Hopefully Elin had a credit card in her wallet.

Vesper was silent for a few moments. "I see. Where are you now?"

"I'm in . . . my car. And I'm parked . . . um—"

"Never mind." Another pause. "I have an extra bedroom. You are welcome to stay here."

"Oh, you don't have to—"

"Somehow I think I do." Vesper gave directions to her home, located in Bells Flats, a settlement about ten miles from downtown Kodiak at the end of Womens Bay. The fog had grown thicker as she'd been on the phone, making the passing cars crawl by. She returned to the road and joined the vehicles moving at a snail's pace.

She almost missed the turnoff to Rezanof Drive West and had to swerve at the last minute, making the truck behind her hit his horn. The fog had reached cotton-batting density, and she was reduced to stopping at each mailbox to read the numbers.

The house itself was all but invisible when she finally pulled into the driveway. She had a vague impression of a single-story rancher with a detached garage.

Vesper came outside as soon as she pulled up. She was accompanied by two young men in their late teens, though one appeared to be slightly older. Both had black hair, round faces, almond-shaped black eyes, and unsuccessful attempts at a mustache.

Vesper tucked Murphy's arm in hers and ushered her to the door. Once inside, Vesper released her arm so she could kick off her shoes and add them to the impressive pile by the door.

"May I have the keys to your rig?" Vesper asked.

She bit her lip. "Um, why?"

Vesper just held out her hand.

Slowly she placed the key in Vesper's palm. Vesper, in turn, handed it to one of the young men, who promptly left.

Oh, Lord, did I just make a big mistake? Murphy wiped her damp hands on her jeans.

Vesper pointed to the battered kitchen table. "Coffee?"

Caffeine was the last thing Murphy needed in her over-stimulated state, but she didn't want to be rude. After all, she could be spending the night huddled in the Walmart parking lot hoping that neither Hunter nor the police would find her. "I'd love a cup."

The spotless kitchen smelled of Pine-Sol and fresh coffee. Vesper placed a thick white mug of the steaming brew in front of her, followed by a mismatched creamer and sugar bowl. Murphy clutched the mug. "Where are you taking the SUV?"

The woman's broad, flat face creased in a smile, and she patted Murphy's arm. "Your rig will be safe. We're just making sure no one is unduly interested."

The young man soon returned, nodded at the old woman, and joined the other youth in the living room. Although the television was on, neither looked at it. Instead, they bent over their cell phones with rapt attention, thumbs flying.

Murphy sipped the thick coffee, then quickly added cream and sugar.

"You were there when the car exploded," Vesper said. It wasn't a question. Vesper folded her hands on the table, waiting.

"How did you know about the car bomb?"

"It's all over the news. They believe two people died. And you were there."

"Why do you think that?"

"You reek of smoke and gasoline. You have a streak of soot on your chin. There's a small cut on your neck, and I would venture to say you have more. And your eyes keep darting around the room as if someone might jump out at you at any moment."

Murphy opened and closed her mouth, then mutely nodded.

"Take off your jacket."

She did as she was told. Vesper seemed to be a woman who always got her way.

The blood on her arms had smeared and coagulated. Without speaking, Vesper stood and moved to the sink, where she wet some paper towels. She pulled a pair of tweezers from a drawer, a bottle of alcohol from a cupboard, a box of Band-Aids from her purse, and a tube of antibiotic from the bathroom. She placed everything on the table.

After sitting, Vesper grabbed her arm and started cleaning the wounds.

The alcohol stung like crazy and several of the glass shards were deeply embedded, but Murphy clenched her teeth and remained silent.

It seemed like eons passed as Vesper cleaned and bandaged her arms, but it was probably only an hour. When the older woman finished, she cleaned up the table and poured another cup of coffee. She sat once more, removed her glasses, and casually began to clean them. "Now, Murphy, who is trying to kill you?"

CHAPTER 23

Murphy hesitated only a moment before telling Vesper everything—about her mission to find out what happened to her sister, Clinton Hunter, the earring, the deaths of Vasily and his caretaker, the fire and murder of her landlady, Salmon Run Lodge, the messages, Ruuwaq Island, the skeleton, Operation Fair Cyan—everything tumbled out of her mouth. She was exhausted when she finished, and convinced Vesper would think she was crazy.

The woman listened to her without interruption, her gaze never leaving Murphy's face.

When Murphy finally stopped talking, Vesper took an oversize tattered Bible off the kitchen counter.

"I'm not a religious person, Vesper."

"Nor am I, child, nor am I. I am a believer, however." She put her glasses on. "I bet you pray when things get bad, though." She opened the Bible and found a passage. "In His grace, God has given us different gifts for doing certain things well. That's from Romans 12:6. The Bible names about twenty spiritual gifts, but that's not an exhaustive list. Some are talents we naturally have—"

"I'm sorry, but—"

"Child, I'm trying to tell you something important. You have a special talent, a rare gift. People open up to you. They tell you their thoughts, dreams, hopes, and, most significantly, their secrets." Her gaze drifted to the window, curtains open to the gauzy fog beyond. She stood and pulled the curtains closed, then remained standing with her back to Murphy. "My own grandmother had such a gift, as did other members of my family. She called it soul searcher."

"But I don't search anyone's soul. I don't know that I believe in a soul."

Vesper turned around and smiled. "Whether you believe in your soul or not, you still have one, and you and I will need to talk about it one day soon."

"But—"

Vesper held up a finger. "That's not open to debate. If you're going to offer up foxhole prayers, you need to know who's listening. Where was I? Oh yes. The term *soul searcher* doesn't refer to your ability to search inside another person. Only God can do that. You cause them to examine their own lives, to reveal the deepest, hidden reaches of their hearts. And they tell you. Different cultures call it by different names, but it's acknowledged around the world. It was a powerful gift in my grandmother's day. It's a massive power today."

Murphy took a sip of cold coffee to wet her dry mouth. "I don't know what you mean."

"Look there." Vesper nodded toward the living room where the two young men were still bent over their devices. "Those are my grandsons. I love them to death, but we seldom have a conversation lasting more than a sentence or two a day. They're always on their phones, checking for messages, texting someone. The cell phone is an extension of their hands. And it's not just my grandsons. Go to an airport, bus station, or doctor's office where people are waiting. How many are talking to each other?

They're not. They're looking at some digital contraption. And the worst? Go to a restaurant. You'll see entire tables where no one is even looking at the others, let alone talking. It's as if that digital shorthand they're getting from someplace else is more immediate, important, and fascinating than the person in front of them. Conversation is dead. Human interaction is all but extinct."

Murphy nodded.

Vesper sat at the table and leaned forward. "But you . . . you look at people. Really look at them. And in your eyes, they see someone who is listening."

"I try."

"You do more than that. Your ability to hear what people—what strangers—are saying, and to let them know you care, is rare enough to be considered a gift. It's almost irresistible to know someone who listens."

She looked down. "I don't consider it a gift."

"But you know how to use it. Give me your glasses."

She handed them to Vesper.

The woman peered through them. "Just as I thought. Plain glass." She handed them back.

"They make things . . . easier." She put the glasses on. "Your grandmother must have had terrific insight into herself."

"No, that's the strangest part of the gift. She could get anyone to talk, but she couldn't use it on herself. She had no clue what made herself tick." She rubbed her arms as if chilled. "And now I suspect others have recognized your gift and are using you. Some might even think you're a liability and need to be silenced. You know too much."

"But I don't know anything! A bunch of people died on an island ten years ago. A dead Nazi had a connection to Denali Stewart's dad over seven decades ago. It's public information!"

"You have come here for a reason. You need to put the events into perspective, to get to the bottom of what's been going on for over seventy years."

"But—"

"No excuses. You'll not be safe until you unravel the threads. The boys will help you." Vesper glanced into the living room. "Lord only knows they need to do something besides stare at those little screens," she muttered.

"I don't even know where to start."

"I'm just an old woman." Vesper stood and started pulling food out of the refrigerator. "And I only went through the eighth grade at school, but I'd say you have to start at the beginning." She piled the food next to the stove and picked up a spatula.

Murphy put her head in her hand. "The beginning. That would probably be the Quonset hut on Ruuwaq Island. Somewhere around 1941. It would really help to have my notes, and access to a computer."

Vesper drummed her fingers on the counter. "I think I may have something better." She raised her voice. "Boys? Andy? Adam?"

The two young men reluctantly put down their phones and entered the kitchen. "Yes, Grandma," they said in unison.

"Go invite Uncle to dinner."

Andy—or was it Adam?—threw up his hands. "Ah, Grandma, you know he's gonna talk our ears off—"

"Scoot!" Vesper pointed the spatula at the door.

They headed for the front door.

"Uncle has trouble with short-term memory. He's hard-pressed to recall if he brushed his teeth, although he never forgets to eat." Vesper went back to cooking. "But his long-term memory is amazing, especially about the war."

"Excellent. Do you need help with dinner?" Murphy asked.

"No. I need you to take a shower and get into some clean clothes. You're a skinny little thing. If you don't mind boys' clothes, I'll find something for you to wear."

Murphy followed the woman across the living room and down a hallway to a bathroom decorated in shades of pink with a selection of Avon and Mary Kay products.

Vesper grinned wickedly. "Keeps the boys from using it instead of their own. If they're even tempted, I dry my underwear on the shower pole. A few old-lady bras dangling in front of them works far better than any sign I might post. Towels in that cabinet. Help yourself."

The shower felt wonderful, although the soap stung her sliced arms. She washed her hair in cucumber-scented shampoo, scrubbed her face with melon-infused soap, and liberally cleansed herself with pomegranate shower gel. She felt like a salad.

Her own clothes were gone when she stepped out, replaced with a pair of boys' slate-green cargo pants, black T-shirt, and dark-red zip-up sweatshirt. She left her hair down to dry.

Vesper stopped stirring a pot of spaghetti sauce when she entered. "That's better. You look like you're twelve, but a clean twelve. You can set the table. There'll be five of us." She pointed to the kitchen table, then to a cupboard full of mismatched dishes.

Set the table. If she survived all this, she'd be well qualified for a job as a waitress.

Table set, she stepped into the living room.

An old man wearing Coke-bottle glasses, a light-blue dress shirt, navy vest, and khaki pants sat in a teal-green recliner speaking to the boys in Alutiiq. His sparse gray hair was combed back. He stopped speaking when she entered.

"Uncle," one of the boys said, "this is . . . um . . ."

"Murphy," she said. "How do you do?"

"*Cama'i.* Hello." His singsong voice was guttural.

"You speak Alutiiq." Murphy took a seat on the sofa.

"Not many of us left dat do." He gestured at the boys with his hand. "We have ta hold on ta what is left, to pass it on to da young people. I remember—"

"Uncle." Vesper poked her head into the room. "Tell Murphy about the war." She winked at her. "Tell Murphy about your father. Tell her about Castner's Cutthroats."

CHAPTER 24

The old man leaned back in his chair and stared at the ceiling. "You are a young girl. Maybe dey no longer teach dis in school. Do you remember da date of da Japanese attack on Pearl Harbor?"

"Of course. December 7, 1941."

"Dat's very good, um . . ."

"Murphy."

"Just six months later to da very day, June 7, 1942, da Japanese invade Alaska. But just three days later, the United States Navy said it no happen. The government buried da truth of da Aleutian occupation and da battles for Kiska and Attu for long time." His gaze drifted from the ceiling and rested on her face. "Are you sure, little girl, you want ta look at dat dark time?"

"I think I have to."

He resumed his study of the ceiling. Vesper softly hummed in the kitchen while the fragrance of garlic toast drifted in the air. The boys were once again absorbed by their cell phones.

"Dis generation"—he nodded at the boys—"no seem ta want ta know. Dey do not care about their culture, their heritage, da sacrifices of their ancestors. You seem to care . . . but I am ramblin' now. You see, where was I?"

"Kiska and Attu."

"Yes. Attu is da westernmost island of da Aleutian chain. Kiska is in da same area. Da Japanese planned ta bomb Dutch Harbor, farther up da Aleutian chain, where da army and naval base was located. Dey would then occupy Kiska and Attu. Dey figure America would rush to defend da territory, leaving Midway Atoll open ta invasion. Midway was a very important place, half-way tween Asia and North America. But America knew da plan. Dey had already broken da code, you see. The Japanese secret code. They no go to Alaska. They rushed ta Midway instead. Dat battle was considered da turning point in da war in da Pacific."

"Dinner is ready," Vesper called from the kitchen.

Adam and Andy shot to their feet and raced out of the room. Murphy stood, moved to Uncle's chair, and held out her hand.

He grunted and took it. "Dat is a good girl." He was probably no more than five feet tall. He slowly limped to the kitchen and took a seat at the head of the table.

A huge steaming pot of spaghetti, an overflowing bowl of tossed salad, and a loaf of garlic bread rested on the surface. It looked to be enough food to feed a small village.

Her mouth watered. She hadn't realized how hungry she was.

Vesper reached for her hand, as did one of the boys sitting next to her. They bowed their heads.

She quickly did the same.

"Lord," Vesper said, "bless this home, this meal, these people. Guard and keep Murphy safe and lead her to the answers she needs. In Jesus's name, amen." They all let go of hands and reached for the meal.

No one spoke while an amazing amount of food was consumed, mostly by the grandsons.

"Uncle." Vesper broke the silence. "I have been listening to you. I need you to tell Murphy about your father."

He nodded. "What you want ta know?"

Vesper sighed and turned to Murphy. "Have you ever heard of the Alaskan Combat Intelligence Platoon, also known as Alaskan Scouts and Castner's Cutthroats?"

"You mentioned Castner's Cutthroats. But no."

"They were a special commando unit made up of Eskimos, Aleuts, American Indians, trappers, fishermen, even prospectors. They were handpicked for their ability to survive the Alaskan wilderness. And they were trained to kill. Hand-to-hand combat."

"Da, and my dad was one of dem." Uncle beamed. "He sneak into Japanese camp, spy on dem. Dey go by submarine, come up from da water, and go to land on rubber boats."

Murphy tried to hide her impatience. This background wasn't helping. "And this relates how to Ruuwaq—"

"Ruuwaq? Ruuwaq!" Uncle pushed back from the table, his brow furrowed.

Vesper reached for him. "Tell her about Ruuwaq, Uncle. Tell her about the rats."

A low gasp left Murphy's lips.

Uncle stood. "Thank you for da meal, Vesper."

"But, Uncle—"

"I want ta think about it." He gave a slight bow and limped out of sight to the front of the house. Vesper followed him, and Murphy heard them speak quietly for a few moments. The front door opened and closed.

Vesper returned. "I'm afraid that's all he's willing to share tonight. I've only heard the rat story once, when I was very little, from his dad. I was hoping he'd repeat it because it involves Ruuwaq Island."

"Will he come again?"

Vesper barked a laugh. "He'll come as long as there's food

involved. Come, child, let's get you to bed. We'll tackle this beast in the morning."

She wanted to argue, to point out she was wide-awake, but the hot shower and a big meal, combined with the horrors of the day, had finally caught up with her. "Sounds good."

"Boys, clean up the kitchen." Vesper led her down the same hall, this time opening a door opposite the pink bathroom. "It's my office. I'm afraid all I have is a futon . . ."

Murphy waved away the comment. "I'm grateful for any kind of bed."

Vesper nodded and quietly closed the door.

"And a friend," she whispered.

———

The house loomed ahead of her, the rusty truck on her right. She picked her way forward through the garbage-strewn, overgrown yard. She held something in her hand. A pistol.

The pale-yellow light from the window bobbed and twisted with the moving foliage. Her movements were clumsy, sluggish.

Cries came from the house. Strident, grating, abrasive cries. The cries grew louder.

Murphy opened her eyes. Her pulse hammered in her ears. The screams of the seagulls continued. It took a moment to figure out where she was. At Vesper's house. Hiding.

Her watch said it was 5:00 a.m.

Sleep was out of the question. Silently she dressed and crept down the hall to the kitchen. Gentle snores came from behind one door. Wallpaper-ripping stereo snores from behind another.

Vesper had left a note taped to the coffeepot. *Coffee set up. Push the bottom left button.*

She wondered if Vesper would consider adopting her.

A quick search of the kitchen turned up a spiral notebook and a pencil. She hoped her hostess wouldn't mind her using them. Vesper's words floated in her head. *You know too much.*

What did she know that would make her a liability?

And who was aware of her soul-searcher ability and could be using her?

The second question was the easy one to answer. Ryan Wallace. The so-called journalist. The one who talked to her about Reinhard Heydrich and Operation Fair Cyan. She wrote Ryan's name at the top of a page, then *Heydrich* and *Fair Cyan*. He'd also mentioned a date, July thirty-first. From seven thirty-one to today. She circled the date. They were only in June, so this had to refer to something from a previous year. She could follow up on that.

The coffee finished perking. She poured a cup, added cream and sugar, and resumed her list.

Her sister's voice in the back of her mind piped up, *Don't forget Bertie.* Bertie had recognized her ability—her *gift*, as Vesper had called it.

"No," Murphy whispered. "Bertie is in the clear. She isn't using me."

But she was using you. Admit it. Bertie wanted you to report on Zinkerton. She wanted information on the case even after Zinkerton was dead.

Bertie couldn't be involved. She was in a hospital bed in Anchorage.

Right next to a phone. She could communicate with anyone she needed to.

Murphy wrote down Bertie's name and added *call her today.*

What about Butch? She jotted down the pilot's name. What had he said about Ruuwaq? She concentrated until she could hear his voice again. *I don't often hear the name of Ruuwaq. There's a small book of legends. A skinny little thing.* She underlined *Library.* What was the author's name? Wallace? No, that was Ryan. "Jonathan Wilson," she said aloud as she wrote it down.

Denali was possibly aware of her ability to get people to talk. He'd commented on it. But with his disability, he could easily be ruled out of planting bombs, shooting Vasily and Irina, stabbing Zinkerton, blowing up the Quonset hut, blowing up Elin and the priest . . .

Wait. He had said something strange when they were looking at the photos on the wall. *I blame myself that they're gone.* Why would he blame himself for a fishing accident that killed his daughter and son-in-law? Survivor's remorse, or something more sinister?

She wrote his name.

The torn photo that she'd copied implied a link between Denali and Ruuwaq. And what about the name Olga had mentioned? Leif B. Murphy circled that name.

The sweet scent of strawberries and vanilla preceded Vesper. "You're up early."

"Couldn't sleep. Much. By any chance do you have a charger that would fit my phone?"

"Let's see." Vesper checked the connection, rummaged around in a junk drawer, and pulled out a match.

"Now I'm in business." Murphy plugged in her phone. She had seven missed calls, all from Joshua. Checking to see if she was safe, or to arrest her?

"You could use my cell." Vesper poured a cup of coffee, then wiggled the pot at her.

Murphy held up her cup for a refill. "It's not safe to use your phone. Your name would come up."

"True." Vesper sat at the table, cupping her mug. "I have to start thinking like . . . like the killers."

"Speaking of which, I'll need to find someplace else to stay. I'm endangering you and your family."

"Let's jump off that bridge when we get to it." Vesper tilted the spiral notebook until she could read what Murphy had written. "Looks like a trip to the library, a phone call, and an internet search are in order. Don't know what to do with that name."

"Really, Vesper, please don't get involved. I was wrong to come here and drag your family into it. I—"

"Murphy, I don't know if you set something in motion or if you just fell into this mess, but whatever you're involved in, I have a very bad feeling that the truth of it is bigger than anyone realizes."

Murphy cleared her throat. "Why do you think that?"

Andy and Adam sauntered in and immediately raided the refrigerator. They each grabbed a Mountain Dew, popped the tab, took a gulp, and trudged into the living room. She didn't need to look to know they were busy on their phones.

Vesper waited until they were out of earshot. She tapped Murphy's list. "Reinhard Heydrich, Operation Fair Cyan, Quonset hut on Ruuwaq? This looks like World War II. The operative words there are *world war*."

CHAPTER 25

B oys, I need your help," Vesper called into the living room. The two young men with matching frowns ambled into the kitchen. "Murphy here needs you to do an internet search."

The frowns became smiles. "All right!" Andy—or was it Adam?—said.

"Murphy, what do you want them to look up?"

Both took seats at the kitchen table, fingers poised over their cell phones.

"Some important event that occurred on July thirty-first," she said. "Year doesn't matter."

Two heads bent over their phones. The younger one spoke first. "In the year 432—"

"Well . . ." She smiled. "Let's start more recent. Say the start of World War II. Around 1941."

The answers came quickly. She wrote them down.

"German U-boats sink or damage twenty-one Allied ships that month."

"Germans kill a thousand Jews in Minsk, Belorussia."

"The last train out of Mechelen heads out to Auschwitz."

"*Brigadoon* closes at Ziegfeld Theater."

She set down her pen. "I'm pretty sure that's not what I'm looking for."

"How about this?" the older one said. "In 1948, President Truman dedicated Idlewild Airport in New York."

"Nope," she said.

"An anti-Chinese uprising in Tibet?"

"Don't think so."

"Ah, this has got to be the answer." The younger one grinned. "The first exhibit of bongos at the Cleveland Metropark Zoo." He began pounding the table as if it were a drum.

"Bongos are also a deerlike animal," Vesper said dryly. "Keep looking."

"In 1964, the Rolling Stones concert in Ireland stopped after only twelve minutes because of a riot."

Murphy just stared at him.

"The Guns N' Roses song 'Appetite for Destruction' was released?"

"Thank you both," she said. "I think I've exhausted that lead."

The young men stood, helped themselves to the refrigerator again, and strolled to the living room. Vesper sighed. "They make up in enthusiasm what they lack in common sense." She checked her watch. "The library won't open until ten. You keep working while I make breakfast. I'll have the boys drive you over and get that book you need."

"I can drive over—"

"Nope." Vesper grabbed an oversized carton of eggs from the refrigerator. "I heard your name on the news this morning. The police are looking for you. You didn't tell me a detective and Father Ivanov died in the car explosion."

"I didn't? I guess I thought you knew."

"I do now." Vesper broke some eggs into a bowl. "They didn't show your picture, so there's some good news, but . . . well, you might need to turn yourself in. You didn't do anything wrong, so I'm guessing they just want to talk to you about what you saw."

Murphy thought of Hunter. He'd be watching the police station, hoping she'd do just that. "Let me call my friend Bertie. She's in law enforcement. She can maybe put in a good word for me." And tell her what to do about Hunter. One thing for sure, Murphy needed to move on from Vesper's place. If the police decided she was a suspect, Vesper could be charged with harboring a fugitive.

Her phone had enough charge for a short call. She unplugged it and stepped out the kitchen door. The backyard of the house faced the woods with no other houses in view. The day was cool with weak sunshine and a slight breeze.

She dialed Bertie's direct line. "Hey, Bertie."

"Thank heavens you're all right! The car bomb must have exploded when you were on the phone with me. It was all over the news. Is it true both Father Ivanov and Elin were in the car?"

Murphy clutched the phone tighter. "They were beyond help. There were three separate explosions."

"Are you safe? I don't think you should be at Salmon Run Lodge anymore."

"I'm not. I'm with . . . a friend."

"Hello?"

"I'm right here, Bertie."

"No, not you, Murphy. Someone is in my room. Behind this silly curtain. Hello?"

A chill went down Murphy's spine. "Bertie, ring for the nurse."

"Hello? Hello?"

"Ring for the nurse, Bertie!"

"You!"

Clang.

The phone must have fallen. Murphy heard distant heavy breathing. A dull thumping sound. Silence.

"Bertie?" Her voice trembled. She disconnected, then scrolled through her call list until she came to the number of the hospital. It took a full minute to reach the switchboard operator.

"I . . . um . . ." She gulped air and started again. "I was on the phone with Bertie Fisher. Something happened, um, something went wrong."

"Who is calling, please?"

Murphy hung up and stumbled backward into the house. The boys were just getting up from the table, now covered in dirty dishes.

"Murphy! What's wrong?" Vesper helped her sit, then shooed her grandsons out of earshot.

"Bertie. I think I just heard someone murder Bertie."

Now Vesper took a seat. "Oh, Lord." The words were exhaled. Her gaze drifted to her grandsons in the living room.

"I have to go." She stood on unsteady legs.

"No." Vesper tapped the notebook. "How close are you to solving this?"

"I don't know. I don't know!"

Vesper called her grandsons to the table. "Boys, Murphy here has to stay out of sight for a day or so. Don't tell anyone, I mean *anyone*, she's here—"

The younger one looked chagrined. "Um, I put it on Snapchat."

"What? *Why?*"

"The guys were talking about the bombing. I'm sorry, Grandma."

Vesper jumped to her feet and peered out the window. "When?"

"This morning."

Vesper pulled the curtain shut, then spun and looked at each of them in turn, eyes wild.

"Do you have family you could visit?" Murphy asked.

Vesper nodded mutely.

"Then it's time for a visit."

Vesper blinked and the wild look left her eyes. "Yes. Boys, go pack. When you're done, Andy, go switch license plates between Murphy's rig and the junker in the garage."

"Those plates are expired."

"Don't argue. Peel the current date off her plate and put it on the old one. Adam, after you're done grabbing your stuff, go to the library and check out a tiny book on local legends by Jonathan Wilson. Check them all out if there's more than one. Go."

The boys left.

Vesper picked up the phone and dialed. "Uncle, a favor. Can you drive Murphy to Arlene's house out on Pasagshak? Yeah, that's the one. I'll pick you up there after I get some groceries. Because I want you to tell her about the rats and Ruuwaq Island."

CHAPTER 26

Vesper hung up. "Uncle will drive you."

"Pasagshak?" Murphy asked. "Isn't that where the Pacific Spaceport Complex is located? And Fossil Beach?"

"There's also a small residential community a few miles from there." Vesper opened her purse and found a key ring that held a large number of keys. "I house-sit for a friend when she travels, which she does a lot. You can stay there for a few days. Maybe the police will catch the bomber in the meantime."

The older grandchild entered. "Packed. On my way to the library."

Murphy put out her hand. "Wait . . . um—"

"Adam."

"Adam. Are there phone books, old phone books, at the library?" She tapped the name Leif.

"Don't know. Probably. Or online."

"Could you look up a name for me? This would be about ten years ago. First name of Leif. Last name starts with a B."

"Sure. I guess." He sauntered out of the kitchen.

She caught Vesper's expression. "I know, a long shot."

Vesper made a few phone calls while Murphy cleaned the kitchen. Arrangements made, the woman bustled off to pack. Andy gave Vesper a thumbs-up on the switched license plates.

Vesper returned with a small overnighter bag and a larger suitcase and handed the overnighter to Murphy. "The clothes you were wearing when you got here are clean. You'll also find some toiletries and odds and ends."

Murphy's eyes blurred, and a giant lump formed in her throat. When she could speak, she asked, "Why are you doing all this for me?"

Vesper smiled and patted her on the cheek. "Lord's working on you. For the record, I hold to Hebrews 13:2. 'Do not neglect to show hospitality to strangers, for thereby some have entertained angels unawares.'"

"I'm hardly an angel."

"You took care of my granddaughter when I needed help. I don't soon forget."

The crunch of gravel announced a visitor. Vesper peeked behind the curtain. "Uncle's here. I'll need to give him something to eat before you go. Why don't you work on your list in the living room? He won't take long."

Uncle—Murphy wondered if he even had a first name—tottered into the house and headed straight for the kitchen. With the notebook on her lap, Murphy returned to her notes.

What do I know that would make me a liability?

She knew the skull in the Quonset hut matched the photograph of Denali Stewart's father. The photograph could have been from Ruuwaq. But the only person she'd told about that was Bertie. And Bertie might have been murdered. Could Bertie have confided in someone?

Maybe Murphy had seen something inside the Quonset hut when she'd looked around that last time, something important. A clue.

Wait, she hadn't followed up on the metal object on the

203

skeleton's body. That photo was still on her phone. She returned to the kitchen and picked it up. Dead.

"Vesper, could I take that charger with me?"

"Sure." Vesper glanced out the window. "Odd."

"What?" Her voice was shrill. She tried again. "What's odd?"

"A gray truck has driven slowly past the house twice now."

Clinton Hunter? "I have to go."

"I think you're right."

A car engine roared, followed by squealing brakes.

Vesper put a hand on Murphy's arm and kept her from bolting. "That's Adam back from the library."

The young man entered and handed Murphy a small book and a scrap of paper. She read the paper. *Leif Bjorkman, 324 W. Shoreline, Apt. 3. Leif H. Berg, 1252 S. Kodiak Way.*

"The librarian helped me. Got anything to eat before we go, Grandma?"

"You can eat on the way."

———

The young men left first in a battered pickup. Vesper backed Elin's SUV out of the garage and turned it around for Uncle. The weather was cloudy, with a chill wind and the smell of wet earth.

Vesper gave Murphy a big, tearful hug. She returned it. The older woman had placed a blanket and pillow on the floor in the rear, with a second blanket to cover her. "God bless you. Keep your head down. I'll join you as soon as I get the groceries. Arlene has an attached garage. Here's what you need to open the door. Park this rig inside and stay indoors."

Murphy stared at the slip of paper as she crouched on the floor of the vehicle and Uncle bumped down the lane.

"Uncle? Could we take a slight detour?"

"Vesper say I drive you directly."

"How about a detour, then we could go to a drive-through? Grab some lunch." She held her breath.

"McDonald's?"

"Sure."

"Subway?"

"If you'd like."

"KFC?"

"Of course."

"Where da ya want to go?"

She sighed with relief. "Let's start with 324 West Shoreline."

Uncle drove with one foot on the gas and one on the brake, jerking the SUV forward and backward. He often pushed both pedals at the same time. She was getting carsick.

The address belonged to a low-income apartment complex. Uncle parked on the curb. She jumped out, eyes scanning the unit numbers. Several children playing on the scrappy lawn stopped and stared at her. She hurried to the nearest building.

Apartment 3 was on the ground floor. A snow shovel, an empty bucket, and a single running shoe sat outside the door. In response to her knock, a small man in a wifebeater answered. He wore red flannel pajama bottoms and was barefoot. "Go away, kid, I ain't buyin' no cookies." He shut the door firmly.

She ducked back into the car, heart racing. Olga said Leif had been like a father figure to Denali. That man was middle-aged. Try again.

"Dat did not take long. Can we go eat now?"

"Soon. We need to visit 1252 South Kodiak Way." She huddled on the floor, occasionally pushing herself up to check their progress. They drove in the direction of Fort Abercrombie before

205

pulling onto Kodiak Way, a gravel drive. Deeply rutted driveways, most of which were not marked, peeled off from it into the woods. After driving back and forth and counting, they finally turned into an overgrown path and up to a small blue house with white shutters. Toys, bicycles, a swing set, and an empty wading pool filled the yard.

Her heart sank. An old man wouldn't live here. Before Murphy could walk to the front door, a plump, black-haired woman with a baby on her hip came out. "Can I help you?"

"I'm looking for Leif Berg."

She frowned for a moment, then smiled. "The old man we bought this house from."

"Do you know where he moved to?"

"Oh, gosh, I think he went into a nursing home or something. That's been, let's see, Rickie was just a baby, so over ten years ago?" She gently bounced the baby. "It took us almost a year to figure out his security system on the house. Everything was coded, but he didn't write down the code anywhere."

"That sounds like the right person."

"We tried to just guess, but he'd actually set traps that locked down all the windows. What a mess! We finally got a company to just remove everything. Cost us a bundle."

"Thank you." Murphy returned to the car. "One more stop?" she asked Uncle.

"KFC?"

"No. Do you know of any nursing homes around here?"

"Ya. The nursing home at the top of the hill." He nodded his head in that direction.

"Drive there."

He twisted around and stared at her for a moment, then backed out of the driveway. She didn't dare sit on the floor until they were out of the woman's sight. It probably looked strange enough that she got into the back seat.

After several wrong turns, Uncle finally found the right road. They passed a cemetery filled with the distinctive Russian Orthodox crosses with three crossbeams.

She averted her eyes. Across the street was Perkins Headstones and Memorials. She memorized the name.

The sign in front of the nursing home said Providence Kodiak Chiniak Bay Elder House. It was an attractive, single-story beige structure with cream-colored trim. The location was spectacular, with Three Sisters Mountain on one side and Chiniak Bay on the other.

Murphy leaned forward from the back seat. "Uncle, I don't think we're going to get much information if I simply go in and ask for someone who may or may not be a patient. Would you be offended if I claim we're looking for a place for you?"

"Are we going to eat afterward?"

"Sure. We'll go to all your favorite places—McDonald's, Subway, and KFC. Okay?"

"Okay den!"

"Just don't say anything, no matter what I say. Just smile."

"Okay den!" He smiled, revealing missing upper teeth.

"Wonderful. Let's go." She helped him out of the SUV and to the front door, then into a small foyer with a second locked door beyond. An open three-ring binder indicated she should sign in. She scrawled an illegible name, then waved at a mature nurse watching them from a nurses' station. The woman opened the inside door. "May I help you?"

"Hi. My name is . . . Mary Andrews and this is . . . my uncle."

"Okay den." Uncle nodded at the nurse.

"The family is thinking about finding a place for Uncle and

I've heard so many great reports about this place." They moved to a spotless open area. A woman in a pink floral housedress with a walker was making her way toward a grouping of chairs, where a second woman was reading.

"Did you have an appointment?" The nurse had a friendly face and a name tag that read Frances Schwartz, CNA.

"No. I'm sorry, Frances. I was hoping to pick up a brochure and have the family look at it."

Uncle smiled. "Vesper say we no stop, you know."

She leaned close to the nurse and whispered, "Vesper was his wife. Died five years ago. He still acts like she's alive." Frances gave a knowing nod.

"I see. Well, you'd really need an appointment—"

"Also, we thought maybe, since we're already here, we could see Uncle's dear friend from the war, Leif Berg. It's been at least ten years . . ." She held her breath.

The woman's face creased with a smile. "Leif Berg? There's a name I haven't heard in a while. I just loved that fellow, in spite of his OCD! What a sweetheart."

Loved. Past tense. Murphy's shoulders slumped. "So Leif has passed away?"

"Yes, poor soul. He was quite old, as I'm sure you knew. He died suddenly nine years ago, in the fall."

"Oh dear." She raised her voice as if Uncle was hard of hearing. "I'm sorry, Uncle, you won't be able to see Leif today." She patted his arm.

"Okay den."

They turned to go.

"Wait." The nurse chewed her lip for a moment. "I do have a photo of Leif. When there's no family, I try to keep something to remember each of my people." She blushed slightly. "I call the residents 'my people.' They're like family to me." She raised her voice slightly at Uncle and spoke slowly. "Would you like to see a photo of your friend Leif?"

"Okay den."

Frances moved behind the desk and pulled out a bottom drawer full of files. After a few moments, she stood and flourished a photograph. She placed it on the counter in front of Uncle.

It was the same image Murphy had copied from the lodge, the one with the faint outline of a Quonset hut in the background. But this photograph showed two men. And one of them was the spitting image of Denali.

CHAPTER 27

Murphy gasped and grabbed the counter. With a trembling finger, she pointed at the dark-haired man. "Who is this?"

Frances snatched up the photograph. "I thought you said your uncle was Leif's friend."

"He is. It's just that he looks so young in this photo I hardly recognized him. And standing next to him must be his . . . friend Paul Stewart?"

The woman relaxed. "Leif actually referred to Paul as a colleague."

"The photo looks like it was taken during World War II. Isn't that a Quonset hut behind them?"

"Yes."

"Did he ever tell you where this was taken?"

"There's something written on the back."

Murphy turned the photo over. Someone had scrawled a short sentence. The words were almost illegible.

"'Our own private . . .' What's that word?" She handed it to the nurse.

"I'm not sure. Cywinard? Cyuinard? He never mentioned the location, so I'm not even sure this is the name of a place."

Uncle tapped her on the arm. "Vesper say—"

"Okay, Uncle, let's get you some lunch." She smiled at Frances.

"Thank you for your time." Murphy took Uncle's arm and headed for the door.

"Wait."

She froze.

The nurse caught up with her. "You forgot to pick this up." She handed Murphy a brochure.

Murphy took it, hoping her face didn't reflect the relief she felt. "Thanks again."

Frances followed them to the door, then watched as they walked to the car. Murphy opened the passenger side for Uncle.

"I will drive." Uncle shook his head.

"I know, but that nurse may be watching. Just let me get us out of sight. I'll turn the SUV around."

He reluctantly slid in. She checked for Frances out of the corner of her eye as she got behind the wheel. The nurse *was* still watching.

She drove past the cemetery, then pulled over. Uncle took the driver's side and Murphy lay down on the rear floor.

Uncle proved his memory to be sound. They picked up sandwiches at Subway, fries and a soda at McDonald's, and a box of extra-crispy chicken tenders at KFC. She paid for it with Elin's forty-seven dollars, reducing the balance to fifty-seven cents.

The combination of the serpentine Pasagshak road and Uncle's erratic driving made Murphy sick.

Concentrate on something else. Like rats.

"Are we far enough out of town that I can sit up on the back seat?"

"Police car behind us."

A jolt went through her. If the officer stopped them and asked for the car registration . . . or ran the plates and found out they were expired . . . "How close is he?"

"Not real close."

She drew her knees up to her chest.

Please don't stop us.

"Ah!" Uncle drew in a sharp breath.

"What?"

"Police turn around."

She waited until her heart rate returned to normal. "Uncle, please tell me about Ruuwaq. What's the story your father told you about the rats?" He didn't answer. Was he going to stonewall now? "Vesper wanted you to tell me."

He tapped the brakes a bit harder than usual. Her head slammed into the back of the seat. He'd better start talking or she would start puking. She reached up and opened a window. The fresh air helped.

He finally spoke. "My father was with Castner's Cutthroats in da beginning. 1942. Da navy needed an air base closer to da Japanese, so they looked at Adak Island, 'bout 240 miles away. But dey did not know if da Japanese were there also. So dey sent thirty-seven Cutthroats to look. Maybe kill any Japanese."

She sighed impatiently. Uncle started driving again.

"The navy then hide a submarine. Dat is not an easy thing to do."

She straightened. "Why did they hide a submarine?"

"Dey wanted everyone to think it sank. Dey report it missing in August. But it was not missing. It was to do things in secret." He made a *shhhh* sound.

Finally. "What was the name of the submarine?"

"I do not know."

"And what was the sub supposed to do?"

"First dey delivered supplies to the island. Ruuwaq."

"Supplies?"

He didn't answer for a few moments as he put the SUV through a series of tight turns. "Maybe for da men there."

"What men?"

"Don't know. We are almost there."

She rose until she could just see out the window. A river filled with fishermen ran parallel to the road. Beyond that, a spit of land faced Pasagshak Bay. Houses with million-dollar views of the ocean perched on the slice of land. Craggy snowcapped mountains rose in the distance. The mountains lining the road were dense with trees.

Uncle signaled a turn. They bumped across a bridge, then turned right. He pulled in front of a small white house with a brown metal roof. A car was already parked in front. Vesper flew outside. "I was terrified when you weren't here! What kept you? Get inside, get inside." She hustled Murphy up a wooden walk and into the house.

"I'm so sorry, Vesper. I needed to check one or two things out."

"We went to Subway. And McDonald's." Uncle gave her a toothless grin. "And KFC! It was okay."

Vesper slumped onto a white sofa covered with nautical-themed, light-turquoise throw pillows. "Thank the Lord. I'd convinced myself that they found you."

"We were careful," Murphy said.

Vesper rubbed her broad face. "Uncle, would you park her rig in the garage? I've already put the groceries away." He left.

"Thank you," Murphy said. "It seems I owe you—"

She held up a hand. "Don't fret. Did Uncle tell you about the rats?"

"Not quite. He talked about the submarine and supplies."

"He needs to tell you the whole story. While he's taking care of the car, let me give you the tour." The owners had decorated the house in a beach theme. Thick sea-grass area rugs covered gray tile that resembled aged driftwood. The walls were mint green with a white-painted cathedral ceiling. The eat-in kitchen featured white cabinets and a Caribbean-green granite counter. One bedroom with a king-size bed had French doors opening to the ocean.

Vesper waved her arms around the room. "You have internet. The computer is over there." She indicated an iMac on a built-in white desk. "There's pretty good cell service out here." She pulled open the Roman shade on the nearest window. "The house next door is for sale. The folks in the one beyond that are gone this time of year. You shouldn't be disturbed, but stay out of sight anyway."

"Where does this road go?" Murphy indicated the route they'd used that continued beyond the beach house.

"More homes, but it dead-ends."

Murphy wasn't sure she liked being in a place with only one way out.

Uncle came in through a door in the kitchen carrying Murphy's sack of clothes, Elin's purse, and the remnants of the chicken tenders.

"Uncle, finish your story."

He dumped the sack and purse on the table, kept the chicken, and strolled to the living room. "Where was I?" He settled on a seashell-patterned, padded wicker chair. Vesper and Murphy took a seat on the sofa.

"Ruuwaq," Murphy said.

He took a bite of chicken and chewed thoughtfully. "After dey deliver da supplies to Ruuwaq, da navy want to get da Japanese off da other islands. First dey send in two Cutthroats, my father and another one. Dey send them to Kiska in da submarine. Dey deliver a box there. My father not told what was in da box, but he know it was something alive. There were air holes, you see."

"Rats, maybe?" Murphy guessed.

"Yah. This be early July 1942. Dey were to go on da submarine, then get in da rubber boat and take da box to Kiska. Secret. Dey were to open it and get away quick." He shook his head. "But when dey opened da box, da rats were dead. Six of them."

Murphy looked at Vesper. "Why would they send rats?" Vesper shrugged.

"There are already a lot of rats on da islands," Uncle said. "Seems silly to me."

"Uncle, why were the rats dead?"

"Father did not know. He said dey have plenty of food and water. My father did not want to be blamed. When dey ask him about the box later, he say everything fine. So dey bombed Kiska for three weeks, to be sure all were dead. But the Japanese got da last laugh. Dey left da island in da fog weeks before da bombing."

"How many got off the island?"

"Over five thousand soldiers. Only da dogs were left. My father tell dis story once. I tell dis story once. Now rat story is done."

"Where did your father get the rats?"

"Ruuwaq."

CHAPTER 28

Vesper stood, helped Uncle to his feet, and moved to the door. "We have to get going." She opened the door. "Stay in touch." She opened her mouth as if to say something else, then ushered Uncle through, closing the door behind them.

Alone. She took a quick inventory of food. Vesper had brought enough to feed not only herself but both grandsons and Uncle.

Moving to the porch off the bedroom, she sat for a few moments. She'd been on just such a beach with her sister so very long ago.

Dallas held up her long skirt as she waded in the softly lapping water of the ocean. Her sandals were in her hand, and her hair was tucked behind her ears. She wore the earrings Murphy had purchased for her.

"Sis." Dallas moved closer to the shore so Murphy could hear. "Did you get a chance to do what I asked?"

"Not yet. I've been slammed at work."

"Well, if you get a chance . . ."

"Sure. What are sisters for?" She smiled at Dallas.

Murphy entered the house, took the sack of clothing to the bedroom, and dropped it on the bed. She removed the spiral notebook

216

and library book on legends. Time to link everything together. After plugging in her phone and turning on the computer, she strolled from the windows to the doors, locking everything. House secure, she sat with the books at the kitchen table.

She scanned the table of contents, not knowing if anything would be useful. Ravens, origins of the wind, bears, black whale. Which one was about Ruuwaq? Opening the book, she skimmed the stories. She paused at the one about the black whale.

When I was a little girl about five years old in Old Harbor, my father was off hunting on Ruuwaq. Mother said we could play. I was walking along the shore with my little brother. The fog clung to the water so I could not see very far. All of a sudden the fog lifted in one area and I saw a big black whale. The whale had a hat on his head and on that hat was another hat, but much smaller. I waved and said, 'Hi, Mr. Whale.' It did not answer but went away. My brother saw it too.

A black whale with two hats? She moved to the computer and typed in *WWII submarine images*. One photograph in particular showed a sub with a conning tower. To a five-year-old child, seeing part of a sub in the fog might make her think of a whale, something she knew. Could she have seen the submarine Uncle mentioned, the one that the navy hid? The one doing things in secret? Old Harbor was not terribly far from Ruuwaq.

Murphy's computer inquiry on missing submarines from WWII brought up fifty-two names. One name jumped out. Grunion. Missing off Kiska. Cause unknown.

A prickling sensation occurred between her shoulder blades. So far the story was falling into place.

She opened the notebook and found the page where she'd

originally circled the name *Leif B.* She now had a full name for the man . . . and a mystery. The man Frances identified as Leif Berg had to be Denali's father. His resemblance to the young Denali was startling.

And if her photographic superimposition was accurate, the skull in the Quonset hut belonged to the blond man in the photo, identified by both Frances and Denali as Paul Stewart. Denali had commented on the awkward composition of the photo, claiming his mother had cut the damaged part away.

So either Denali's mother had an affair with the dark-haired Leif Berg, or Leif Berg was the blond man, and Paul Stewart had taken his identity. Murphy was inclined to go with the latter possibility. The name Leif Berg indicated Scandinavian heritage.

The sun had set and the long twilight had started. How safe would it be for her to turn on the lights? After opening a few drawers, she found a flashlight that worked. She made sure the kitchen blinds were tight, sat, and turned it on. Murphy turned to a clean page, then picked up her pen. She had a lot of suppositions, guesses, and assumptions, not a lot of facts.

Bertie's voice played in her head. *Hey, Murph, you're not looking to make a case. You're looking to stay alive.*

"This is all coming together."

What is? her sister asked.

"Leif and Paul were colleagues on Ruuwaq during the war. Leif died on Ruuwaq Island on April 1, 1946, when an earthquake brought the mountain down on his Quonset hut and a tsunami flooded the island."

Can you prove that?

"The skull and facial superimposition fit. If I'd taken a photo of the image Frances had . . . Wait!"

What did you just remember?

"I took a second photograph on the island—the metal piece on the skeleton's body."

Show me, her sister's voice whispered in her mind.

Murphy turned on the phone and quickly found the image she sought.

The metal was eight-sided with a loop at the top. Whatever had been on the surface was too worn to see. Metal. Medal. A military medal? She moved to the computer and typed in *octagonal medal.* The answer came quickly. The Navy and Marine Corps Medal, awarded for heroism. At the bottom of the page was a list of recipients by war.

She found Leif Berg's name.

"There it is, Dallas. Confirmation."

So the real Leif Berg died in the Quonset hut.

"Right. Paul must have gone when the tsunami struck."

He could have been washed away.

"Then who is the dark-haired man in the photo, the man Frances knew as Leif? I think at some point, Paul found out about Leif. He returned to Ruuwaq, maybe even found his body." She stood and paced. "Paul decided to take his identity . . . but he needed to 'die' so his family wouldn't look for him. The body found on Afognak had been dead for two months . . . badly decomposed. All Paul had to do was place his dog tags on the body. No one would look for him. Free as a bird."

I don't know, sis. Wouldn't anyone recognize Paul and know who he was? Can you draw a timeline?

"Good idea." She drew a table on the tablet. "Since Leif won that medal, there should be more information on him." She typed his name into the computer search engine. If he died nine years

219

ago in Kodiak, he should have had an obituary in the paper. She found it. "Okay, this says Leif Havelock Berg was born in 1918." She started filling out the chart.

Date	Event
1918	Real Leif born.
1946	April 1, real Leif dies. Age 28.

"Now I need to get Denali's birth in here." She typed his name. Impressive. He was on Wikipedia.

Date	Event
1918	Real Leif born.
1946	March 23, Denali born. April 1, real Leif dies. Age 28.

"That would mean the real Paul was with his wife the summer before Denali was born."

And the only description and photo of Denali's father came from his mother.

"Right. Denali said his mother cut the photo because of mildew. But I bet she knew, or suspected, Paul had skipped out on the family."

Lucas told you Denali's mother wasn't buried near Paul because she was mad at him. Maybe during his last visit they had a fight?

"In either case, Paul decided to ditch his family, or at least his wife. According to Leif Berg's obit—which would have been Paul—he worked for the government until he retired to Kodiak Island."

Date	Event
1918	Real Leif born.
1946	March 23, Denali born. April 1, real Leif dies. Age 28. Paul assumes identity.
1946–1985	"Leif" works at Fort Detrick, later at Deseret Test Center

"*Paul Stewart, 1918–1946.* His wife died in . . . 1971. So if he came back to Kodiak, no one would know what he looked like. But if Olga was correct, he did return. She mentioned Leif became like a father figure to Denali."

Ironic.

"No kidding."

Date	Event
1918	Real Leif born.
1946	March 23, Denali born. April 1, real Leif dies. Age 28. Paul assumes identity.
1946–1985	"Leif" works at Fort Detrick, later at Deseret Test Center.
After 1985	"Leif" moves to Kodiak, befriends his son.

She thought for a moment. "I wonder if he was the one who remade the family headstones. More irony in marking the resting places of the family he abandoned." Denali had mentioned something from the past was found in the family cemetery.

He could have returned for something. Or someone.

"Or to do something. Whatever the reason, ten years ago five bodies turn up on Ruuwaq. Denali's daughter and son-in-law die. He has the accident that kills his wife and puts him into a wheelchair. And Leif and Denali have a falling out. That's a whole lot of coincidences."

Dallas had nothing to say to that. Murphy glanced around the empty kitchen, then rubbed her arms.

Maybe she could call someone. Hear a friendly voice. She picked up her phone.

Joshua had left more messages. She couldn't help herself. She played the last one.

"Hey, Murphy, listen, I know you're scared. Please call me. I can help you."

She stopped the message, then clutched the phone to her chest and rocked back and forth. "Joshua, Joshua," she whispered. "I'm in so deep. I do need help."

Her sister pushed into her brain. *You can't trust him. You can't trust anyone. Look what happened to me.*

"What did happen?" she whispered.

You have to get rid of Clinton Hunter.

"What do you mean?"

You know. You have Elin's Glock. You have a mission.

———

Murphy woke on the floor, clutching her necklace. The cold tile had seeped into her side. She shivered and stood, wincing at her stiff muscles. She must have slipped.

A scratching came at the front door.

She froze.

More scratching.

Silently she padded to the window overlooking the front porch.

A springer spaniel scratched at the door again. In the distance, a voice called, "Here, Riley! Come on, girl."

A woman holding a flashlight walked toward the house, still calling the dog.

Murphy spun around. Blinds were open in the bedroom. If the woman peeked in . . . She dashed to the room. She could see the woman clearly now. Murphy dropped to her knees and crawled to the backside of the bed. Reaching up, she snatched the sack of her clothes and pulled them to the floor.

"Bad dog, Riley! You need to come when I call." *Clump, clump, clump.* The woman was on the wooden porch just outside the window. The dog whined.

"What is it, girl? No one is home. At least I don't think . . ." *Clump, clump, clump.* Footsteps moved down the porch toward the garage.

Murphy shoved the sack under the bed, then scurried to the kitchen. A quick peek gave her the bad news. The woman's flashlight was penetrating a window in the garage.

The dog barked. It could hear her moving in the house.

She pressed against the wall.

A knock sounded at the door. "Hello? Arlene? Are you home?" More knocking.

Murphy remained motionless.

"How odd," the woman said. The footsteps crossed the porch to the bedroom again.

Was there a mark on the perfectly made bed to show where the sack had been? She could barely catch her breath.

"Come on, Riley, let's go home."

Had she gone? More importantly, would she return?

Murphy crept to a window and looked out. The woman was strolling down the beach, dog now in tow. She exited the front door as quietly as possible and hurried to the edge of the garage, where she could see the woman's progress.

Murphy counted the houses. One. Two. Three.

The woman turned into the fourth house.

Had she seen Elin's vehicle in the garage? Was she now calling the police? Murphy moved to the same window the woman had looked into. She couldn't see anything. Blackness.

But the woman had a flashlight.

She sprinted into the house, snatched the flashlight, and returned to the garage window. The light illuminated the back side of a shelving unit filled with boxes.

Disaster averted. For now.

Her cell phone was vibrating across the counter when she returned. She picked it up and checked the caller ID.

Bertie Fisher.

CHAPTER 29

Murphy swallowed and stared at the screen. Bertie was dead. Wasn't she? She'd heard the woman die.

What if she was wrong and Bertie had merely dropped the phone? Or she was right and the killer now had Bertie's phone? She'd never know unless she answered. She reached for it.

The vibration stopped.

Murphy snatched it up, answered, then listened for a moment. Dial tone.

Slowly she placed it down.

It rang again. She grabbed the cell and connected. "Bertie?"

A woman answered. "No. I'm sorry. This is Nurse Johnson. Bertie suffered a stroke. She's . . . not doing well."

"I thought . . . I thought she was dead."

"No. She's a fighter, but she's in and out of consciousness. I'm calling because prior to the stroke, she asked me to mail an envelope to you, which I've done. You should have it tomorrow morning at the latest."

"Thank you. Would I be able to speak with Bertie?"

"I'm afraid not. Maybe in a few days."

"Where did you send the envelope?"

"The address was for a Salmon Run Lodge." The nurse disconnected.

Murphy reached for a chair and dropped heavily into it. Bertie was alive! And the envelope would have to be information about Dallas. She'd have to go to the lodge to get it.

Fool. How did she know this wasn't a trap? Anyone could have picked up Bertie's phone, especially the killer, and found someone to read a script of what to say.

Could she take the chance? Bertie *had* told her she was getting the information on her sister.

A plan formed in Murphy's mind. The mail and packages came in the morning and were left on the side table in the living room. The house would be open during the day. She knew Olga's and Denali's routines. If she timed it right, she could snatch the envelope when they were busy. She could park at the private landing field and approach the house on foot via the trail.

It just might work.

As for how she would drive through Kodiak without the police spotting her, a quick internet search turned up the great news that a cruise ship was due to dock in the morning. Lots of tourists. Lots of chaos.

Murphy stood in the bedroom doorway staring at the glorious king-size bed. She'd bet her favorite #10 flat brush that it was a pillow top. Unfortunately, the blinds were open, and should that snoopy neighbor return, she'd notice closed blinds or a sleeping stranger in the bed. Murphy would have to sleep on the couch.

She snuggled up with a turquoise pillow embroidered with a sea horse, then tucked a striped blanket around her legs. The sofa was reasonably comfortable. All she had to do was close her eyes . . .

The house loomed ahead of her in the trees, the rusty truck perched on her right. She picked her way through the garbage-strewn, overgrown yard. She clutched a pistol.

The pale-yellow light from the window flashed on something moving. She stepped closer. More movement. Then one head rose. A rat. She took aim and shot it.

Another rat appeared on her left. She fired at it. Three more appeared, then five, then the yard was full of rats, swarming her. She fired again and again, but each rat she hit created three more. She screamed.

Murphy opened her eyes. She was soaked with sweat. Gray dawn touched the edges of the blinds. Mint walls surrounded her. The beach house. No rats.

After her breathing returned to normal, she rose and headed to the kitchen for coffee. Then a shower. Horrible dream. She hated rats.

Rats.

Warm water poured over her head and ordered her thoughts. Laboratory rats. Experimental rats. Rats in a box taken to Kiska Island. Lucas said his great-granddad was a medical doctor. *Like a scientist.* There was only one reason someone would hide a submarine, build a facility on a remote and obscure island, and place two men there with rats.

Biological weapons.

Murphy shut off the water and swiftly toweled herself dry. She knew the word on the back of the photo Frances had showed her. Not *Cyuinard.* He'd written *Our own private Gruinard.* She dressed, grabbed her cup of coffee, then sat at the computer and typed in the name. A webpage devoted to the island came up.

"British military scientists used Gruinard Island, located off the coast of Scotland, for biological weapons testing during World War II. Using sheep, the scientists tested anthrax—"

Anthrax! Did Paul Stewart and Leif Berg infect the rats with anthrax and send them to Kiska as a weapon? No. In the close confines of a submarine, the rats would have infected the crew.

She read on.

"The anthrax spores, however, proved to be too hearty to use as a weapon, causing contamination for decades. Gruinard Island had to be extensively decontaminated in the 1990s and was uninhabitable for almost fifty years."

But anthrax might explain the five dead men on Ruuwaq Island. If they'd accidentally landed on a WWII biological warfare site . . . No, that wouldn't work either. Vasily had come across them shortly after they'd died. He wasn't infected. Nor were she and Bertie when they'd explored the island.

Ryan mentioned Reinhard Heydrich had died of botulism. The Nazi officer was connected to Paul Stewart in a letter that also noted Operation Fair Cyan. Maybe Operation Fair Cyan was the United States developing botulism.

Enough speculation. She had a mission to fulfill.

———

Murphy watched the beach for snoopy neighbors with dogs. A cold wind blew in from the bay with intermittent rain showers, undoubtedly keeping the woman inside.

Only one way to discover if the police were waiting to ambush her. Get in the rig and drive. She grabbed a rain jacket and Elin's Glock and purse, then got into the SUV.

The road was less than seventeen miles from Pasagshak Bay to the town of Kodiak. Clutching the steering wheel with white-knuckled hands, she checked every passing car to be sure they didn't slow down. Rain made it difficult to see cars and passengers clearly, which was a plus for her.

You're walking into a trap.

Bertie would want her to have the information on her sister. Who else would know about that?

Her thoughts flittered around like a crumpled newspaper in a strong wind.

The town buzzed with the cruise-ship tourists scurrying around under umbrellas. She slid down in the driver's seat as far as possible as she drove through. Her grip didn't loosen until she was through town and driving out Spruce Cape Road. No traffic passed her on this drizzly day. She drove slowly, looking for a turnoff that might lead to Salmon Run Lodge's private airfield.

She almost missed it. An overgrown, rutted lane led from the road. After pulling off, she drove a few hundred feet before a chain with a No Trespassing sign on it stopped her. This had to be the place. She parked, making sure the vehicle was out of sight of the main road. If she'd figured right, the airfield would be empty. She could cross it, find the path leading to the lodge, wait for a time when everyone in the house was gone, and retrieve the package from Bertie.

The lane opened up to a primitive airfield—mowed grass with a tattered windsock—and a gray metal-sided hangar on the far side. Pulling her rain jacket tighter, she crossed the field to the hangar and scanned inside. A de Havilland Beaver—possibly the same plane Jake had flown to Ruuwaq—was parked inside next to an older Ford diesel truck with a snowplow mounted on the front.

The trail leading to the lodge and cemetery started near the hangar. She followed it until she reached the fork. From there, she crept through the spruce and underbrush, watching. If the package was a trap sprung by Clinton Hunter, he'd be watching the lodge, waiting for her.

When she reached the equipment shed, she ducked inside. Through the dirty window she could see the front of the lodge. Olga and Lucas walked down the stairs and got into a parked car. Olga had been carrying a sheet of paper. Murphy would bet that was the grocery list for the week. Excellent. She'd have at least an hour, possibly two.

Once the SUV pulled out of sight, she headed for the woods around the lodge. If Denali was in the living room, he could easily see any approach from the front or this side of the building. The kitchen, on the far side, offered good access.

She could feel the ticking of passing time as she worked through the woods. Rainwater soaked her jeans and the bottom of her sweater. Her hands were freezing.

No light showed from the kitchen, but she scouted the room through the windows before approaching. She slipped through the door and shook off the rain, then listened for the sounds of Denali's wheelchair or the padding of his dog. Silence. The room smelled of fresh coffee and cinnamon. She thought of Elin on the first day she arrived and swallowed hard.

A quick peek through the door showed the living room empty. A large manila envelope rested on the table.

Go now.

She dashed through the door, snatched up the envelope, and peeked inside. Newspaper articles, police reports.

A voice came from near the stairs. "I've been waiting for you."

CHAPTER 30

Murphy spun around.

Denali rolled closer, pulled back the blanket over his legs, and lifted a pistol aimed at her midsection. "Move away from the door."

She did as directed, gaze never leaving the gun. Maybe she could lie her way out of this one. "I'm . . . I'm sorry I missed work yesterday and this morning. I saw both Elin and Father Ivanov die in the car bombing. I was mentally screwed up . . . I needed some time—"

"Stuff it, Murphy. For all I know, you set the bomb." He lifted his chin toward the stairs that led to her room. "The police are actively looking for you. They've been all over your room looking for evidence, and I overheard them talking about reconsidering you as a person of interest in the arson at your landlady's place."

"But—"

"Save your protests. Tell me what you've learned in your snooping."

"What? I don't know what you mean."

He pulled the trigger. A chunk of log wall flew off and nicked her hand, drawing blood. "Don't lie to me. The next shot will be in the knee. What do you know?"

She dropped the envelope. Headlines poked out. "Serial

Killer . . ." Her legs were rubber. "Your father, Paul Stewart, must have returned from a trip off Ruuwaq and found his partner, Leif Berg, dead. He saw that as a chance to start over, to walk away from his family. To walk away from you."

The pistol wavered a bit, then steadied. "She was barely twenty-one when she got married and became pregnant with me. My mother told me my father wanted her to end the pregnancy. She refused."

"So Paul didn't want to be a father, didn't want the responsibility. He needed a way out. He knew if he simply disappeared, your family would keep looking for him, so he faked his own death. The family accepted his ruse, and in June of 1946, they buried that body from Afognak Island in the family cemetery. Paul Stewart took the identity of Leif Berg."

"Go on."

Put it all together. You have nothing to lose but your life. "During the war, Paul and Leif worked on a biological weapons project, Operation Fair Cyan, on Ruuwaq Island. It was a top-secret project. So secret that the government hid the use of a submarine, the *Grunion*, to supply the Quonset hut and conceal the work."

"Very impressive. I suppose your buddy Ryan told you about Fair Cyan."

"He's not my buddy. Where is he, by the way?"

"Gone."

She didn't like the tone of his voice. She risked a glance out the window.

"Don't look to be saved by Olga either. She won't be back for hours."

She could make a run for it. She'd certainly get away from him. The bullet was another matter. "I've told you what I found out. Now you tell me what happened to your father after the war."

232

He glanced down at his gun for a moment, then swiftly returned his focus to her. "What he did after the war was despicable. Have you ever heard of Unit seven thirty-one?"

"Seven thirty-one?" Of course. She had thought Ryan meant July thirty-first. He hadn't clarified what he meant.

"The Japanese conducted human experiments in Pingfan, near Harbin, Manchuria, from the 1930s to 1945. They used Russian, Chinese, Korean, and even US prisoners of war. Men, women, and children, all referred to as 'logs,' were experimented on. Thousands died."

Her stomach heaved and head buzzed. She didn't want to hear more.

"The work they did was equal to what Dr. Mengele performed on prisoners in Auschwitz. The Japanese studied the effects of frostbite, bubonic plague, syphilis, cholera—"

She threw up her hands. "Wait! Why isn't this common knowledge?"

"Two reasons. The US government was so anxious to get their hands on the research and keep it from the Russians that they let the perpetrators go free in exchange for information. No war trials. No crimes against humanity. No Nuremberg. In fact, most of those responsible in Japan went on to positions of great respect and honor. They prospered. Because America buried the truth."

"And?" she asked faintly.

"All the people they experimented on died."

She took a half step back.

He raised his pistol.

She froze. "Why are you telling me all this?"

"I didn't want to. I wanted you to go away."

"*You* poisoned the sandwich."

"And you gave it to my dog. I almost shot you then."

"Why try to kill me?"

"There wasn't enough in the sandwich to kill you, just make you sick. Just make you go away."

She shook her head. "You could have fired me."

"Olga took a shine to you. She would have wondered why I'd fired someone who finally knew how to set a table. She would have found you and brought you back. And there would have been questions."

"But *why*? What did I do?"

"You made people talk." Denali shifted the gun. "Sooner or later, someone would have talked."

"About what?"

His eyes narrowed and lips pulled against his teeth. "You want to know about dear ol' Daddy? He relished the research of the Japanese in Unit seven thirty-one. When he went to work as Leif Berg after the war, first at Fort Detrick, later at Deseret Test Center outside of Salt Lake City, he couldn't wait to get his hands on the Unit's work at our own biological weapons locations. He was a big part of the cover-up. He was one of the principal scientists who reviewed the results of the Japanese experiments. He used their research to develop more biological weapons, worse weapons." His face had turned red. Spit gathered at the corner of his mouth. "Dad was the mastermind behind the 1950 simulated germ warfare attack in San Francisco, one of the largest human experiments on unsuspecting people."

"I don't—"

"You don't have to believe me. It happened. Of course, I only found all this out much later."

A blast of rain pelted the windows on the side of the lodge. Denali glanced out, then to his left.

She followed his gaze. The wall of family photographs. He

seemed to be studying the one with his daughter and son-in-law, then he shifted his focus to the Distinguished Service Medal.

"So to keep your family reputation from being tarnished by the truth about Leif Berg's real identity, you had someone blow up the Quonset hut. You had someone murder all those people. Zinkerton to get the evidence. Vasily, Elin, all of them. But I know something—"

"Shut up." He lifted the gun. "You were in the middle of an investigation that would have identified all those bodies, the skeleton. With modern DNA testing, how long would it have taken to figure out *my father*, not Leif Berg, was obsessed with killing people in the worst imaginable ways? And the confession of Vasily? What would happen if the families of the five men who died on Ruuwaq found out they died because of the work done there—my father's work?"

"How did they die?"

"They had to have been exposed! Don't you see?"

"After all those years—"

"The publicity, the lawsuits, would have caused me to lose the lodge. And Lucas would lose his inheritance."

"Wouldn't your grandson want to know?"

"No! My grandson will never know, because all the evidence is going away. My mother hated my father, and my father destroyed everything he touched. But Lucas will never feel that pain. It's a simple decision. Get rid of you, get rid of the last witness." He looked over her shoulder. "Jake, it's time. Make sure you're far out to sea before you drop her body."

She started to turn.

Sharp pain. Blackness.

CHAPTER 31

Cold. Wet. Murphy's head thrummed in pain. Face against something hard. Hands stuck. She blinked. What a strange dream. She'd wake up anytime now.

She tried to make sense of what she was seeing. Blinking didn't seem to help. Something sticky caught her eyelid. A round shape, dark, in front of her face, looked like . . . a tire?

The tire moved away. The coldness stayed. She squirmed to find a better place, but her feet were together . . . tied together? She was outside the house, by the pickup.

No. No. That's not real.

Reality smashed into her brain. Denali. The pistol. His last words. *Jake, it's time. Make sure you're far out to sea before you drop her body.*

Jake was preparing the plane. Of course. Uncle Jake. Denali's half brother—and obviously the appointed hit man for the family—but why would he take the chance by killing her?

His words came back to her. *They don't pay me enough to climb cliffs.* Money. Jake could stand to inherit a fortune when Denali died. Of course, he'd have to kill Lucas.

And now she was going to be murdered. *Lord, Lord, I don't want to die. Not today. Please help me.*

Jake approached. *Or was it Hunter with a knife?*

She couldn't get her mouth to work, to scream, to beg for mercy. He reached for her. She rolled away and kicked at him.

Jake just laughed. "Spunky little thing." Stepping over her, he lifted her effortlessly under his arm.

She flailed and kicked.

That just made him laugh harder. He opened the door to the plane and tossed her in like a rag doll.

She rolled on the green shag carpet.

Air wouldn't fill her lungs. She tried screaming again. All that came out was exhaled air. *Hut, hut, hut.* He pulled a burlap bag over her face and tied it around her neck. She couldn't breathe. She couldn't . . .

———

The noise. A loud, deafening roar. Ground rocking under her. Stink in her face. She opened her eyes. Fabric, burlap, covered her head.

He's here, with the knife. Focus.

She was in the plane. In the air. Her head was pounding. She was going to die.

If Vesper was right and she had a soul, God was soon going to meet it.

Was it going to hurt? Would she feel every bone in her body snap when she hit the water from . . . three thousand feet? Five thousand?

She had failed her mission. She hadn't found her sister. And now no one would ever find her. Tears burned Murphy's cheeks.

The plane engine slowed. After a sudden rushing sound, the engine roared louder. Her ears popped. The plane rocked, then leveled. A hand grabbed her jacket and pulled her upright.

This is it, God.

The hand fumbled with the rope tied around her neck. He must want to see her face, her fear, her horror.

Well, she wouldn't let him. The burlap came off. She spit in his face.

Ryan pulled away and wiped off the few drops she'd managed to get out. He reached over and placed headphones over her ears and adjusted the microphone. "That wasn't nice. Here I go saving your life, and you spit on me."

Frantically she searched the tiny cabin. "Where's Jake?"

"Jake, I'm afraid, met the fate he'd planned for you."

"What do you mean?" She tried to keep her voice from squeaking.

"I mean I've been keeping an eye on you." Ryan returned to the pilot's seat. "When Jake strolled down the trail with you thrown over his shoulder like a bag of flour, I figured I needed to step in. But if I hadn't taken off in the plane, Denali would have known something was wrong. I just gave Jake a whack on his head, tossed him in the copilot's seat, then took him skydiving. Without a parachute."

"He's dead?"

"Oh yes." He banked the plane sharply. Murphy braced herself on the floor.

"But . . . why not just hand him over to the authorities?"

"You have no idea what's at stake. Suffice to say, in this case I am the authority."

"Can you fly this plane?"

"Of course. It's a bit tricky because it's set up for someone who is crippled—"

"You mean this is Denali's plane? Not Jake's?"

Ryan came back to her. Her stomach flipped at the sight of

the knife in his hand. "The man is perfectly capable of getting around. Now, if you'd turn around, I'll cut the ropes and explain everything."

She rolled onto her side so he could reach her wrists. The pain of returning circulation in her hands made her eyes burn. "Thank you."

"You're welcome. Here." He handed the knife to her. "Cut the rope off your ankles, and if you can manage it, come up here."

After slicing the ropes, she massaged her legs and feet until the tingling passed, then gingerly felt the aching lump on her head. Her hand came away bloody.

Blood. Her nightmare kept rearing up in her mind, but she was awake. She wiped her hand on her jeans and crawled to the copilot's seat. "Just who are you? And don't tell me that cockamamy story about being a journalist." She reset her headphones over her jumbled hair, carefully avoiding the tender area. Her glasses were missing.

"So you figured that out. I work for the government, an agency with a bunch of letters—"

"CIA? NSA?"

"Something like that. Denali's dad, the man who called himself Leif Berg, was on our radar for years. He 'retired' in 1985 and came here." His fingers made quotes around *retired*.

Kodiak Island appeared in the distance, surrounded by fog. Ryan must have flown quite a way out into the Gulf of Alaska to make sure Jake's body would never wash up on any shore. She rubbed her arms.

"Are you cold? I can turn up the heat."

"Yes, please. Why did you say it like that? He didn't really retire?"

"He left under a bit of a cloud. He'd been working in biological

239

weapons, one of the top scientists. Of course, our government would vehemently deny we had any such projects. After all, we signed the 1972 Biological Weapons Treaty."

"But we continued to develop them."

"Of course, as did most countries. The Russians had massive stockpiles and were actively developing more. Think about it, Murphy. Disease is the perfect weapon. The origins can be concealed, so there's no smoking gun. It's efficient. During the 1918 Spanish flu pandemic, fifty million people died worldwide in two years. We can never predict how any given virus may mutate into something more virulent naturally—influenza, AIDS, Ebola, even Zika. So if we decide to, say, thin out a population, or to wipe out a town harboring terrorists, we can introduce a biological weapon and no one would have a clue."

He turned the plane to follow the coastline. The rain had stopped for the moment, but more fog was moving in. Below was Potatopatch Lake, then Mission Lake. Her landlady's blackened remains of a home was a blight on the beautiful shoreline.

"Do you want to know how easy biological weapons are to cover up?" Ryan glanced at her. "In July of 1975, in a town on the banks of the Connecticut River, thirty-nine children and twelve adults were diagnosed with juvenile rheumatoid arthritis. Two years later, doctors traced the symptoms to the deer tick and named it Lyme disease after the town. Hardly anyone put the sudden outbreak of the previously unknown disease to the proximity of Plum Island."

"What was Plum Island?"

"Home of biological warfare testing site Lab 257."

Despite her aching head, she felt chilled.

"Anyway, back to Leif. He was always a loner, independent, and they thought he might have been working on his own projects.

When he returned to Kodiak, we figured he might be looking for an investor or even someone interested in buying his work, like a foreign government. We believed he'd hidden his early research in the area. So we watched him. When he made contact with his son, we made it a point to put both him and the lodge under constant surveillance."

"Surveillance!"

"Yes."

"Why didn't you simply go in with a search warrant or something? Or go through all his things and search the lodge? Or the cemetery?"

"Leif was known for keeping his work under the tightest security. He was pathological about it. His psychological profile indicated he'd go to great lengths to protect his work, including destroying it. We'd have to find his materials, figure out what security or code he used, and bypass them on the first try. Get anything wrong and, *boom*, nothing left."

Murphy almost commented on the inefficiency of the government but decided the timing was bad.

"The surveillance told us where you'd hidden your notes. We knew you'd copied Denali's photographs. And most of all, we knew about you, Dakota."

Her face grew warm. "Seems everybody knows who I am."

Salmon Run Lodge appeared on the horizon. "Duck down for a moment. I'm pretty sure we're too far away for anyone to see who's flying, but the presence of two people might raise alarms."

She ducked. He wagged the wings of the plane.

She grimaced. Ryan, pretending to be Jake, had just sent the signal to Denali that he was successful in killing her. She stayed low until they landed and taxied to a stop.

"Why did we land here? Couldn't we have flown to the mainland?"

"Not enough fuel. Help me get the plane into the hangar."

They quickly moved the plane and closed the hangar doors.

"Now what?" she asked.

"Is your rig over there?" He indicated the small road she'd parked on.

"Elin's SUV is."

"Let's go." He quickly trotted across the airfield and into the trees. She raced after him and unlocked the SUV. Ryan took the key from her and got behind the steering wheel. She slipped into the passenger side. After the roar of the plane, the silence was almost a vacuum.

He stared forward for a few moments, tapping his lip with his finger. She remained silent and watched him. He finally looked at her, then did a double take. "You look quite different without your glasses."

"Yes." She made eye contact. "What's going on?"

He blinked. "Here's the deal. You need help, and I can help you, but I need some information from you first."

"I've given you information."

"You've learned more about Denali's father than you let on. I want to know everything."

Her mind scrambled. More? As far as she could tell, he knew everything about Paul Stewart that she knew. "Um, if I did that, what can you do for me?"

"I can get you identification so you can get off Kodiak. And money." He noted her expression. "Oh yes, I know about your stolen purse."

"Well—"

"I'll get you a plane ticket to anywhere you want to go."

"So—"

"And I know where you can find your sister and her escaped convict boyfriend, Clinton Hunter."

CHAPTER 32

Murphy caught her breath. "Where? Where!"

"They're both here on Kodiak."

"Dallas is alive." The words were an exhale of air. Murphy's vision blurred. Her nose burned. *Alive!*

"They've been hiding out, but finding and keeping an eye on people is what I do."

"Wait. Wait a minute. She's been hiding *here*?"

"Of course."

"But she wouldn't do that. She would have contacted me—"

"You've been a hard person to find. Maybe she tried."

Murphy shook her head violently, then immediately regretted it. "And Hunter—"

"Is with her. The two lovers reunited."

She tried to speak, but nothing came out for a moment. "No! That can't be true. Dallas wouldn't fall in love with a murderer."

"Maybe he brainwashed her. Did you ever think about that?" His voice was soft.

She continued to shake her head, though slowly. "No. No. No. Wait! If you knew where he was, why didn't you turn him in?"

"Murphy, listen carefully. If I turned him in, your sister

would still be under his spell. She's waited for him all these years. She'll wait forever to be with him. She isolated herself from you. There is only one way to set your sister free. And only you can do it."

"I . . . I don't know what you mean."

"Yes. You do."

Murphy shivered in spite of the blasting heat. "You're saying . . ."

"Do you want your sister home? Do you want to see Dallas's face again, hear her voice? Do you want to be with her? Think about how close you were, how much you've missed her. She must be freed from the demon who has her ensnared. She is powerless on her own. Only you, Murphy—it's all up to you."

She closed her eyes. All around her, everything was empty, hollow. It hurt to breathe. "Me?" She looked at Ryan.

Ryan nodded. "You have to kill him."

Murphy brought her knees up to her chest and wrapped her arms around them. "I have to kill Clinton Hunter?"

Save me, her sister murmured in her brain.

"Yes. You have to save your sister by killing Clinton Hunter. Do you have a gun?"

"Elin's Glock."

"When I give you their address, what are you going to do?"

She hesitated. "Save my sister by killing Clinton Hunter?"

"Say it again."

"Save my sister by killing Clinton Hunter."

He glanced at his watch. "Good. Then after you tell me everything, and you take care of Hunter, both you and your sister will have plane tickets to leave Kodiak and money to live on. Do we have a deal?"

"Yes."

The SUV was parked in front of a small bungalow.

She blinked. She didn't remember Ryan starting the SUV, or moving, but they were no longer at the airfield. "Who lives here?"

"I do."

"Is this where you watch people?"

He turned in his seat and looked at her. "Tell me what you learned, Murphy."

"You heard all that I told Denali, right?"

He nodded.

"There's still a missing part. I know I'm close, but I'd like a little time to put it together."

"Well then, come inside my humble abode. We need to do something for that bump on your head." They got out of the SUV, and he led the way to a wooden door painted dark green. He unlocked it, then immediately moved to an alarm system and deactivated it. The living room was ordinary, devoid of any personal items, and spotless. It felt like a stark motel room.

"What do you need?" he asked.

"Something to write with and on. And some aspirin."

While he went into the kitchen, she wandered around looking for listening devices, cameras, any kind of sleuthing equipment. Not even a television set.

Just a bloody white sheet.

She shook her head clear. There was no sheet. She needed to stay with the present, not the past. Not the nightmare. She'd tell him whatever she could. Then finish her mission. Her sister was waiting for her.

She passed an open bedroom door. Maybe Ryan wasn't with the CIA or FBI. Maybe he was a dirty old man who had saved her and was now planning on collecting a reward . . .

"Ryan, do you happen to have any identification on you . . . like government ID or a badge?"

He came back into the living room. "Starting to doubt me already? No, obviously I wouldn't carry official identification saying I'm a secret agent of some kind."

She stepped closer to the door. "How do I know—"

"You don't." He placed a glass of water and two white tablets on the table. "But remember, I found Hunter and your sister, something the police, sheriffs, FBI, you name it, haven't been able to do. And I assume you want that information."

"Yes, I want to know where she is. And I want to kill Clinton Hunter and set her free." Her voice sounded flat.

"Good girl. Here's your aspirin." He opened a drawer in a side table and took out paper and a pen, placing them next to the glass of water. "Sit here and let me look at your injury. You keep shaking your head."

She sat. "I think the bashing I took knocked a screw loose. I keep having mini flashbacks of my last encounter with Hunter. They usually come in a dream."

He stood above her and gently parted her hair. "Ouch. That looks painful." He moved to the kitchen, pulled out some paper towels, then wet them at the tap. Once again he moved her hair, then dabbed at the wound.

She winced.

"Sorry. I don't think you'll need stitches." He finished cleaning up her head.

She tossed back the aspirin and washed them down with a gulp of water. Hopefully the pain would go away soon.

She looked at the blank paper. What did she really know that no one, at least not Ryan or Denali, knew? Rats. The dead rat story. Okay, follow the rats.

She wrote *Ruuwaq laboratory rats → dead rats in box.*

She pictured the rat on the island, the one she'd hit with a rock. *Current rats on island.*

One other reference to rats nagged at her. What was it? She clicked the retractable pen. It was on the edge of her mind. From visiting the island? The lodge? Rat . . . dog! Rat terrier. The identified victim, Eddie, was going to breed "rat killers." He must have had a terrier with him. She'd found part of the collar.

She wrote *Dog killed rat.*

"Ryan, can some animals, say a rat, carry a disease and not die from it?"

"I believe so. Why?"

"Just thinking out loud." If the rats from the experiments performed in the 1940s were turned loose, or got loose, and stayed on the island . . .

But how did those men die? Vasily hadn't died there. Nor had she and Bertie. So the disease wasn't airborne, or transferred by anything that was contaminated. *Think, Murphy.* But if a rat had been bitten or consumed by a host, and the host had caught the disease . . .

She pictured Denali staring at the family photo wall. The photo of his daughter and son-in-law on their boat . . . with a cat.

Her pen slid across the paper. That meant . . .

"Ryan, I think I know what happened."

He pulled a chair up to the table. "I'm waiting."

"As you know, more than ten years ago, Paul Stewart returned to Kodiak under his assumed name of Leif Berg. He made friends with his son, Denali, although Denali didn't know right away that Leif was his own father."

"We knew Leif was discreetly making inquiries about some of his work," Ryan said dryly. "Looking for buyers. He was also getting up in years. He was eighty-seven ten years ago. I suspect he didn't want to end up in a VA hospital."

She thought of the spotless, pleasant elder-care home he'd gone to. "His last days were more than comfortable. So now let's go back to 1942. Leif and Paul sent infected rats from Ruuwaq to Kiska in order to transmit a disease to the Japanese occupiers. Why not just bomb them?"

"Part of the reason for that was the extensive underground tunnel system the Japanese had dug. Bombing would be only so effective." Ryan leaned forward.

"I didn't know that, but it makes sense. So I think the plan was to kill or make as many of the enemy sick as possible, bomb the remaining soldiers, then invade."

"Right." He tapped the table. "But it was their first big failure. The rats didn't infect anyone. When Leif and Paul found out, they continued to work on biological warfare until they closed the lab down in 1946."

"The government closed it down before the earthquake and tsunami?"

"The two events happened almost simultaneously." He glanced at his watch again. "I'm sorry, but—"

"You have to get back to your surveillance and I need to get to the point."

He gave a motion for her to continue.

"Everyone thought the experiment was a failure because that's what they were told. But the rats died in transit. An accident."

He sat up straighter. "What? So the experiment could have been a success?"

"Apparently it was."

"That changes everything," he said slowly.

"Now fast-forward to ten years ago, and let's look at what

happened. Five men with a half-baked plan to get rich quick are shipwrecked on the island along with a dog. A rat-killing dog." She said that last part deliberately to be sure he got it. "They die horribly. Shortly, and I mean within a day, another man, Vasily, arrives there. He is unharmed."

"Right."

"If those rodents were left over from the lab, maybe turned loose or got loose, allowed to breed, living without predators, but infected . . ."

Ryan ran his hand through his hair. "Maybe they'd been specifically bred to be immune. They passed on this trait. They were carriers. And along comes a dog that kills one or two. I see where this is going. Everyone dies because the dog infects them, then the dog dies, but not anyone who comes later because there is no intermediary host."

"That's how I see it. I don't know how long it took for the dog to get sick, or how the dog gave it to the men, because we don't know how long the men were on the island before they died. The next event is the one I'm guessing even more about. Someone else comes along and burns the bodies, getting rid of the evidence."

"So far, so good."

"And many years later, Bertie and I travel to Ruuwaq, again without getting sick, let alone dying, because we don't have a dog. Or a cat." She took a deep breath. This had better be good, or she'd never get such a chance to save her sister and kill Clinton Hunter. "I've put a few things together."

He gave a go-ahead sign with his hand.

"I believe Jake was keeping an eye on that island for the family. An alternative theory is that Jake used to be a spotter for a fishing fleet, so he could have seen the bodies then. He tells Denali. Leif somehow finds out. Leif knows the significance of those bodies—he knows his work on the island was a success. Suddenly he has the ultimate weapon—a biological weapon that he can sell to the highest bidder." She looked at Ryan. "And the US government is at the head of the line."

Ryan's eyes narrowed.

"Leif tells Denali to get rid of the evidence. If anyone finds the bodies, there will be questions. Leif pushes all the right buttons, telling Denali that his family's reputation is at stake. So Denali sends the people he trusts most to clean up the island, the ones who would never betray the family."

"His own daughter and son-in-law. Yes."

"Lucas's parents do as they are told. But they have a cat."

Ryan nodded. "And that cat caught a rat and became infected, and things ran their course."

She circled the word *rat*. "That's the way I see it. And the virus would work quickly. Lucas's parents probably died the same terrible death, maybe even on their way home from the island. Denali would have blamed Leif. He was so distraught he got in a car wreck that crippled him and killed his wife. Everything could be laid on Leif and his work. I don't know if Leif ever confessed his real identity."

"Good job. Seems like you covered most of the bases."

"Not quite." She placed the pen on the paper. "Leif goes into a nursing home and dies suddenly."

"Most unexpected. Yes. We'd just about concluded the deal."

"Did it occur to you that he might have destroyed his notes? That he had nothing to offer?"

"No. He wanted the money too badly." Ryan nodded.

"So the trail goes cold, as in cold for ten years."

"We had people in place, keeping an eye on things."

"I imagine. People like Olga?"

Ryan didn't answer.

"Whoever was watching the family and waiting for a break must have heard about Vasily and his revelation, but this person was much lower on the food chain. So you show up. As you already said, you're the authority. You were sent in to negotiate the deal with . . . Denali?"

Ryan didn't answer.

"I'd guess, given what happened to Jake, you came to clean up any loose ends."

"Let's just say I create plausible deniability for the US government should anything go south." He smiled, but his eyes remained hard. "I didn't expect Vasily's murder, or how fast the cover-up would occur."

"Ruuwaq?"

"Yes. The other night when you mentioned a rat on the island, either Denali or Jake knew they had to destroy the last evidence of Leif's work."

"The last living evidence. The island was scoured of life."

Ryan folded his arms. "I don't suppose you have an idea about where Leif hid his research notes?"

She bit her lip. Lucas's words came back to her. *I overheard Grandpa say he'd find it here, but when I asked, he only said "something from the past."* "I think I might, but I need to make a phone call."

Ryan frowned but brought her a landline. "Do you know the number?"

She shook her head. He pulled a phone book from the desk drawer. She quickly turned to the yellow pages, found the number, and dialed.

"Perkins Headstones and Memorials."

"Hi. I need to . . . make an appointment with someone to . . . ask about a headstone. Do you do custom work?"

"Custom work is our specialty. What were you thinking about?"

"I recently saw a series of headstones that I found very interesting. They were ordered about ten or more years ago by my . . . uncle, Leif Berg. Did you do that work?"

"Our company did. Those headstones have gotten quite a few inquiries over the years."

"I imagine they have. Is the stonemason—"

"Everyone always asks that question as well. The man died shortly after he completed the work. Single-car accident. He died a few days later in the hospital."

"Oh, I'm so sorry. Did he die of his injuries?"

There was a moment of silence. "No one's ever asked that question." His voice grew distant. "Hey, Jim, what was it Ralph died of?"

A distant voice called, "Some kind of infection. No, wait. Botulism."

"I see. Thank you."

"But if you're interested—"

She hung up and looked at Ryan.

He gave a half shrug. "We looked at the tombstones. We looked at everything. There was just no way to pin down the location, and even if we had that, with his obsession with security, Leif would have coded everything and set booby traps for anyone foolish enough to try to get around his codes. It's one of the reasons he was fired from the Deseret lab."

"I thought you said he retired."

"Let's say he left under a cloud. One of his booby traps blew the hand off a coworker."

"I believe he used the headstones at the family cemetery. The man who did the work died in the hospital—"

Ryan waved her words aside. "We know that! A car accident. That proves nothing."

"He died of botulism. The same way Reinhard Heydrich died."

Ryan fell silent for a few seconds. "Well I'll be. That solves one mystery. I don't suppose you've worked out exactly where in the cemetery, and how to get to it without triggering Leif's trap?"

"No. Not yet."

"That's unfortunate. As I mentioned before, if we get it wrong, *boom!*"

CHAPTER 33

Ryan sat across from Murphy at the table. "You've kept your part of the bargain. Write this address down." He recited an address in Bells Flats. The house was less than a half mile from Vesper's home. She'd been so close.

"When you're . . . done, come back here. I'll have the money, airline ticket, and identification ready for you."

She nodded. "Okay, but the car, Elin's car. Aren't police going to be looking for it?" She held up the piece of paper she'd written the address on. "To get here, I have to drive right through the center of town. The cruise ship has already departed."

"If you wait until it gets dark, or at least darker, I can create a diversion."

"What kind of diversion?"

He patted her hand. "One that keeps the police from looking your way. Let me worry about that. Did you want to get some rest? You still have a few more hours before it's dark."

"I can't sleep. I'm too wound up."

"You'll have the house to yourself. If I'm going to get your money and tickets and cause some mischief, I need to get going." He looked at his watch. "It's 1130 hours. The sun will set at 1300 hours. Wait half an hour. 1330. Then go. Got that?"

"Yes."

He waved and left.

The aspirin helped, moving the headache from a throbbing ache to a distant pulse, but her brain was fuzzy and vision off. She glanced around the spotless house. He probably had surveillance cameras here and was watching her.

So what? He'd know she'd snoop.

Starting with the kitchen, she examined every cupboard, drawer, the refrigerator, stove, closet, and microwave. All she learned was he didn't cook. Or eat here. The living room was equally barren of personal items, as was the bedroom. Not even clothes in the closet. She ended up in the living room feeling uneasy and restless.

Feeling uneasy was normal. What did she expect? He was some kind of secret agent.

She'd see Dallas soon. After so long, she'd be able to talk to her sister, laugh, share secrets. The hollow feeling would leave. Everything would be like it was before . . . before Clinton Hunter. She would save her sister by killing Clinton Hunter. Save her sister by killing Clinton Hunter. Save her sister by killing Clinton Hunter . . .

She blinked. The words pounded in her head like a drumbeat. She'd been pacing the floor, chanting.

"I'm not a killer," she said out loud.

You're not killing. You're saving. Rescuing, Dallas whispered over the thumping words.

Don't kill. Call the police, a tiny voice murmured.

The police failed me, Dallas whispered back. *The judicial system failed. All those women are dead. I need you to save me. Kill Clinton Hunter.*

"I will." She had the mission. And it was time.

She secured the house, fumbling with the lock. As she turned to the car, she stumbled. Maybe that blow to the head gave her a concussion. The cotton batting in her brain thickened slightly. She got in the car. The driver's side crowded her, the computer open beside her . . .

She scolded herself aloud. "Stop, Murphy. There isn't an open computer. You're in an SUV." Her words were slurred slightly. *Focus on the mission.* She made sure Elin's gun was loaded, then placed it in her lap. If the police stopped her . . .

She'd passed Lily Lake when she heard the sirens. The closer she got to downtown, the louder and more numerous they became.

Driving by W. Marine Way, she spotted the fire. Flames engulfed one of the boats in the marina. Police and fire trucks converged on downtown. "Good work, Ryan," she whispered.

Bells Flats was about ten miles from town. Her heart hammered in her chest, pounding along with the throbbing in her head. The headlights bounced off patches of dense fog covering the almost empty two-lane road. The rain, for now, had ceased. She saw the sign up ahead. S. Russian Creek Road. The sign dissolved into another sign. *Parker Lane.* She blinked and the sign changed back.

She slammed on the brakes. Was that a trick of the fog? Was she overtired?

When the sign didn't shift again, she turned right. Now where? Holding up the slip of paper with trembling hands, she reread the address and directions. The closer she got, the more the landscape warped. Russian Creek Road was rural, small homes set far back on large lots . . . Now it was a low-income bedroom community. Parker Lane. Neglected older homes built closer together. Run-down. She pulled over and rubbed her eyes, then glanced around.

She spotted the number next to the door of a house on her right. A rusted truck, windows shattered, sat up on blocks on an overgrown lawn.

Tugging her coat closer in the cool fall air, she took out her flashlight and pistol. A dog barked in the distance, soon joined by a second. She watched where she put her feet, weaving between the discarded toys, trash, and hunks of grass.

At the front door she peeked through the small sidelight.

A coffee table lay on its side, one leg broken off. The stained brown sofa was slashed, with stuffing spilling onto the floor. Graffiti was spray-painted on the walls. In the center of the room sprawled a bare mattress, discolored and worn, with filler leaking from the ticking. A filthy sheet covered someone dozing, tangled hair sprawled across the mattress.

Murphy's gut tightened at the stillness of the body.

With her gun steady in front of her, she reached for the doorknob. Unlocked. She opened the door, swinging it wide to be sure no one was hidden behind it, and stepped inside.

He stood across the room. Hunter.

His mouth moved, but she could hear no sound.

She raised the pistol.

He put up his hand.

She pulled the trigger.

CHAPTER 34

Murphy winced at the blast of the pistol. The smell of gunpowder clogged her nostrils. Still holding the Glock in front of her, she went to the body under the sheet. She reached for the corner and lifted it, then pulled it back.

Her sister. Hair sprawled from her ruined face.

No. Not her sister. Pillows.

What?

The room shimmered around her. Murphy found herself on the floor, not knowing how she got there.

Clinton Hunter lay crumpled in the corner, a handcuff on one wrist holding him to a steam radiator.

Handcuff?

Murphy closed her eyes.

Her sister's lifeless body barely looked human.

The floor rocked, the light dimmed, a shrieking hurt her ears. The screaming should stop. Someone stop the screaming. Murphy took a deep breath and the screeching ceased. It had come from her. She put her hand over her mouth. Muffled mewing replaced the screams.

She opened her eyes. There was no body. Only pillows.

Her mind was whirling, pieces of shattered mirrors twisting

around. Her sister. Hunter. The house. The gun. Her badge. The blood.

"Murphy?" a voice whispered from the corner. "Murphy."

She hadn't killed him. She stood and tottered to his prone body. Blood seeped from his shoulder, soaking his shirt. His skin was waxy and pale. "Murphy," he said again.

Why wouldn't Hunter stay dead? How many times must she shoot him? She raised the gun and took aim at a point between his eyes.

"It's me, Murphy. Look at me. It's Joshua."

Hunter's face metamorphosed. "Joshua?" No.

"Murphy, focus. You're remembering. It's confusing. But I'm Joshua."

She looked down at her pants. They turned black. Uniform pants. She wore a standard-issue duty belt. The room shifted again. The walls were black with mold. The shag carpeting green.

She turned, stumbled over the pillows, fell. The room spun. She crawled forward until she reached the wall. The black mold was gone, replaced by off-white paint. Pulling herself to her feet, she looked around the room. A broken mirror hung above a small table. She crept to the mirror, holding on to the wall for support. Her face was fragmented. She moved closer. Closer. Until only her eyes showed. Her pupils were small. She blinked and her mind began to clear.

Finally, she remembered.

She'd gotten the call on her radio.

"Unit 23, please do a welfare check on 225 Parker Lane."

"10–26 in fifteen." Murphy yawned and turned her patrol car toward the seedier section of Anchorage. She'd only been back from vacation for a few days and was trying to readjust to working the graveyard shift.

She pulled up to a dilapidated house. A rusty truck rested on blocks on the overgrown, garbage-strewn front lawn. A pale-yellow light from the window bobbed and twisted with the moving foliage.

Tugging her coat closer in the cool fall air, she took out her flashlight and pistol. A dog barked in the distance, soon joined by a second. She watched where she put her feet, weaving between the discarded toys, trash, and hunks of grass.

At the front door, she peeked through the small sidelight.

A coffee table lay on its side, one leg broken off. The stained brown sofa was slashed, with stuffing spilling onto the floor. Graffiti was spray-painted on the walls. In the center of the room was a bare mattress leaking filler from its stained and worn ticking. A filthy sheet covered someone dozing, tangled hair splayed across the mattress.

She tapped on the door. "Hello? Police. Please open the door."

The figure on the mattress didn't stir.

Murphy's gut tightened at the stillness of the body. She turned off the flashlight, returned it to her duty belt, then triggered the mic attached to her shoulder. "This is Unit 23. I have a person down with an unknown status. Requesting backup at 225 Parker Lane. Please acknowledge."

"Ten-four. Backup to 225 Parker Lane."

She knocked again. "Police. Hello. Are you all right?"

No movement.

With her Glock steady in front of her, she reached for the doorknob. Unlocked. She opened the door, swinging it wide to be sure no one was hidden behind it. "Hello? Police."

She stepped into the room, glanced around, then approached the figure.

Harsh breathing behind her.

She twisted backward.

Something gleaming flashed across her face.

A million bees stung her forehead and cheek. She staggered, almost dropping her gun.

A man with a knife lunged at her again, aiming toward her heart.

She pulled the trigger. Again and again. Her brain finally registered she was dry firing. Sucking in a shaky breath, she released the magazine of her Glock. Empty. She reloaded another magazine.

Her face was on fire. Hot blood streamed down the front of her uniform. Holding a hand over her wound, she advanced to her assailant. He was dead. She bent down and checked his pulse, but the dilated pupils in his wide-open eyes told the story. So did the ruined chest where she'd pumped seventeen rounds.

She caught her breath. She knew him. Clinton Hunter. Her sister's boyfriend.

Slowly raising her gaze, she looked at the prone figure on the floor. "No," she whispered. "Please, God, no."

Murphy's legs were water, unable to support her. She dropped to her knees and crawled. A fly buzzed past her and landed on the body's exposed ear. A delicate ear with a carved earring. She recognized the piece of jewelry. She'd bought it for Dallas when they'd vacationed on Kodiak Island.

Gently she pulled the sheet away. Her sister's open eyes stared upward, mouth open in a silent scream.

Murphy's head hit the floor.

"Murphy, do you hear me? Murphy, help."

The voice was muffled, distant.

"Murphy, please, you have to help me."

She opened her eyes. The room was sideways in front of her prone body. The carpet reeked of mold. In front of her were pillows on a stained mattress. Beyond that, Joshua was staring at her.

"Murphy?" he whispered.

She pushed to her knees and the room straightened. Her head rang from hitting the floor. Wait. Jake had hit her on the head. He tried to kill her, throw her out of an airplane. She waited until the flurry of thoughts settled, then got to her feet.

Another vision crowded in. Had she really tried to kill him? "Joshua?"

"It's me, Murphy. Help me."

She had to get him to a hospital. Staggering over, she saw the handcuff. He was cuffed to a radiator. Her hand went to her side to retrieve the key.

No duty belt. No key. She wasn't a police officer anymore. Anymore? Who was she? Where was she? The room swirled.

"Murphy, can you hear me?" Joshua's face was gray.

She was in a house in Kodiak. Not Anchorage. "Yes. I shot you. I thought you were—"

"Don't worry about it now. Do you have a cell phone?"

"No."

"Get your gun. Shoot the links of the handcuff, then drive me to the hospital. Can you do that?"

"Yes."

Her pistol lay where she'd dropped it. She picked it up, moved to his side, and fired at the links. They popped apart. She reached for him and helped him to his feet. Almost crumpling under his weight, she slowly helped him to her car. She started the engine and turned toward town. Joshua was barely conscious.

"Joshua, I'm so sorry. I thought you were Hunter. I thought my sister . . . I'm so confused."

"Murphy, listen to me. The guy who lured me here—"

"Wearing glasses, brown hair?"

Joshua nodded.

"Ryan Wallace. Works for the government."

"He set you up. He called me and said you needed help and would meet me at that house. When I arrived, he was waiting with a gun. He arranged the mattress, saying it would look like we were having an affair."

She felt her cheeks growing warm. She remembered the aspirin. "I wonder if he drugged me."

"He's playing with your mind."

"He expected me to empty my magazine into you."

"But you didn't, Murphy, remember that. Remember your name."

"Dakota Murphy Andersen."

"And what is today's date?"

She had to think about that question. "Um, June twelfth."

"Good," he whispered. "Where are you?"

"Bells Flats. Kodiak."

"And where are we going?"

"To the hospital. Because I shot you. I thought you were someone else."

"Where do you live?"

The road rippled in front of her. Different places flashed in her mind, images coming faster and faster. "I don't know."

Her sweat made the steering wheel slippery, and she gripped it with white-knuckled intensity.

"Keep talking to me, Murphy. Don't lose yourself. Where did you go to school?"

"Undergraduate at University of Washington, MFA at the Rhode Island School of Design, Rhodes Scholar," she said automatically.

"Rhodes Scholar?" He gave up a low chuckle. "Impressive. And before that."

"What do you mean?"

"Where did you go to college before U of W?"

She gripped the wheel even tighter. "AA in Law Enforcement from the University of Alaska–Southeast."

"Very good, Murphy. Now"—Joshua's voice was barely a breath of air—"think about everything that happened since you graduated from the University of Alaska. Recall working as a patrol officer with the Anchorage Police Department. Remember everything since the night you found your sister's body." His head slumped against the door.

CHAPTER 35

Through blurry eyes, Murphy raced through the fog of downtown Kodiak to the hospital.

She shook Joshua slightly. "Please don't die. I didn't mean to shoot you."

She slammed on the brakes in front of the emergency room, jumped from the car, and burst through the door. A startled nurse looked up from a clipboard.

"Help me! Outside, he's dying." She tore back to the SUV and opened the passenger door. Joshua started to topple from the seat. She caught him but was shoved aside by a large male nurse.

"We got this." He eased Joshua onto a stretcher with the help of two other nurses. "Come inside and give us the information on this man, please." His voice was firm.

Surrounded by medical personnel, the gurney flew through the doors. Her last glimpse of Joshua was the top of his dark hair disappearing through an inner door.

They would take about five seconds to agree he'd been shot. Less than a minute after that, someone would come looking for her.

She bolted for the SUV and took off. She drove without lights until she was a block away from the hospital, then flipped them on.

Adrenaline had flooded her system. Her heart raced. Her hands were numb and sweat soaked her bloody clothing. Where should she go? She'd probably killed Joshua. She was already wanted for car theft. Probably for planting the bomb in Father Ivanov's car. And don't forget the arson on her landlady. Denali had tried to kill her.

And Ryan had set her up. He could have given her another car, but he wanted her to be found, to be arrested and charged with arson, murder, car theft, you name it. Why?

The code. When she said she didn't know the security code, she was no longer useful to him. Ryan's chilling words came back to her. *When my dog couldn't work anymore, my dad shot him. He said when something's no longer useful, it's time to get rid of it.*

She slammed on the brakes, then quickly looked around to see if anybody had noticed. The street was deserted. The digital readout on the dash said 2:00 a.m. She had to find someplace to hide out before the sun came up, someplace to think about what Joshua said.

Someplace to plan.

She'd dropped the pistol when she helped Joshua to the car. Whatever she did, she'd have to find some way to protect herself. The house out on Pasagshak was a tempting refuge. She could shower, change clothes, think in silence, but over ten miles of exposure on a two-lane road would mean certain discovery.

She realized she was driving on the road that led to the back side of Salmon Run Lodge and its private landing field. Airfield. Something tickled her mind. Something to do with the airfield. Certainly the dense foliage on the rutted road would hide this car. The police would be actively searching for her. Probably the state troopers as well. She'd bet Ryan called in gunshots in Bells Flats. Police and troopers would converge on that house soon if they hadn't already.

She passed the turnoff twice before finding it. Switching off the lights, she eased the SUV into the trees.

In the distance, sirens screamed.

She nudged the SUV faster into the underbrush, wincing at the cracking and scraping.

The sirens approached.

She slammed on the brakes, jammed the SUV into neutral, and turned the engine off.

The police were almost there.

She darted out and sprinted ahead.

A patrol car roared past, lights flashing.

At the edge of the airfield, she paused until she could stop shaking. Already a hint of dawn allowed her to see across the landing field to the hangar. Hangar. What did she know about it? Lucas had told her that Jake had an apartment in the hangar. That's what she was trying to remember. And Jake wouldn't be returning to the apartment any time soon. Or ever.

But Ryan told her he killed Jake. How could she trust anything he said? He could be in league with both Jake and Denali to get the information about the biological weapon.

She'd just have to assume everyone lied to her.

The fog clung to the ground, looking like a giant brush had painted a layer of gouache over the landscape. The dampness wrapped around her. She trotted across the field, watching for any movement. More sirens wailed in the distance.

If they found Elin's car, they'd quickly find her. When she reached the hangar, she circled it. On the far side, away from the path leading to the lodge, she found a series of windows and a door. The door was locked. Though the interior was dark, she could make out a kitchen and living area.

If Ryan lied about murdering Jake, Denali's half brother could be asleep in a bedroom.

She moved from window to window, peering in. The last one in the row showed an empty bed.

Did she really want to be cornered in Jake's apartment?

A dollop of rain struck her head and made up her mind. She'd have to seek cover.

The rain increased as she ran to the open door of the hangar. She hoped Jake had left the inside door to his apartment unlocked. He had.

Once inside the apartment, she locked the door and flipped on the lights. She'd have to find a flashlight and get rid of the overhead illumination, but first she needed to not crash into things. She quickly closed the window shades, then turned and examined the room. Several doors opened off the main living quarters. One led to a bathroom with a large mirror over the sink. She turned on the light, then darkened the rest of the apartment. The sliver of light under the bathroom door shouldn't show from the outside with the shades drawn.

Standing in front of the mirror, she stared into her eyes and whispered Joshua's words. "Think about everything that happened since you graduated from the University of Alaska. Recall working as a patrol officer with the Anchorage Police Department. Remember everything since the night you found your sister's body."

Screaming. There had been so much screaming.

The officer yanked her to her feet and shook her, then slapped her. Murphy stopped yelling. Her legs gave way and she started to slump. He grabbed her before she fell and hustled her outside the house and onto the rotting porch.

From a distance she heard him on the radio. "I just arrived at 225 Parker Lane. Officer down. Two down inside the house. Possible homicide. Adult victims are male and female. Possible gunshot wounds. Send crime-scene techs and roll medics."

She drifted on a blank void, drifting away . . .

"Hey there, are you okay? That's quite a cut." A gentle hand lifted her face. "Can you tell me your name?"

Murphy looked at the man and blinked with the one eye not stuck closed with blood.

She was on her back, strapped down.

"Poor kid. She doesn't look old enough to be a cop." A woman's face appeared above her.

Bertie's face.

Murphy shook her head violently and was rewarded with a shooting pain from her injuries. Bertie had been there when Murphy found her sister. Bertie had been the crime-scene technician.

When she first met Bertie on Kodiak, Bertie would have recognized her immediately. Bertie had wanted her to come and work for the crime lab. Return to law enforcement. She'd offered to find out what happened to her sister. She'd bet what Bertie did instead was find out what happened to her after her sister died.

"What did happen?" Murphy asked her reflection.

Her eyes gazed back at her. Silly question. She'd gone back to college. Finished her degrees.

"You're skipping parts. What happened before that, and what happened to put you on Kodiak?"

Her mind felt like Swiss cheese, with big holes of time missing.

A voice came from outside the apartment. "Jake? Uncle Jake, are you here?"

CHAPTER 36

Murphy flipped off the bathroom lights.

Outside, Lucas called again. "Uncle Jake?"

Had Ryan told the truth? Was Jake currently floating somewhere in the frigid Gulf of Alaska? Or was Jake merely AWOL?

The inside door to the hangar rattled. "Uncle Jake, please. Dad needs to talk to you." His voice broke.

Why was Lucas crying? Slipping from the bathroom, she raced to the outside door and let herself out. The rain had increased to a steady downpour, and the landscape was cloaked in gray. She pulled up the hood of her jacket and ducked into the woods.

Now what? She was out of ideas.

Something crashed through the brush, coming closer.

She backed away, tripped, and fell.

It was on her before she could stand, pinning her to the ground. Licking at her face.

"Quinn, get off me, you oaf." She shoved the enthusiastic Labrador away.

"Murphy." Lucas stood over her, the tears running down his face mixing with the rain. "Grandpa said you'd left. He said you'd caught a plane off the island and weren't coming back."

She shivered. Denali had told his grandson the truth, just

leaving out the little matter of a mid-ocean drop-off. "As you can see, I'm still here. Why are you crying, Lucas?"

"Ryan has a gun on Grandpa and said he was going to kill him unless I bring Uncle Jake back."

"They're at the lodge now?" She stood, bracing herself on the Lab's rump.

"Cemetery." His voice was a squeak.

"Come here." She opened her arms.

He flew into them, sobbing and clinging to her like a little boy. He was soaking wet and shaking with cold. "What am I gonna do? He's all I have."

She held him until his sobs subsided. She had no doubt Ryan would follow through with his murderous intent. She could pretty well guess why Ryan needed Jake. Ryan must have figured out Leif's code, or how to bypass any booby trap Leif may have left to protect his research. She figured the headstones were the hiding place, but if Leif placed anything under them, Ryan would need an able-bodied person to dig. Denali couldn't from his wheelchair, and Lucas wasn't strong enough.

She needed some time, and someplace dry for both Lucas and herself. "Listen to me, Lucas. You need to go back to the cemetery and tell your grandfather and Ryan that Jake is on his way. Then you need to tell them that you need to put Quinn in the lodge. When you're in the lodge, get on the phone—"

"Ryan cut the phone lines. I saw him do it."

"Are there any cell—"

"No."

"Can you drive a car?"

"No."

She gnawed on her lip. "Sweetheart, I need to get you to safety. Come with me." Lucas and Quinn trailed her across the field to

273

where she'd left Elin's car. She put the Lab and shivering Lucas in the back seat, then went to the rear of the SUV. Elin had a blanket and coat there. She brought the blanket to Lucas and wrapped him in it. "You need to stay here until I come back for you, do you understand?"

He nodded.

She returned to the rear and changed into the dry slacks, sweater, and vest Elin had in her go-to bag, pulling her raincoat over the whole thing. She waved at Lucas, then trotted across the airfield to the hangar. She'd have to hurry or Ryan would come looking for Lucas. In Jake's apartment she found a pair of scissors, leather gloves, and a quart-sized measuring cup. She took the measuring cup to the fuel barrel near the plane and filled the container, then fueled the plane. Ready for a fast exit. Inside the plane's cabin she located the braided twine that Jake had used to hold the burlap on her head. She cut it into two halves. One leather glove became a pouch, with holes poked in the side. She attached the twine on both sides of the pouch, tied a loop at one end of the twine, and fastened a handle on the other.

If she had to fight Goliath, she needed David's shepherd's sling.

On her way toward the cemetery, she collected a number of stones.

She moved off the trail as she neared the graveyard and crept through the woods until she could see the iron fence surrounding the graves. Denali was alone just outside the fence.

She ducked and searched the trees for Ryan.

A slight movement in the periphery of her vision caught her attention. He stood opposite her, watching the trail.

She melted back into the trees. The steady drum of the rain would hide the sound of her moving through the underbrush.

She worked around through the densest brush until she was behind Ryan. Elin's water-resistant clothing was mostly soaked, and the air was cold. She clenched her jaw to keep her teeth from chattering.

Inching her way forward, she stayed low under the dark foliage until she could see the cemetery once more.

Ryan had moved back to Denali, gun pressed to his head. "That grandson of yours had better get back here in the next few minutes or I'm going to start shooting. First your right arm. Then your left." He shot into the air. "That should bring him running."

She clutched the nearby tree. No time.

Ryan was turned away from her. She had one chance. She glided right, until she was clear of the trees and completely behind him. Taking out the sling, she placed a stone into the pouch and started spinning it over her head. Then she deliberately stepped on a stick.

Snap.

Ryan turned, raising the pistol.

She let go of one side of the sling, sending the rock flying.

The stone struck Ryan in the forehead. He dropped to the ground.

She raced over to his prone body. He was unconscious. Good. Killing two people in one day was probably over the top, even for a former police officer. She grabbed his pistol and stuck it in her pocket.

"You!" Denali's face paled. "You're dead."

"Don't you wish." She used the sling twine to tie Ryan's wrists behind his back, then tied him to the iron fence. "The only reason I didn't let Ryan shoot you is for your grandson's sake."

"Where is he? And where is Jake?"

"You tell me. Ryan said Jake was dead, but if so, why would

he send Lucas after him? I'm guessing Ryan's planning on getting that formula from your family one way or another. As for Lucas, he's safe." She straightened. "Now you're going to tell me the truth for a change." She stared straight into his eyes. "Tell me about Ruuwaq."

Denali swallowed twice, hard. "I had to protect my family name. Our reputation. Our home."

"I'm not impressed. Get on with it."

"I didn't know any of this until Jake spotted the bodies on Ruuwaq ten years ago. I told Leif, or at least the man who called himself Leif, about it. I figured he'd be interested because he worked with my dad on that island.

"That was when Leif confessed that he was my father. We agreed that to protect the family name and fortune, we needed to get rid of the bodies." Denali looked away. "He said the men died because they'd become stranded on the island, that nothing was left of his work there. I figured that was reasonable—after all, more than fifty years had passed. So I sent my only child, my daughter and her husband, to get rid of the evidence. They were to burn the bodies, then throw everything into the ocean. They never came back from that trip."

Rainwater trickled down the back of her coat. She shivered. "What biohazard did your father cook up that had our government buddy here willing to commit murder?"

Denali glanced at Ryan. "Leif—I can't think of him any other way—was looking for a way to accelerate the incubation period of a particular virus to make it extremely fast-acting. He also was exploring fleas, ticks, and finally rats as a delivery system. The rats were the most promising. But he thought he'd failed when he found out the Japanese evacuated Kiska with no evidence of disease."

"The rats died before they could be released."

Denali's brows rose. "That was not the conclusion he came to. He thought they destroyed all the remaining rats, but apparently some of them escaped, and generations of specially bred infected rats continued to live on Ruuwaq."

"So what virus did he mutate?"

"Rabies."

CHAPTER 37

Murphy grabbed the iron cemetery fence to keep from falling. "Your father mutated the rabies virus?" She pointed at Denali. "Those five men on Ruuwaq Island, your own family, died of rabies?"

Denali wouldn't look at her. "Essentially one hundred percent lethal. Attacks the brain, so even in the early stages, it renders a person unable to function. Perfect as a military weapon. The incubation period was the problem. Three to eight weeks."

"People can be inoculated, the disease prevented—"

"If you know what you're dealing with. But millions, billions of doses of vaccine aren't available on short notice. In wartime, it could wipe out an entire military division. And here's the beauty of the disease: it can't live long outside a host, unlike anthrax, which contaminates the environment."

"You almost sound like you admired his work."

"Admired it. Hated it."

Ryan stirred and moaned.

"What are we going to do with him?" Denali jerked his head toward the unconscious Ryan.

"What do you mean, 'we'? I'm out of here. You tried to have Jake murder me. Ryan tried to frame me and get me to kill an innocent man. Why did he set Joshua up like that?"

"I suspect it was because your boyfriend was getting in the way. He was frantic to find you, driving everyone crazy."

Her face grew warm in spite of the chilled air. "You and Ryan deserve each other." Murphy pulled her raincoat closer. If Ryan really was an agent for the US government, they'd come and collect him and hustle him off to another assignment. Or whatever super-secret groups do to compromised agents. And Denali's biggest fear was exposure, which she'd be delighted to do. She turned to leave.

"Grandpa!" Lucas ran down the path toward his grandfather. "I heard a gunshot." Quinn beat him to his owner and sat by the wheelchair.

Denali extended his arms to the boy. "I'm okay now that I know you are too."

"Good." A new voice from the trail froze Murphy. "All of you are together."

She knew that voice. But it wasn't possible . . .

Father Ivanov stepped from the trees, pistol held out in front of him. His beard was gone, as was all his priestly clothing. His head was shaved. She would not have recognized him except for his voice. "Murphy, drop the gun and kick it toward me."

She debated pulling it out and shooting him before he had a chance to pull the trigger, but he aimed the pistol at Lucas. "Don't even think about it."

She did as she was instructed.

"You murdered Elin!"

"Yes."

"Who was the other person?"

"A bum. One of the homeless eating at the kitchen. Nobody important."

"Why did you fake your death? And why do you have a gun on me?"

"In a word, fingerprints. I wiped down Vasily's house, but Elin said they'd recovered one set of prints, and she wanted to print me. I couldn't take the chance." He smiled, but it didn't reach his eyes. "So I had to die."

Murphy couldn't believe his logic. "But Elin didn't! You didn't think someone else would identify your prints and know you killed Vasily and Irina?"

"It wasn't about the murders." Ryan slowly rolled to a seated position and looked at Ivanov. "He's a Russian agent. Running his prints would have flagged him to the CIA. Very clever, by the way, to pose as a priest."

"I am a priest. I just have a, shall we say, part-time job."

"You must have heard about the bodies on Ruuwaq," Ryan said.

"No." Ivanov pointed the gun at Ryan. "We, that is, the Russian government, got an offer several years ago to buy Paul's research. For a large fee, of course."

"We got the same offer," Ryan said. "Leif Berg wanted to know if the US government was interested in recovering the biological warfare results from World War II. Of course, considering he was in the military when the work was done, it's ours anyway."

"So Paul," Murphy said, "or as he called himself then, Leif Berg, decided to sell—"

"Not him. He died before we had a chance to work with him," Ryan said. "Jake."

"What?" Denali's face flushed red. "Jake would never—"

"Ah, but I would." Jake casually strolled down the path.

Murphy's heart sank.

"Come here, Quinn," Jake called. "Good dog." Jake took a rope from his pocket and tied the dog to a tree. "I don't want any of you trigger-happy clowns to shoot the only good member of the family."

"How dare you say that!" Denali raised his fist.

"Cool your jets, old man," Jake said. "The whole family is a work of fiction you created to make you feel good. Your drunken wife, your hero father—I know you bought that Distinguished Service Medal on eBay."

"Shut up. Shut up!"

Jake turned his back on his half brother and addressed Ryan. "You said you'd studied Murphy's file carefully. You said she'd buy my death. You claimed she'd see you as a knight in shining armor and would trust you."

"She did," Ryan said.

"But here she is, rather than in jail."

Ryan shook his head. "Heads will roll in the profiling unit."

Jake flicked his hand impatiently. "What did she tell you?"

"Nothing useful."

"Well then, our deal is off." Jake looked at Ivanov. "Now, about your offer?"

"Have you got the formula?" Ivanov asked.

"Have you got the money?" Jake shot back.

"That's what I thought." Ivanov moved a few steps backward until he could easily see everyone. Jake was on his right, near the trail. Denali had moved his wheelchair sideways to the cemetery, and his grandson clutched his shoulder. Ryan sat on the ground, leaning against the fence he was tied to. Murphy was farthest away, on Ivanov's left. "We've suspected, Jake, that you don't have the formula in your possession. Were you going to just point to the cemetery and say, 'It's there'?"

Jake didn't answer.

"We know the research is buried here," Ryan said. "Murphy

clarified that. That's not the issue. Did you find out the code, or how to bypass Paul's booby traps?"

"I need the money first," Jake said.

"Well, I don't need you." Ivanov calmly shot Jake in the chest. Lucas screamed.

Quinn lunged for Ivanov and was brought up short by the rope. He continued to lunge and bark.

Ivanov aimed at the dog.

"No!" Lucas dashed to Quinn and put his arms around the frantic Lab.

Ivanov shifted his pistol to take aim at the boy.

"Stop!" Denali screamed.

"Don't shoot!" Murphy yelled at the same time. She stared intently at Ivanov.

"I won't. Not yet. The kid's too good a motivator to get you to talk. I bet if I shot his dog, you'd be most helpful. If that didn't work, I could shoot his grandfather."

Lucas shuddered. Denali's face was drained of color.

"I'll talk." If she could distract Ivanov, she could injure him with a well-placed rock. Break his nose or hit him in the eye.

"She's bluffing. She told me everything she knew." Ryan jerked his arms, trying to loosen the twine binding his wrists. "She said she didn't know the code. Remember, I studied her file. She's nuts. You know she spent two years in an insane asylum."

Murphy gasped. A floodgate of memories opened into her brain. Being diagnosed with post-traumatic stress disorder. Counseling. Voluntary commitment to the state mental hospital. Finding control and stability. Enrolling in the university. Trying to fill holes in her life.

"Murphy?" Lucas said.

She was sitting on the ground. She had no idea how she got

there. She was soaking wet and so very cold from the rain. A huge empty place had opened back up inside her.

She remembered why she'd come to Kodiak.

"Murphy?" Lucas asked again. "Are you okay? Are you really . . . crazy?"

"No, Lucas, I'm not crazy. I lost my way for a bit, but I'm fine now." She looked at the men. "But all of you are still lost, and morally barren. Denali, you hated your father for his role in developing biological weapons, yet you tried to poison me. You sent your brother to murder me and burn my landlady alive."

"I'm afraid that was my work," Ivanov said. "I needed to keep an eye on you, and to do that, I needed to have you nearby. Remember, I was the one who suggested you get a job at the lodge. It worked."

She blinked. "And Vasily and Irina?"

"My work as well. I would have taken care of Vasily before he had a chance to talk to the police, but the caretaker had already notified them. I also took care of that obnoxious Zinkerton, but the recovered evidence was of no use."

"So, like the Japanese human experiments in Manchuria, you think of people as 'logs.' They justified their torture in the name of war. Ryan"—she looked at him—"you probably justify your actions in the name of national security. And you, Denali"—she stared at him—"you were willing to kill me to protect your pride and reputation." She waved her hand at all of them. "Ultimately, no matter how you justify it, at your core, all of you simply like killing people."

Ivanov shrugged and nodded at Ryan. "In our line of work, we do what's necessary to accomplish our goals. And you will do that for me, Murphy."

"She doesn't know the code," Ryan said.

"That's where you are wrong, Ryan," Ivanov said. "Your culture no longer acknowledges what she is. In Russia, she is what we call an *Iskatel' istiny*. A truth finder."

"What are you talking about?" Ryan asked.

"She finds the truth, the innermost thoughts and secrets of people, don't you, Murphy?" Ivanov looked at her. "I knew it the moment Vasily confessed to you. And most of the time you don't even know what you've done, or that they've told you something no one else knows. Somewhere in that head of yours is the answer—the key to unlocking the code that protects Paul Stewart's research."

She shook her head. "No, I don't have it. I'd tell you if I did."

"Look, Ivanov, turn me loose." Ryan struggled with the bindings. "I have drugs and a few choice techniques for getting her to talk. But I don't think she knows anything."

"You are tiresome. And no longer necessary." Ivanov aimed the gun at Ryan and pulled the trigger.

The blast of the pistol lingered in the air. Ryan slumped forward.

Adrenaline flooded Murphy's system. Her muscles tensed and hands tightened on the sodden grass.

"Stand up." Ivanov waved his pistol.

She stood. Her mind examined then discarded solutions. She had to protect Lucas from that murderous monster.

"You"—Ivanov pointed to the boy—"get over next to Murphy. Stay next to her."

Walking stiff-legged, like he couldn't feel his legs, Lucas made his way over to her.

"I'm sure, Murphy, that Ryan told you about the booby trap that blew the hand off a coworker. Imagine what he'd do to keep the wrong person from getting his life's work. You will open Paul Stewart's grave, or tomb, or wherever it is he's hidden the formula. You'll only have one chance. If you make a mistake, I guarantee the trap he left will kill both you and Lucas."

CHAPTER 38

Murphy's sweat mixed with the rainwater. She put her arm around the trembling child. "If anything happens, play dead," she whispered. "Don't be frightened," she said louder for Ivanov's benefit. "I'll keep you safe."

She moved inside the fenced area, staring intently at each grave. All the headstones came from Paul, claiming to be Leif. Denali said as much to her. Paul's wife had the angel on her grave. Denali's wife had the praying hands. Lucas's parents bore the bas-relief of the Gloucester Fisherman's Memorial. Paul's memorial was the obelisk with the metal plaque and the cast images of an ant, bird, amphibian, cow, turtle, and shark. Carved above were the words *All creatures great and small.*

She remembered Lucas's words. *He studied stuff. I figured out those are invertebrates, birds, amphibians, mammals, reptiles, and fish.*

If she guessed wrong, she'd kill Lucas.

Don't guess, Dallas whispered in Murphy's mind. *You know the answer.*

She returned to the image of the Fisherman's Memorial. Paul's work had killed Denali's daughter, Paul's granddaughter. Would he gift the research to her out of guilt? Or entrust it to the angel on his wife's grave? No. Paul was selfish and greedy. He would have reserved his hiding place for himself. She returned to the obelisk. The squares with the cast animals didn't look solid. She touched the shark. It moved slightly. One chance. One chance.

"Stop wasting time," Ivanov said.

Operation Fair Cyan. She turned the words over in her head. Ant, bird, amphibian, cow, turtle, and shark. They meant nothing. How was she supposed to break this code? The US government had experts on it for years, didn't they?

Wait. Denali had called the shaggy cow a yak. It didn't look like a yak. It looked like a Scottish Highlander cow. Fair Cyan. If yak was a *y*, the *c* would be . . . was that a bird, or could it be a crow? Crow, yak, *a* would be the ant. That left an *n*. What started with *n*? Nurse shark? Newt. All the others were single names. Fair? Was *Fair* part of the combination? That didn't match up with the images. Unless . . .

I figured out those are invertebrates, birds, amphibians, mammals, reptiles, and fish.

With trembling fingers, Murphy reached up and pushed the shark. The square moved inward about half an inch. *Click.* The noise sounded abnormally loud in the stillness. She pushed the newt. *Click.* Ant. *Click.* Turtle. *Click.* She paused to wipe her hand on her pants. Crow. *Click.* Yak. *Click.* Ant. *Click.* Finally newt.

Click. The bronze panel opened fully.

"Move," Ivanov ordered.

She stepped away from the obelisk.

Ivanov approached and reached inside, pulling out two thick notebooks. His face didn't change expression. "Move over there." He indicated a spot near Denali.

Taking Lucas's arm, she went to Denali, avoiding the crumpled bodies of Jake and Ryan.

"You"—he pointed to her—"come with me. I have other uses

for you. Go there." He pointed to a spot farther away from Lucas and his grandfather.

She shifted, watching his expression.

He raised the pistol, aiming at Lucas.

The child's eyes widened.

She lunged.

Ivanov pulled the trigger.

The bullet struck her in the chest.

Searing pain smashed through her brain. She crashed to the earth. Blackness enfolded her.

Ivanov laughed. "How about that? Got two with one bullet."

Her mind went dark.

CHAPTER 39

The throbbing pain in Murphy's chest wouldn't go away. She remained still, hoping it would subside. It didn't. She tried to remember where she was, why she hurt, and why she was cold and wet.

Ivanov! Ivanov shot her. She was probably dead. Being dead hurt.

This is ridiculous. She opened her eyes. Lucas lay underneath her, silent and still.

Was Ivanov nearby, waiting to pump another round, this time into her head?

From this angle, the coast was clear. She pushed off of Lucas's body, grunting. "Lucas?"

The boy opened one eye. "Can I move now?"

"Are you hurt?"

"You squished me."

"Outside of being squished, are you hurt?"

"No."

"We have to find out where Ivanov—"

"A little bit ago I heard a plane taking off from the airfield."

"Ah."

His face was covered in mud and streaked with tears. "I thought you were dead too."

She patted his shoulder. "I'm wearing Elin's Kevlar vest. Getting hit by a bullet hurts like the dickens, though."

She glanced over at Denali, then did a double take. He'd been shot, just like the others. "Listen, Lucas, we have to run from here. More bad people might come."

"Where are we going?"

"For now, run to the car. Don't look back."

"But what about Grandpa?"

She glanced at the man. His head was thrown back, eyes open, staring at nothing.

"We'll get help. Grab Quinn. Go!"

The boy scurried to the dog, untied him, and ran toward the airfield. Ivanov would be confident he'd killed everyone. Sure enough, he'd placed the pistol he'd taken from her close to her hand. He would have planted the second gun near Jake. Yes, she found it there. It would have looked like she'd gone on a shooting spree before being mowed down by Jake.

Two could play at manipulation. She untied Ryan's wrists, wiped down Elin's pistol, and placed it in his hand before aiming at a tree and pulling the trigger. They'd find gunpower residue on Ryan's hand. Doing the same with Jake, she had him shoot a tree in Ryan's direction. Both men were stiffening in the cool day.

She went through Ryan's pockets and took his keys.

Closing the metal plaque on the obelisk, she wiped down the surface with her coat and took off after Lucas. He and the dog sat in the rear of the SUV, huddled under the blanket. The rig was still too hot to drive, but Ryan's house wasn't that far away. Edging out to the road, she drove as quickly as she could. She parked in the rear.

"Where are we?"

"Someplace safe, at least for a few minutes." Using Ryan's keys, they entered the house. Lucas kept the blanket around him. The Lab left muddy footprints on the spotless floor. Good. "Lucas, you might want to lie down and get warm." She pointed to the sofa.

He didn't argue. Both he and the dog sprawled on the sofa and were soon asleep. She was pretty sure he was in shock.

She thought for a few minutes, then picked up the telephone. The receiver clicked a few times before the dial tone. As she suspected, the phone was monitored. Moving to the kitchen so as not to disturb the sleepers, she punched in a number to silence the dial tone. "I know you can hear me. This is Murphy Andersen. Your man Ryan Wallace is dead. You'll find his body, along with Jake Swayne's and Denali Stewart's, in the cemetery where Leif Berg hid his formula."

She heard a tiny intake of breath, then a woman said, "A moment, please."

A smooth male voice came on. "What happened to the formula?"

Priorities. "The last I saw it was in Ivanov's possession."

"I see."

"But I'll tell you where you can find it if you fix things."

"What do you mean by 'fix things'?"

"Call me when it's done." She hung up the phone.

She didn't have to wait long. The phone rang.

"Murphy?" Vesper asked.

Sweat beaded on her forehead and dampened her upper lip. She figured the government kept tabs on terrorist groups and insurgents, but Vesper's call now proved they did an astounding amount of intel gathering on regular citizens.

"Hi, Vesper."

"What's going on? I just got a call from some man saying you need a ride. He gave me an address. I said I wasn't doing any such thing until I spoke with you."

"Um, this isn't a secure line, but yes, could you pick me up? I'll have someone, make that two someones, with me."

"I'll be right there."

Murphy wanted to change into dry clothes, get out of the itchy vest, and take a look at her chest. She bet she had a humdinger of a bruise just below her heart. But she needed to stay on alert.

Twenty minutes later Vesper drove up.

Waking Lucas, Murphy got both him and the dog in the back seat. Vesper took the presence of a dog and a boy in stride. "Now where?"

She gave an address.

Vesper looked at her for a moment, then put the car in gear. They soon arrived at the city cemetery. Murphy got out of the car and walked through the tombstones until she found the one she was looking for. Dallas Andersen. The date of their birth. The date of her death at the hands of the murderer Clinton Hunter.

She'd found her sister.

Vesper approached and stood on the other side of the grave. "Look at me, Murphy."

Murphy did. A small jolt went through her. She stared into the other woman's eyes. "You're a soul searcher too."

"I am. And it's time you took a look at what's inside, eating you up."

"I already did. I looked at myself in the mirror. I remembered almost everything."

"What happened to you?"

Murphy touched the headstone. "I thought I was strong enough to sort out my sister's things. I found her earring, the one she'd lost, the match to the one she'd been wearing when she was murdered. It ripped open the buried memories."

"So you coped by creating an alternate reality."

"Yes. I made up a whole story about my sister and what happened to her, about how Hunter had been in prison, had gotten out. I even wrote a letter to myself saying he'd escaped. I've lived with tissue-paper lies for the past year, trying to find a way to write a different ending to her story."

"You said 'almost everything.'"

"I was in a mental hospital. Voluntary commitment. I remember that too."

Vesper continued to make eye contact.

A memory slammed into Murphy's conscience like a freight train.

Dallas held up her long skirt as she waded in the softly lapping water of the ocean. Her sandals were in her hand, and her hair was tucked behind her ears. She wore the earrings Murphy had purchased for her.

"Sis." Dallas moved closer to the shore so Murphy could hear. "Did you get a chance to do what I asked?"

"Not yet. I've been slammed at work."

"Well, if you get a chance, would you do a quick background check on this guy who asked me out? I just want to be sure. His name is Clinton Hunter."

If she got the chance.

She didn't take the time. And Dallas was forever dead.

Her mission: ask forgiveness from her sister. "I'm so sorry, sis."

Don't be, Dallas whispered back. *You got to the truth.*

She looked at Vesper through blurred vision. "Thank you."

"You're not quite done." Vesper handed her a mirror.

She looked at it, then her. "What . . . ?"

"Look at yourself."

She held up the mirror and gazed at her image. She was flushed, eyes red. Her scar . . .

Her scar was the thinnest of white lines, barely visible. She touched it, then looked at Vesper.

"Scars heal eventually. Even deep ones," she said.

"But it was there for so long."

"The scar will always be there, but now you can know what others really see when they look at you. Just a whisper of past hurt. Not a disfigurement."

EPILOGUE

Three months later

The house on the ocean at Pasagshak was as clean as she could make it with a twelve-year-old boy and large Labrador trooping through every five minutes. True to his word, the man at the other end of the phone had "fixed it." After some negotiations, she received a key to this house, temporary custody of Lucas and Quinn, and a stipend to live on. In return, she told them about Ivanov. She replayed the conversation in her head almost daily.

The same smooth male voice came on the line. "We've taken care of the issues at the lodge."

"By issues, you mean the dead bodies, right?"

"Um . . . yes. A terrible car crash. Now, what happened to the formula?"

"Well, I'd planned to fly off Kodiak myself in Denali's plane. I gassed it up and got it ready."

"Your information doesn't show you have a pilot's license."

Her information? "I don't. Butch showed me how to fly a plane, and I saw a YouTube on it once. How hard could it be?"

He seemed to be speechless.

"Only I made a mistake. I gassed the plane with diesel fuel, just

a little, you understand. The fuel barrels were sitting next to each other. I suspect Ivanov made it a little way before he realized what had happened."

He still hadn't found his voice by the time she disconnected.

Her visitors were due to arrive any moment. She checked to be sure the Lab hadn't gone swimming again and shaken himself out all over the kitchen. Kid and dog were outside, kitchen clean.

A car drove up.

She was suddenly nervous. What if . . . ?

Someone knocked.

She jumped, then hurried to open the door.

Vesper entered, carrying a small box, followed by Bertie in a walking cast.

"Greetings, ladies. I'm excited to hear all the news." Murphy stood aside.

"Bertie has all the news." Vesper grinned. "I'm here to drop off some books for you to read about that soul of yours." She headed for the kitchen table.

"Thank you." Murphy turned to the beaming Bertie. "You're looking good."

"Hey, Murph, whatcha think? I lost ten pounds doing physical therapy."

Pursing her lips, she studied the woman's ample body. "Are you sure? You look more like you've lost thirty pounds."

"That's my girl! Lie to me."

She grinned. "Come on in."

"First the news and a couple of surprises. They found Ivanov's plane, or what was left of it. He tried to land on the side of a mountain. Not successfully. Rumor has it that Leif's notebooks were burned up."

Murphy grinned. "So no one got the formula. Good. You said a couple of surprises . . ."

"Ah, yes." Bertie stepped aside and Joshua appeared. He was leaner than before, but still toe-curling handsome.

Her hand flew to her mouth. Her eyes grew blurry. Her mouth stopped working.

"Hello, Dakota." He studied her face. "I like your hair color. The dark brown didn't suit you."

"Joshua . . ."

"I came here for three reasons." He moved closer with that same fluid grace.

Did women still swoon?

"First, you owe me an apology. It was very rude to shoot me."

"Oh, Joshua, I'm so sorry—"

He put his hand over her mouth, then his lips.

Time froze. Her mind went blank, her legs turned to butter.

His kiss ended. "Apology accepted," he whispered.

Bertie grinned her gap-toothed smile, then jabbed him in the ribs with an elbow. "Show her reason two."

"Ah, yes." He held up his hand. No wedding ring.

"But what about—"

"My four boys. I want you to meet them." He disappeared around the side of the house where they'd parked the car. A moment later, four huge Bernese Mountain dogs flew around the corner, shot past her, and launched themselves onto the sofa. "Meet Travis, Max, Cody, and little Sammy." He was grinning as he followed them. "Little Sammy isn't so little anymore. Sorry about the sofa."

One of them found a seashell throw pillow and was making short work of it. "And the pillow," he added.

Lucas came trotting over from his walk on the beach. Quinn

spotted the dogs wreaking havoc in the living room, barked an invitation, and all five dogs flew from the house and charged the beach.

"Cool." Lucas turned and ran after them.

"And reason number three?" she asked faintly.

"I'm still waiting for you to accept that dinner invitation with me."

She took a deep breath. She really hadn't planned on getting in so deep.

But still, there was this cop standing beside her.

And her future in front of her. "Yes."

AUTHOR NOTE

Dear Reader,

At the suggestion of my agent and editors, I gave poor Gwen Marcey a break. There's only so many almost-drownings, burning buildings, gunfire, wolves, caves, a crummy husband, and cancer a woman can go through before she needs a rest. I do believe she'll be back in the future. In the meantime, I hope you enjoyed the adventures of Murphy Andersen. As in my other books, this one also has a theme of forgiveness, but this time it's about forgiving yourself. Guilt and remorse, if not addressed, can eat away at a person. Let's face it, being human means making mistakes. You can't go back and change the past, but with forgiveness, you can change your future.

I love hearing from you. I read and answer all my emails, so please don't be shy.

God Bless,
Carrie

ACKNOWLEDGMENTS

Ahhh, so we made it through another book, this time meeting Murphy Andersen. The seed of this story came from my husband, Rick. When asked, "Where would you like to go to research a book?" He promptly answered, "Kodiak!" Thank you, Rick, for suggesting this fascinating place.

Placing this novel on Kodiak Island gave me a chance to learn about a little-known location and even less-known history, reconnect with old friends, and meet some new ones. I am grateful to a lot of people. I dutifully noted everyone's names in the book I carried with me for a year. Then lost the book. I apologize to those I have forgotten.

First on my list are Priscilla and Butch Patterson. Yes, there really is a Butch Patterson. Priscilla and Butch met on Kodiak Island many years ago. From Priscilla I got the names of contacts, what to see, and where to stay during our research trip. Butch gave me more names and allowed me to use both his name and his real-life discovery of the oldest plane crash in Alaskan history.

Once in Alaska on Kodiak, Rick and I were shuttled about and treated like royalty by Voni and Rich Harris. Voni is a wonderful writer, and much of the flavor of Kodiak came from her efforts. Thank you!

ACKNOWLEDGMENTS

My friend, neighbor, dog sitter, and massage therapist extraordinaire, Lorrie Jenicek, thank you for the brain storming session and beta reading I subjected you to. Speaking of beta, thank you to my beta readers Kerry Kern Woods, Molly Smith, Gayle Noyes, Kathy Birnbaum, Michelle Garlock, and Trish Hastings.

And now that I'm on the subject of Trish Hastings, a special shout-out for letting me pattern the "Christ's Table" after the Christ's Kitchen that she manages in Victoria, Texas.

All things Russian came from my sister-in-law, Diane Stuart, aided by my niece, Shilo Stuart, and Vartan Kazarov. Russian Orthodox information came from St. John the Baptist Orthodox Church in Post Falls, Idaho.

Back to Kodiak for more thank-yous. Paula Ensign's bed-and-breakfast on beautiful Mission Lake was an inspiration. The folks at Andrew Air gave us a bird's-eye view of the island, Katmai National Park and Preserve, Alaskan brown bears, and even a timber wolf. Thank you to owner Dean Andrew, pilot Scooter Mainero, and guide Devin Downs.

Rhonda Wallace, chief of police in Kodiak, was a delight to meet and provided the insightful information about her department. Additional law enforcement details came from sergeant Cornelius A. Sims, post supervisor, "C" Detachment, Kodiak Post, Alaska State Troopers.

The Kodiak Military History Museum at Miller Point, Fort Abercrombie, was wonderful and a treasure trove of ideas. The nursing staff at Providence Chiniak Bay Elder House were most helpful.

My cop-sounding dialogue came from Melanie Walchek, CCA, Crime Scene Specialist, Surprise Police Department, Arizona.

Pacific Seafood, headquartered in Clackamas, Oregon, allowed me to tour their facilities on Kodiak. I thank the president and

CEO, Frank Dulcich, as well as Mary Schaffhausen and the Kodiak staff.

I am totally grateful to my fantastic agent, Karen Solem, who believes in me even when I doubt. I consider the dream team I have at HarperCollins Christian Publishing as family—the good kind of family! Editors Amanda Bostic and Erin Healy know how to polish my manuscripts until they glow. The rest of the HCCP group, from Jodi Hughes and Paul Fisher to Kristen Golden and Allison Carter, and all the rest of you, bless you, bless you, bless you!

Thank you to Frank Peretti, who started this journey and mentored me through it. And finally, eternal thank you to my Lord and savior, Jesus Christ, in whom all things are possible.

DISCUSSION QUESTIONS

1. Murphy Andersen believes the scar that disfigures her face is the outward reminder of the terrible mistake that mars her soul. Have you ever studied your face in a mirror to see if it reveals your innermost thoughts?

2. I invented the "gift" of being a soul searcher—the ability to get others to open up and reveal their secrets like Murphy does. There are people, however, that do seem to have a similar ability. Have you met any? Are you one of these people?

3. The biological warfare information is, unfortunately, true. What do you think about this?

4. Did this story leave you with the desire to visit Kodiak Island? Why or why not?

5. Uncle had an irreplaceable memory of past events, customs, and traditions. Did you know someone like this? If so, did you try to capture these memories?

6. If you were the casting director for this movie, who would you get to play the parts?

7. If you could describe each of the main characters in one word, what would that be?

8. At the end, Vesper brought Murphy a stack of books to "read about that soul of yours." If you were to put together a reading list for Murphy, what would you include and why?

New York Times bestselling author Frank Peretti says, "*When Death Draws Near* reflects Carrie's way with all things creative: it's engaging, tightly woven, painstakingly researched, and a just plain fun read. Dive in!"

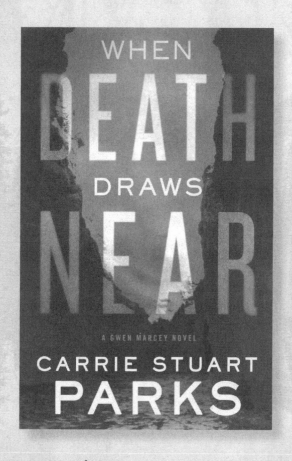

LOOKING FOR YOUR NEXT GREAT NOVEL?

RT Book Reviews gives *A Cry from the Dust* four stars and says, "This is an excellent book that is sure to put Carrie Stuart Parks on readers' radars."

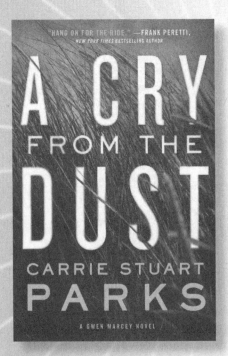

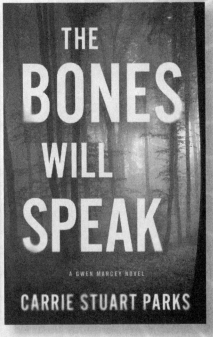

ABOUT THE AUTHOR

Andrea Kramer, Kramer Photography

Carrie Stuart Parks is an ECPA Christy Award and multiple ACFW Carol and Inspy Award–winning author. An internationally known forensic artist, Carrie draws on her extensive experience with actual criminal investigations to write authentic, true-to-life fictional suspense. Carrie lives in Idaho and travels with her husband, Rick, across the US and Canada, teaching courses in forensic art to law enforcement professionals. She has won numerous awards for her fine art and is the author/illustrator of numerous books on drawing and painting.

Website: CarrieStuartParks.com
Facebook: CarrieStuartParksAuthor
Twitter: @CarrieParks